nickelodeon

TEENAGE MUTANT NI
TURTLE

VOLUME 1

RISE OF THE TURTLES

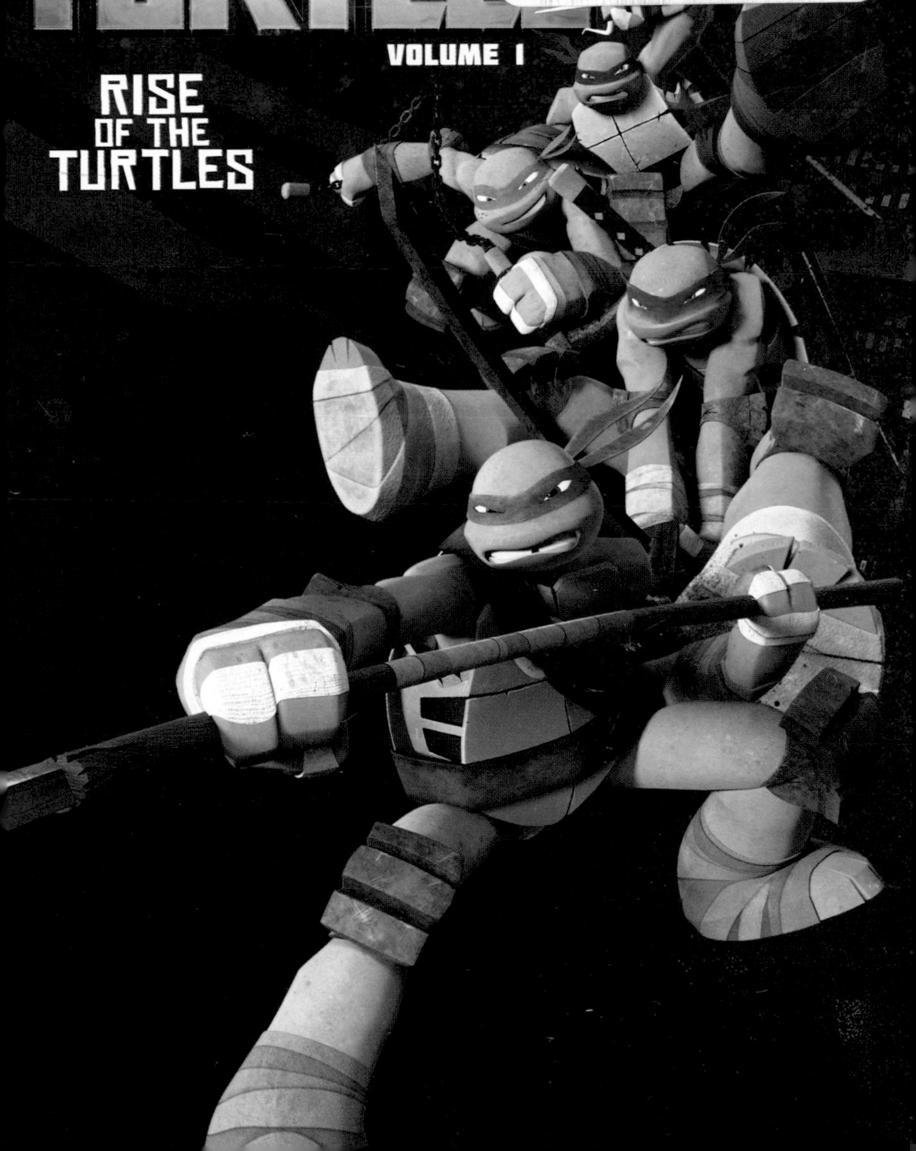

nickelodeon™

TEENAGE MUTANT NINJA TURTLES™

RISE OF THE TURTLES

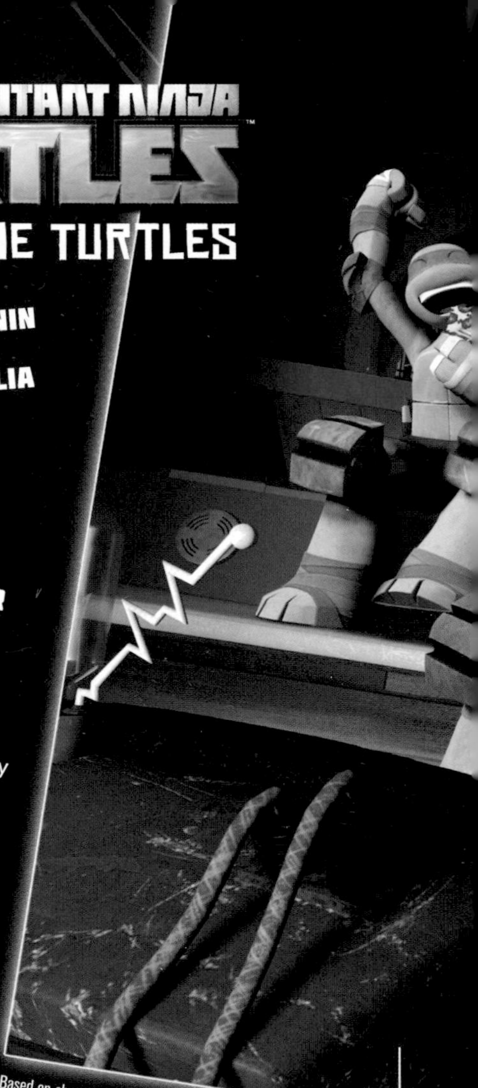

Written by
JOSHUA STERNIN
&
J.R. VENTIMILIA

Adaptation by
JUSTIN EISINGER

Edits by
ALONZO SIMON

Lettering and Design by
TOM B. LONG

Special thanks to Joan Hilty, Linda Lee, and Kat van Dam for their invaluable assistance.

Based on characters created by Peter Laird and Kevin Eastman.

ISBN: 978-1-61377-613-1
16 15 14 13   1 2 3 4

www.IDWPUBLISHING.com

IDW®

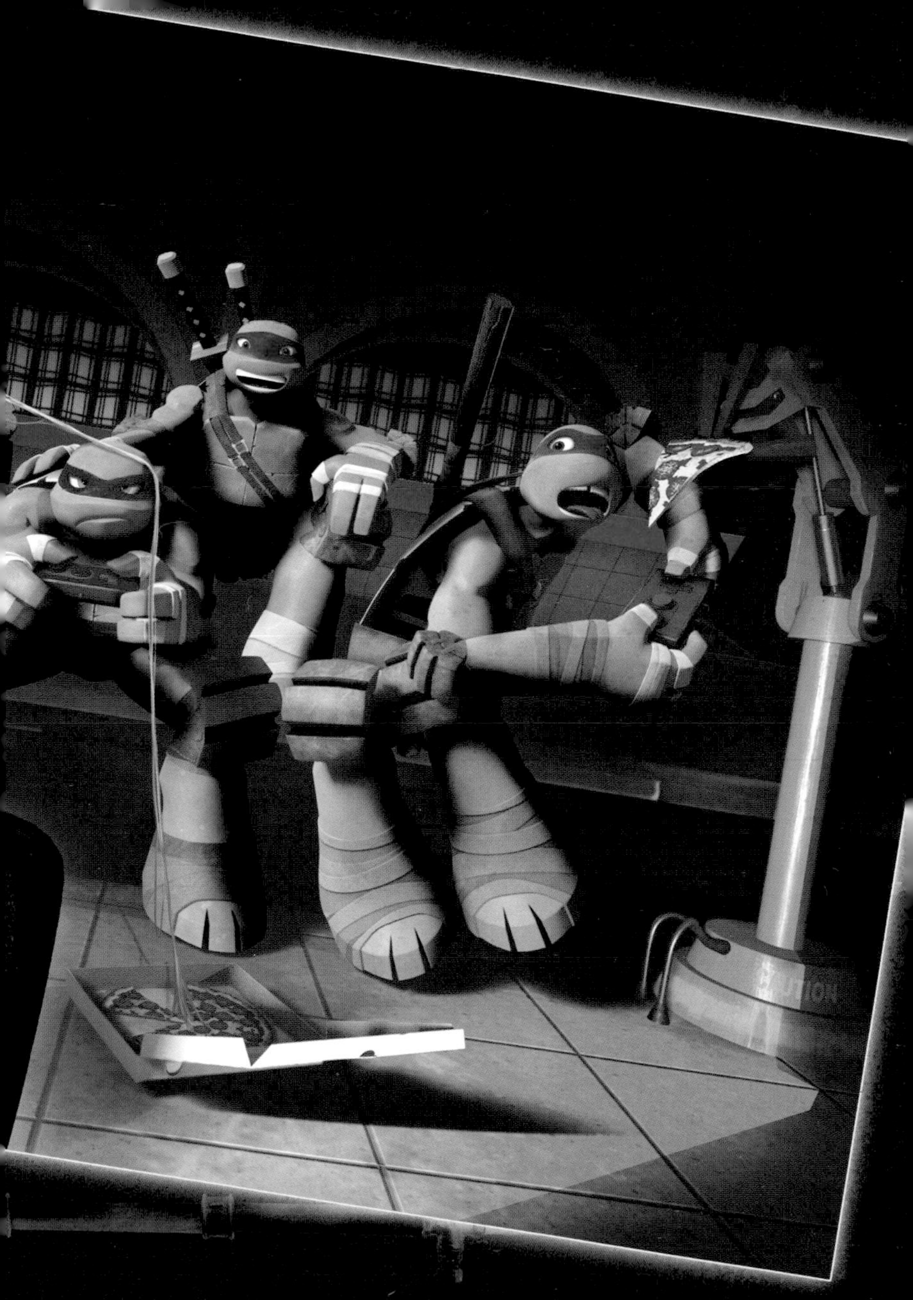

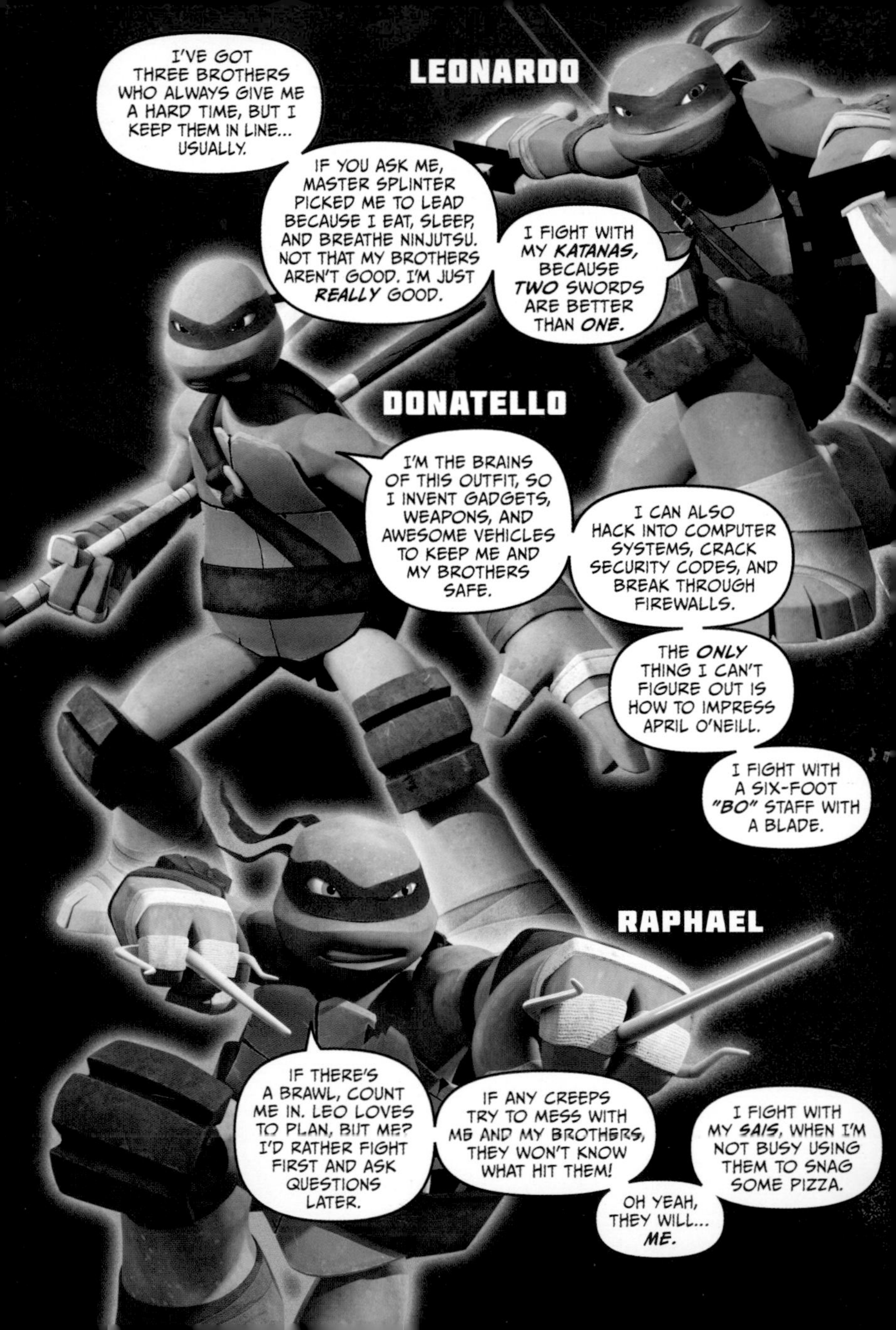
LEONARDO
I'VE GOT THREE BROTHERS WHO ALWAYS GIVE ME A HARD TIME, BUT I KEEP THEM IN LINE... USUALLY.
IF YOU ASK ME, MASTER SPLINTER PICKED ME TO LEAD BECAUSE I EAT, SLEEP, AND BREATHE NINJUTSU. NOT THAT MY BROTHERS AREN'T GOOD. I'M JUST *REALLY* GOOD.
I FIGHT WITH MY *KATANAS,* BECAUSE *TWO* SWORDS ARE BETTER THAN *ONE.*
DONATELLO
I'M THE BRAINS OF THIS OUTFIT, SO I INVENT GADGETS, WEAPONS, AND AWESOME VEHICLES TO KEEP ME AND MY BROTHERS SAFE.
I CAN ALSO HACK INTO COMPUTER SYSTEMS, CRACK SECURITY CODES, AND BREAK THROUGH FIREWALLS.
THE *ONLY* THING I CAN'T FIGURE OUT IS HOW TO IMPRESS APRIL O'NEILL.
I FIGHT WITH A SIX-FOOT *"BO"* STAFF WITH A BLADE.
RAPHAEL
IF THERE'S A BRAWL, COUNT ME IN. LEO LOVES TO PLAN, BUT ME? I'D RATHER FIGHT FIRST AND ASK QUESTIONS LATER.
IF ANY CREEPS TRY TO MESS WITH ME AND MY BROTHERS, THEY WON'T KNOW WHAT HIT THEM!
OH YEAH, THEY WILL... *ME.*
I FIGHT WITH MY *SAIS,* WHEN I'M NOT BUSY USING THEM TO SNAG SOME PIZZA.

MICHELANGELO
I'M DEFINITELY THE LIFE OF THE PARTY AROUND HERE.
I LOVE VIDEO GAMES, SKATEBOARDING, PRANKING THE OTHER GUYS, AND MOST OF ALL, PIZZA!
DID SOMEONE ORDER A SWINGING *NUNCHUK* SMACKDOWN? 'CAUSE I'VE GOT ONE FOR YOU!
SPLINTER
FOR MANY YEARS I HAVE LIVED IN THE SHADOWS, TRAINING MY ADOPTED SONS IN THE WAY OF NINJUTSU.
MY SONS ARE NEARLY GROWN NOW, AND IT IS TIME TO LET THEM EXPERIENCE THE WORLD FOR THEMSELVES.
MY STAFF IS A SYMBOL OF BALANCE.

RISE OF THE TURTLES

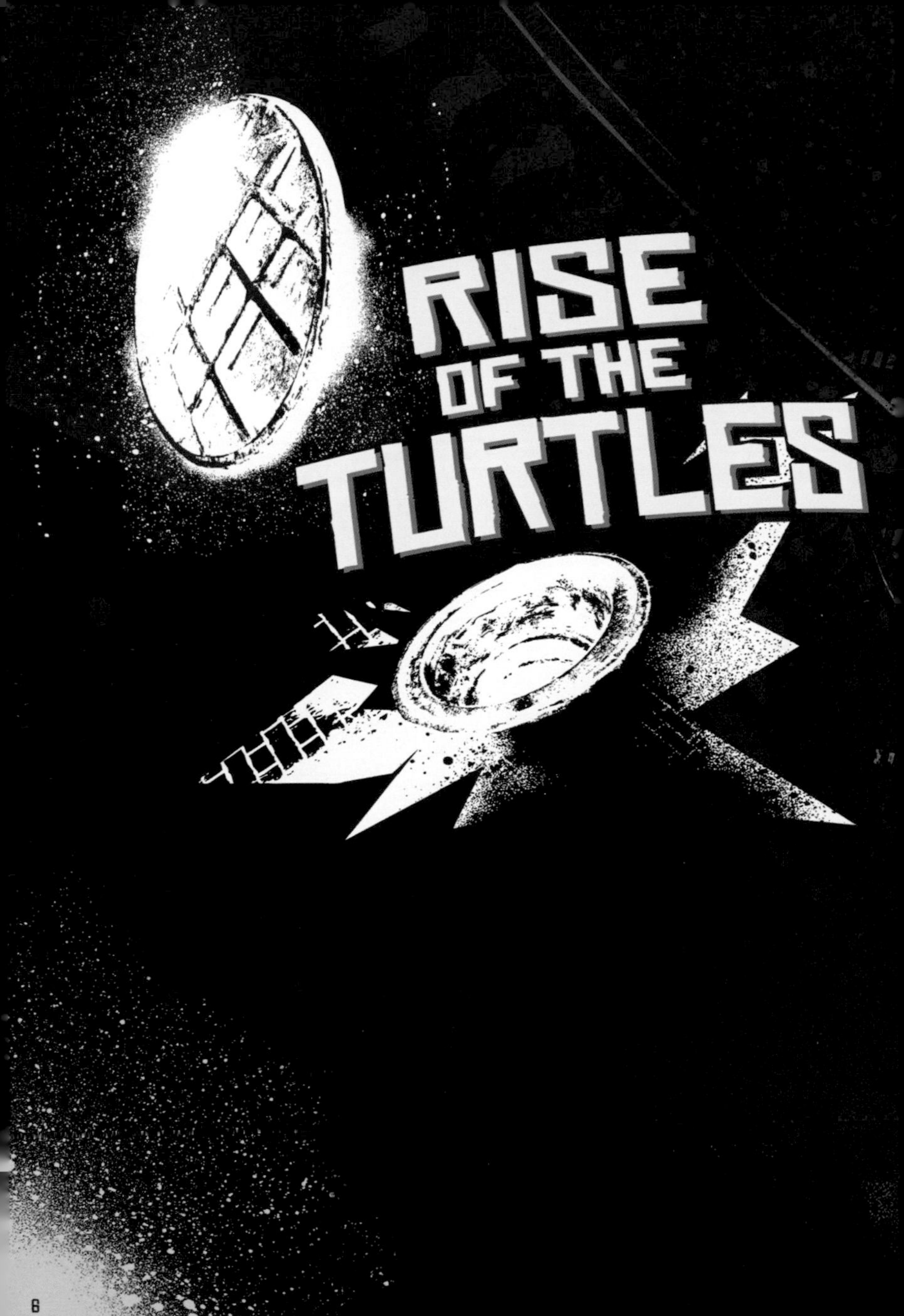

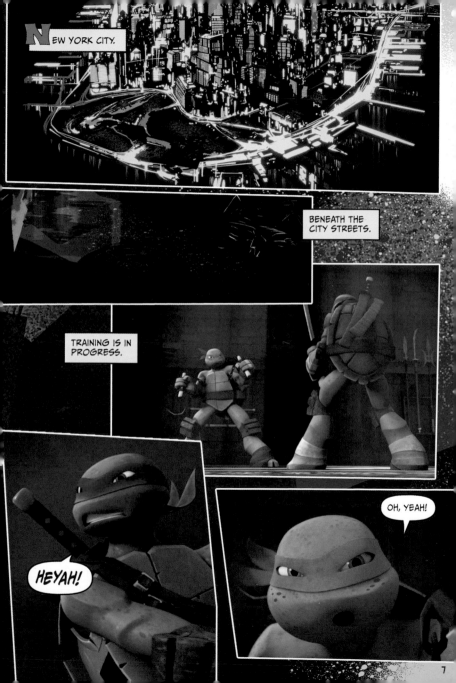

NEW YORK CITY.

BENEATH THE CITY STREETS.

TRAINING IS IN PROGRESS.

HEYAH!

OH, YEAH!

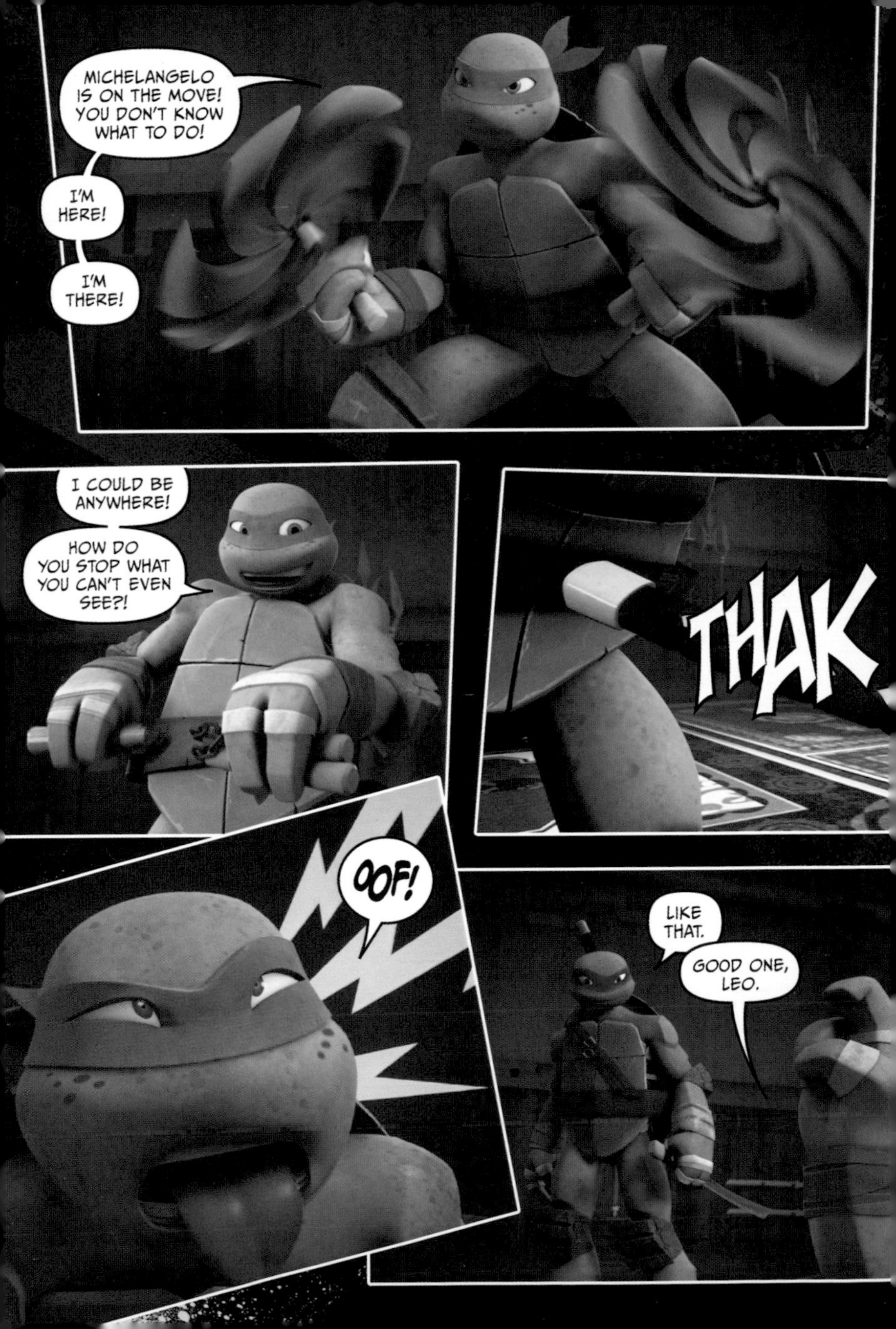
MICHELANGELO IS ON THE MOVE! YOU DON'T KNOW WHAT TO DO!
I'M HERE!
I'M THERE!
I COULD BE ANYWHERE!
HOW DO YOU STOP WHAT YOU CAN'T EVEN SEE?!
THAK
OOF!
LIKE THAT.
GOOD ONE, LEO.

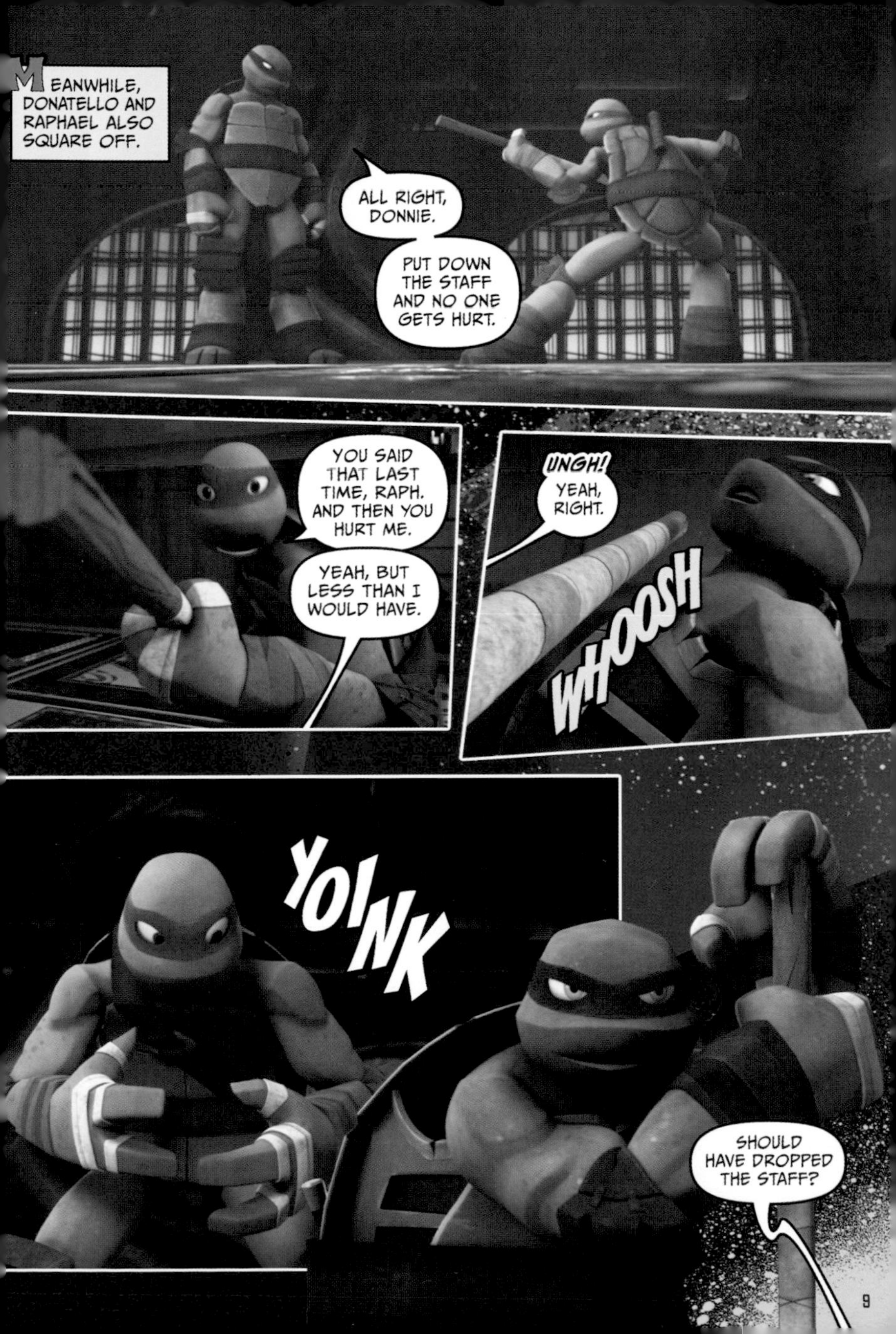
MEANWHILE, DONATELLO AND RAPHAEL ALSO SQUARE OFF.
ALL RIGHT, DONNIE.
PUT DOWN THE STAFF AND NO ONE GETS HURT.
YOU SAID THAT LAST TIME, RAPH. AND THEN YOU HURT ME.
YEAH, BUT LESS THAN I WOULD HAVE.
UNGH!
YEAH, RIGHT.
WHOOSH
YOINK
SHOULD HAVE DROPPED THE STAFF?

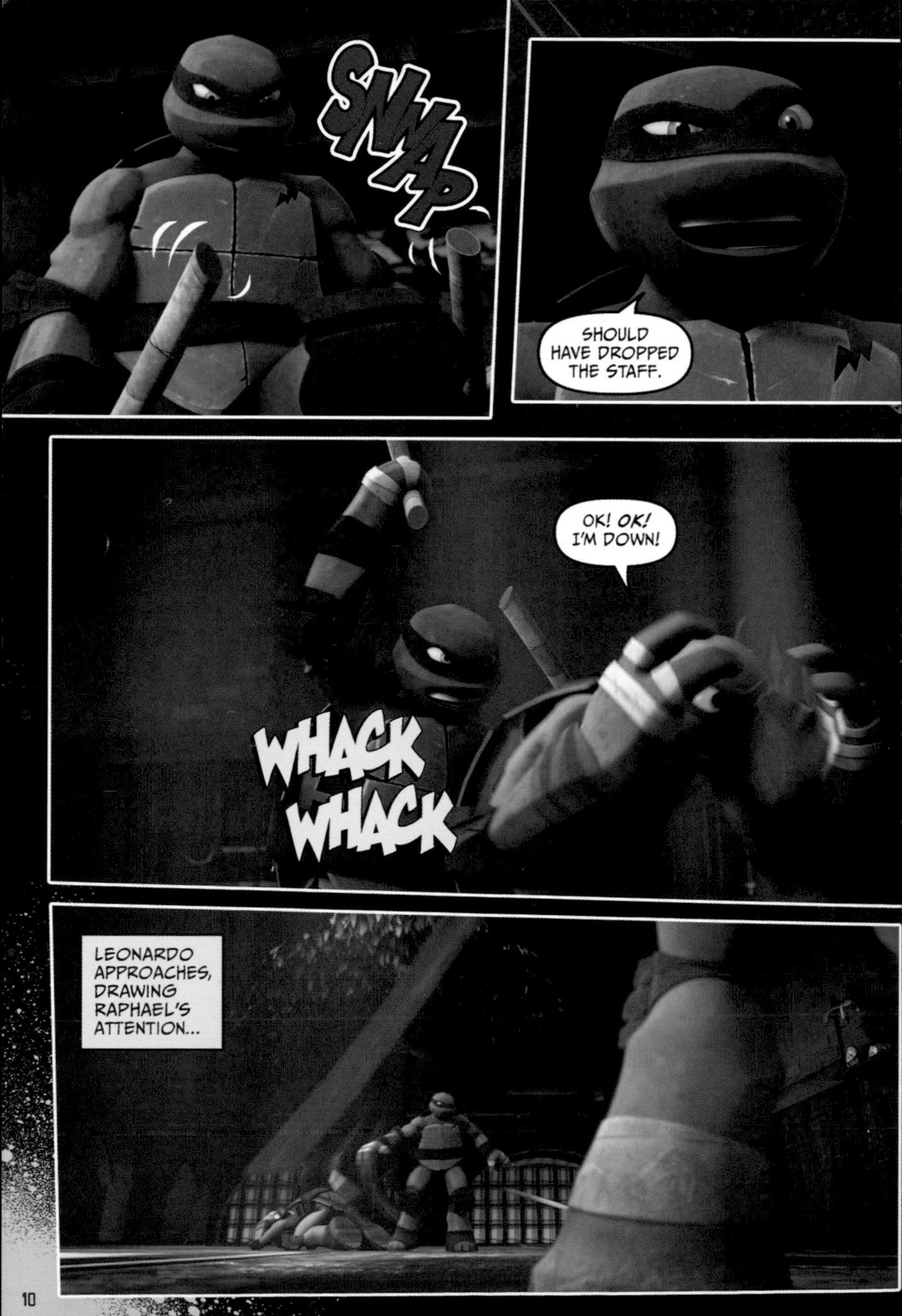
SNNAP
SHOULD HAVE DROPPED THE STAFF.
OK! OK! I'M DOWN!
WHACK WHACK
LEONARDO APPROACHES, DRAWING RAPHAEL'S ATTENTION...

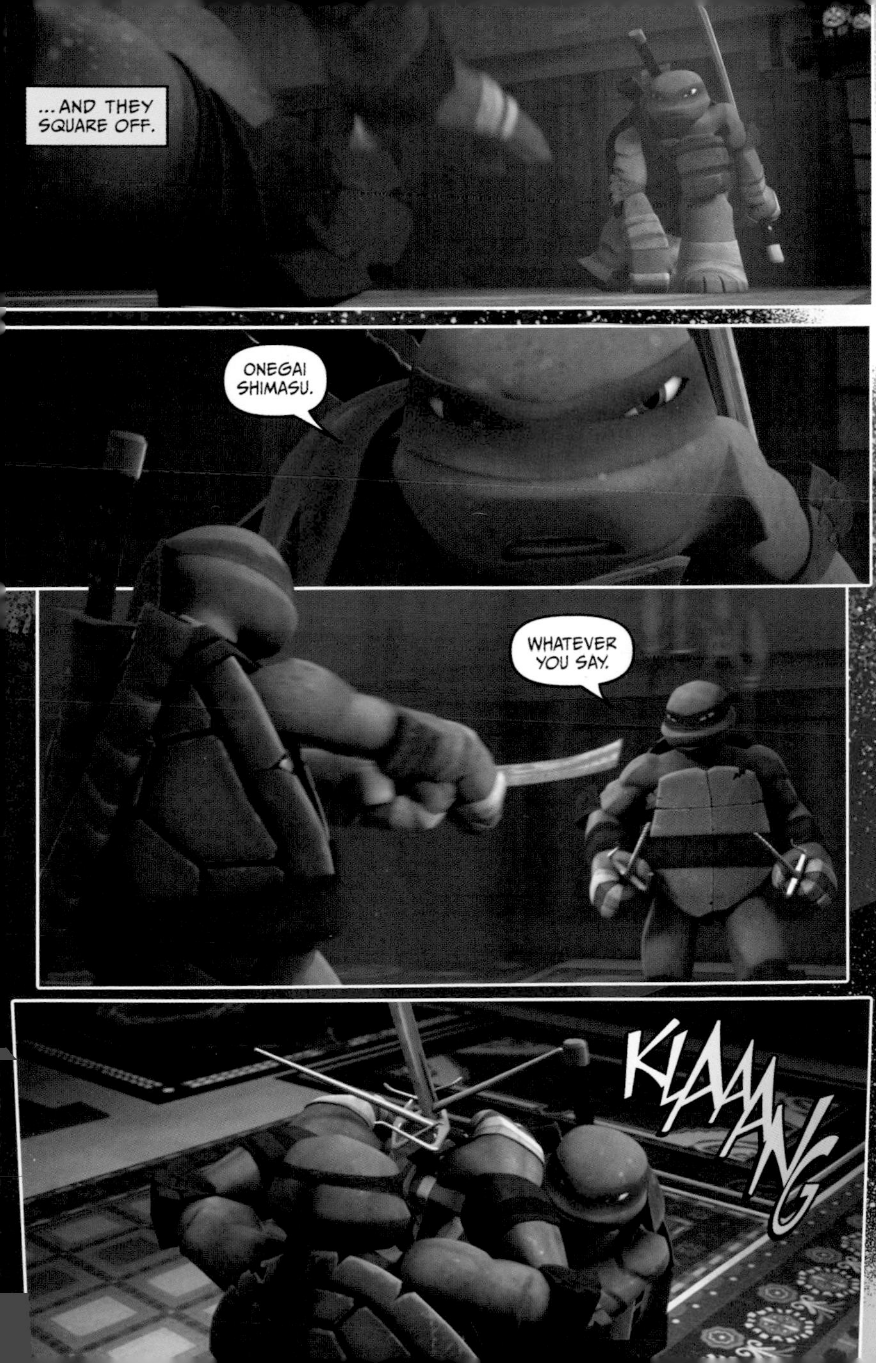
...AND THEY SQUARE OFF.
ONEGAI SHIMASU.
WHATEVER YOU SAY.
KLAAANG

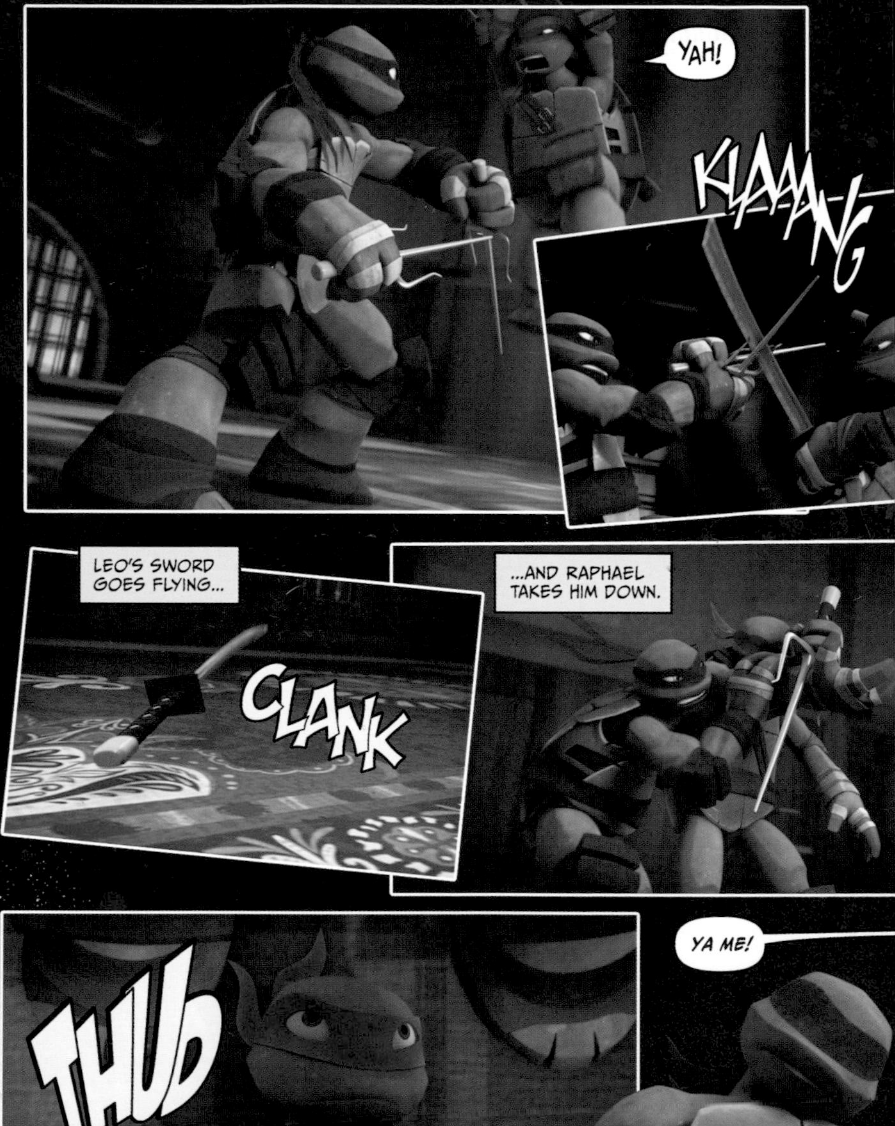
YAH!
KLAAAANG
LEO'S SWORD GOES FLYING...
CLANK
...AND RAPHAEL TAKES HIM DOWN.
THUD
YA ME!

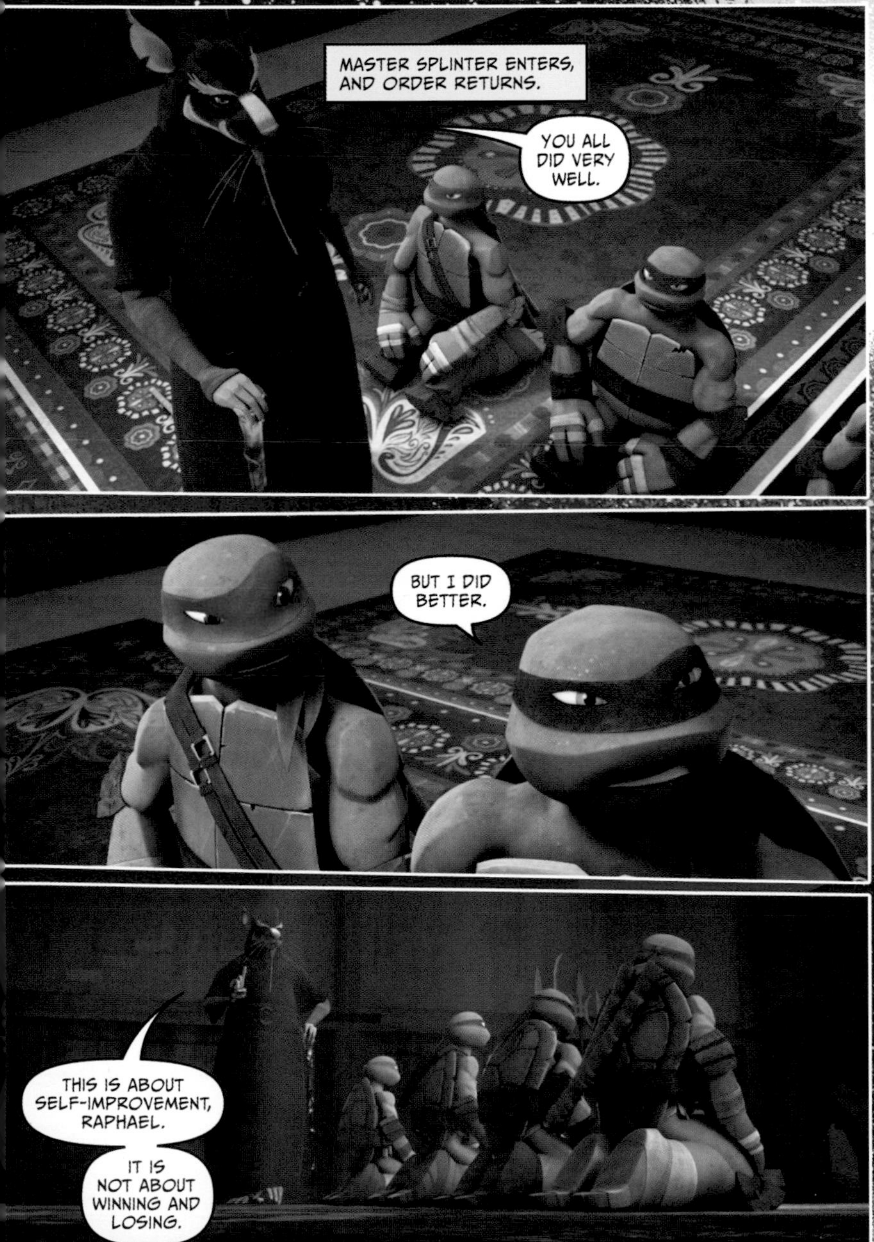
MASTER SPLINTER ENTERS, AND ORDER RETURNS.
YOU ALL DID VERY WELL.
BUT I DID BETTER.
THIS IS ABOUT SELF-IMPROVEMENT, RAPHAEL.
IT IS NOT ABOUT WINNING AND LOSING.

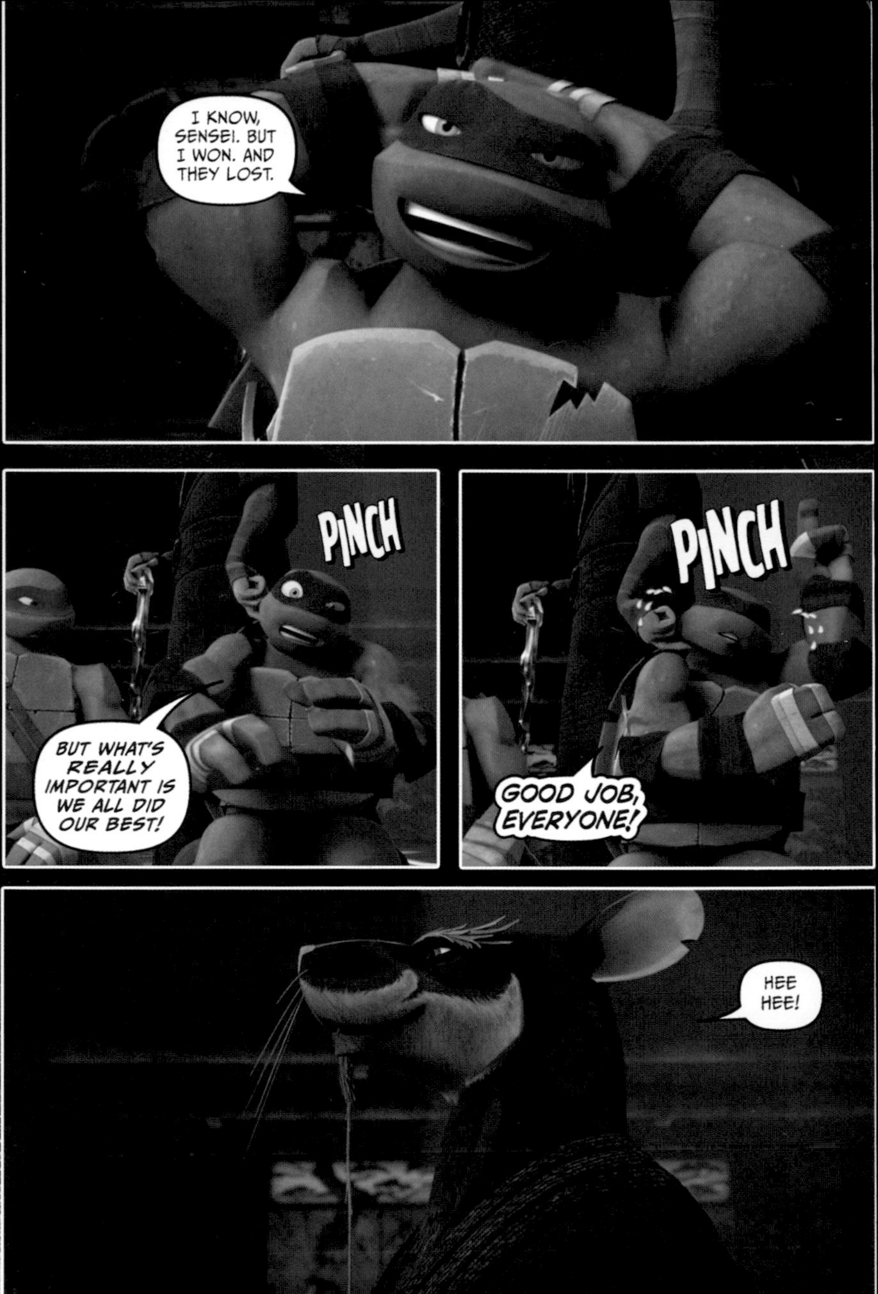
I KNOW, SENSEI. BUT I WON. AND THEY LOST.
PINCH
BUT WHAT'S REALLY IMPORTANT IS WE ALL DID OUR BEST!
PINCH
GOOD JOB, EVERYONE!
HEE HEE!

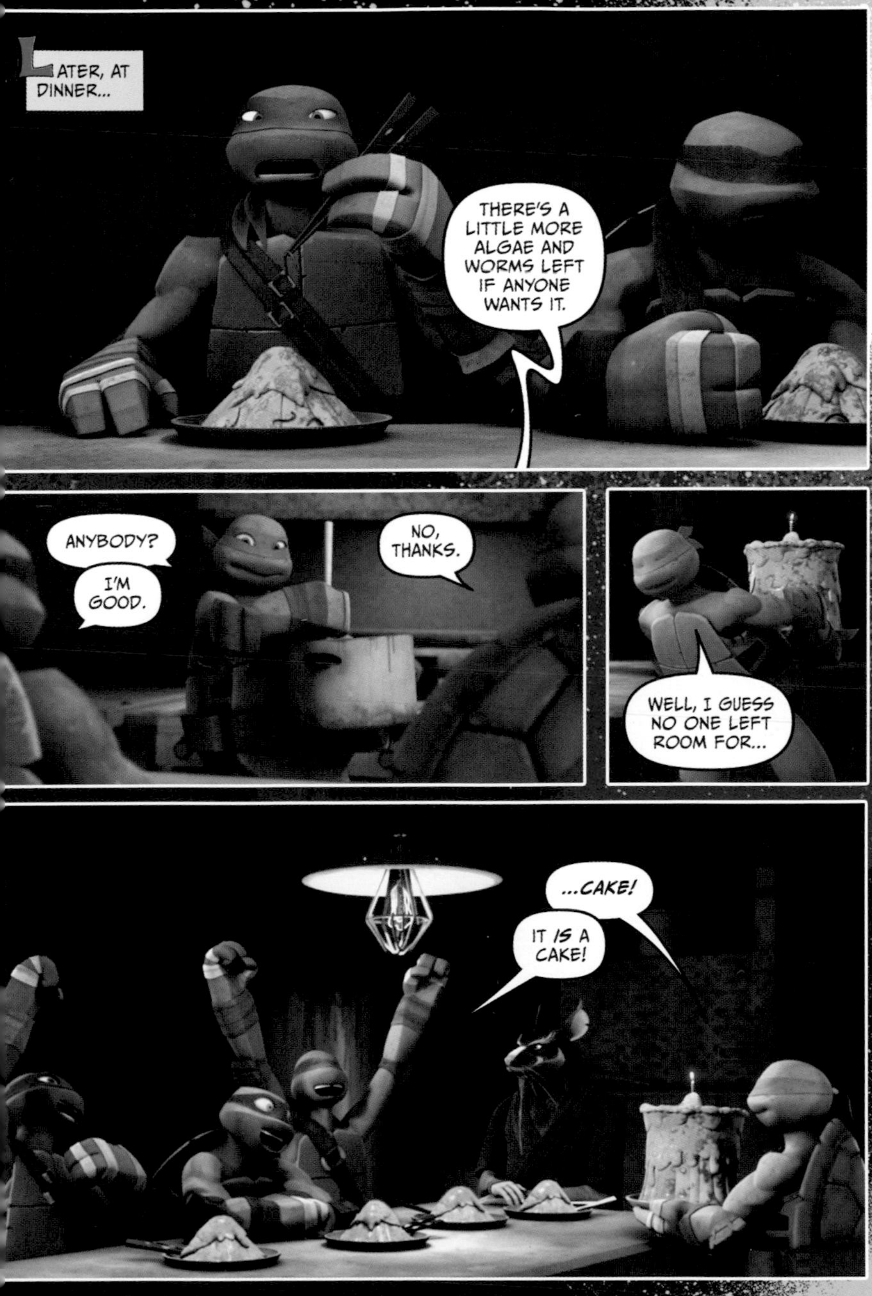
LATER, AT DINNER...
THERE'S A LITTLE MORE ALGAE AND WORMS LEFT IF ANYONE WANTS IT.
ANYBODY?
I'M GOOD.
NO, THANKS.
WELL, I GUESS NO ONE LEFT ROOM FOR...
...CAKE!
IT IS A CAKE!

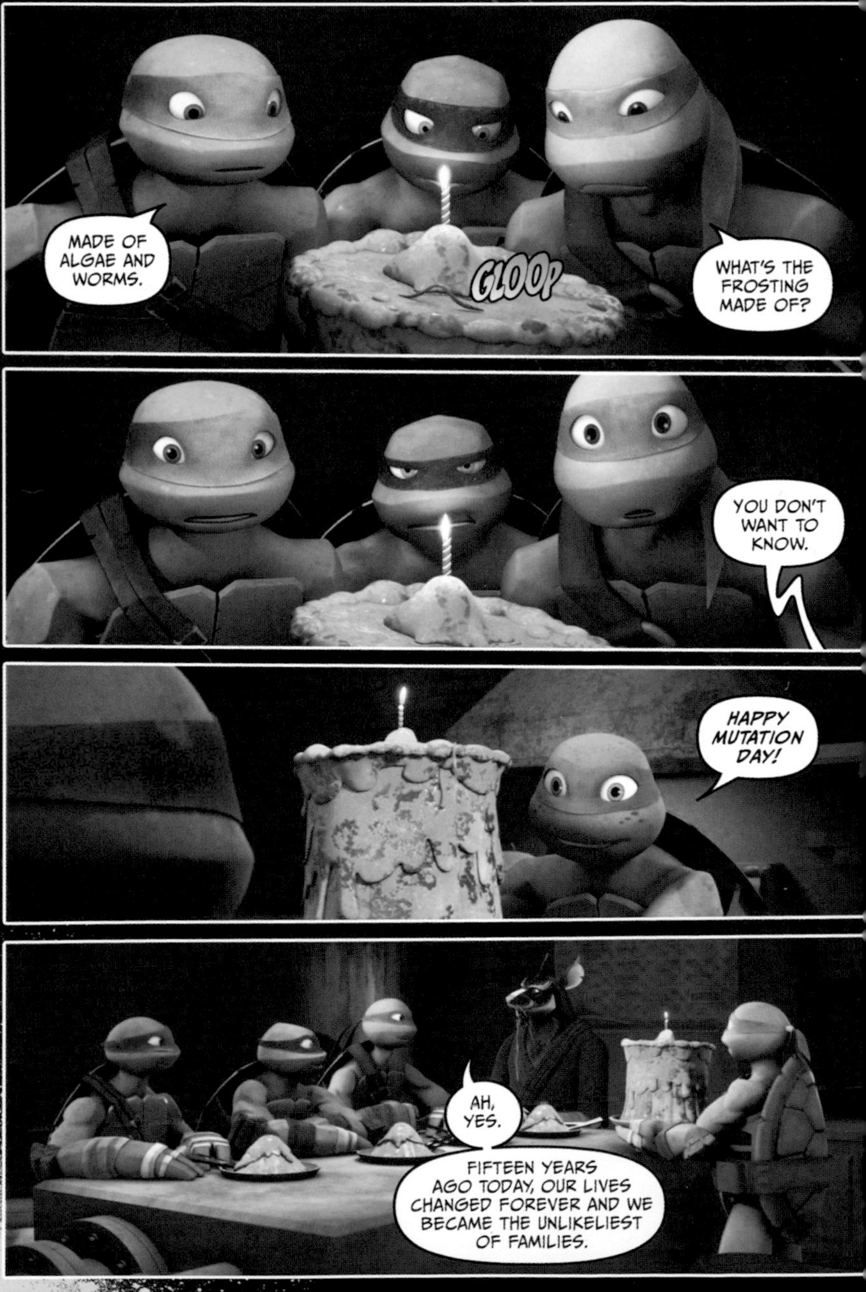
WHAT'S THE FROSTING MADE OF?
GLOOP
MADE OF ALGAE AND WORMS.
YOU DON'T WANT TO KNOW.
HAPPY MUTATION DAY!
AH, YES.
FIFTEEN YEARS AGO TODAY, OUR LIVES CHANGED FOREVER AND WE BECAME THE UNLIKELIEST OF FAMILIES.

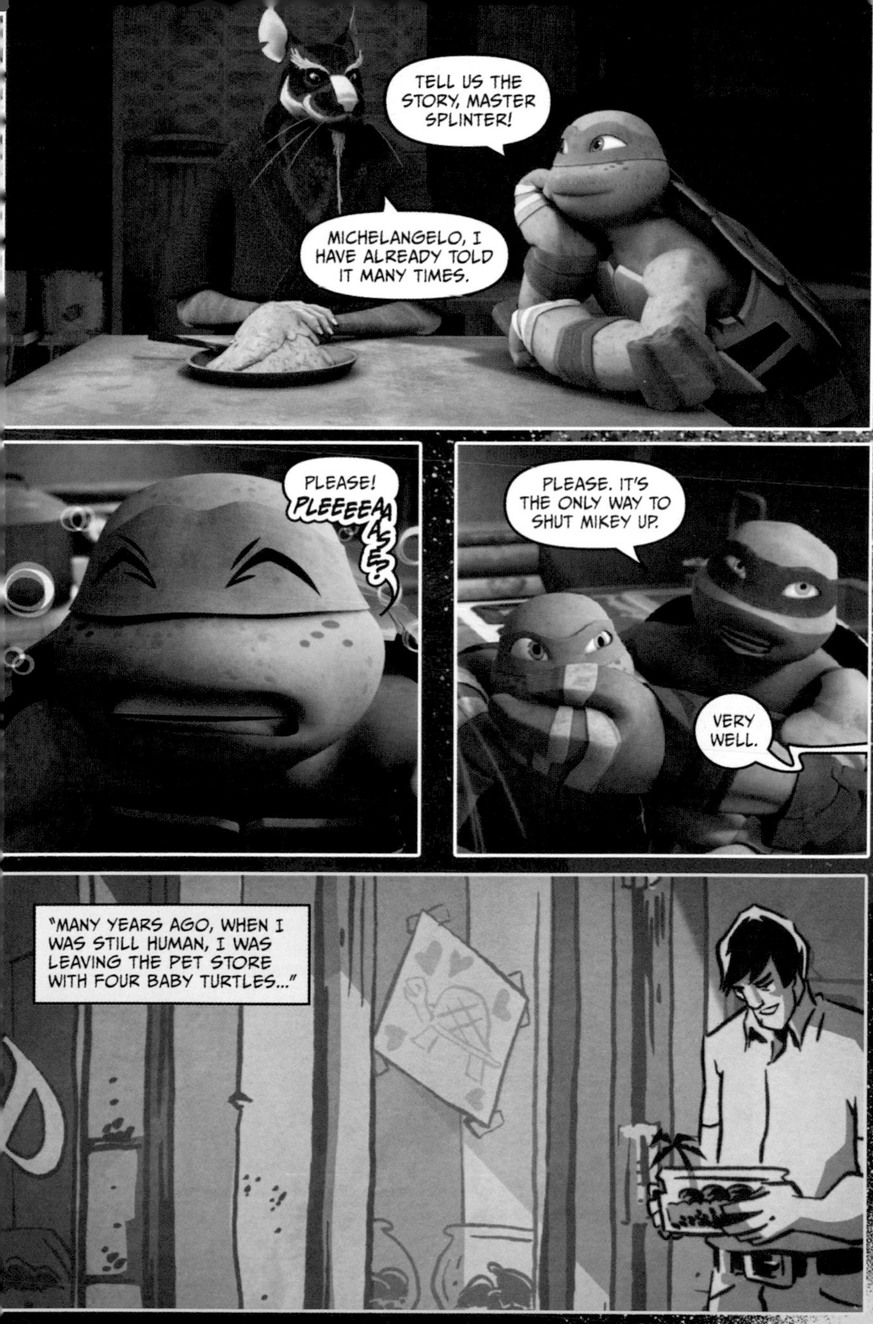
TELL US THE STORY, MASTER SPLINTER!
MICHELANGELO, I HAVE ALREADY TOLD IT MANY TIMES.
PLEASE! PLEEEEEAAASE?
PLEASE. IT'S THE ONLY WAY TO SHUT MIKEY UP.
VERY WELL.
"MANY YEARS AGO, WHEN I WAS STILL HUMAN, I WAS LEAVING THE PET STORE WITH FOUR BABY TURTLES..."

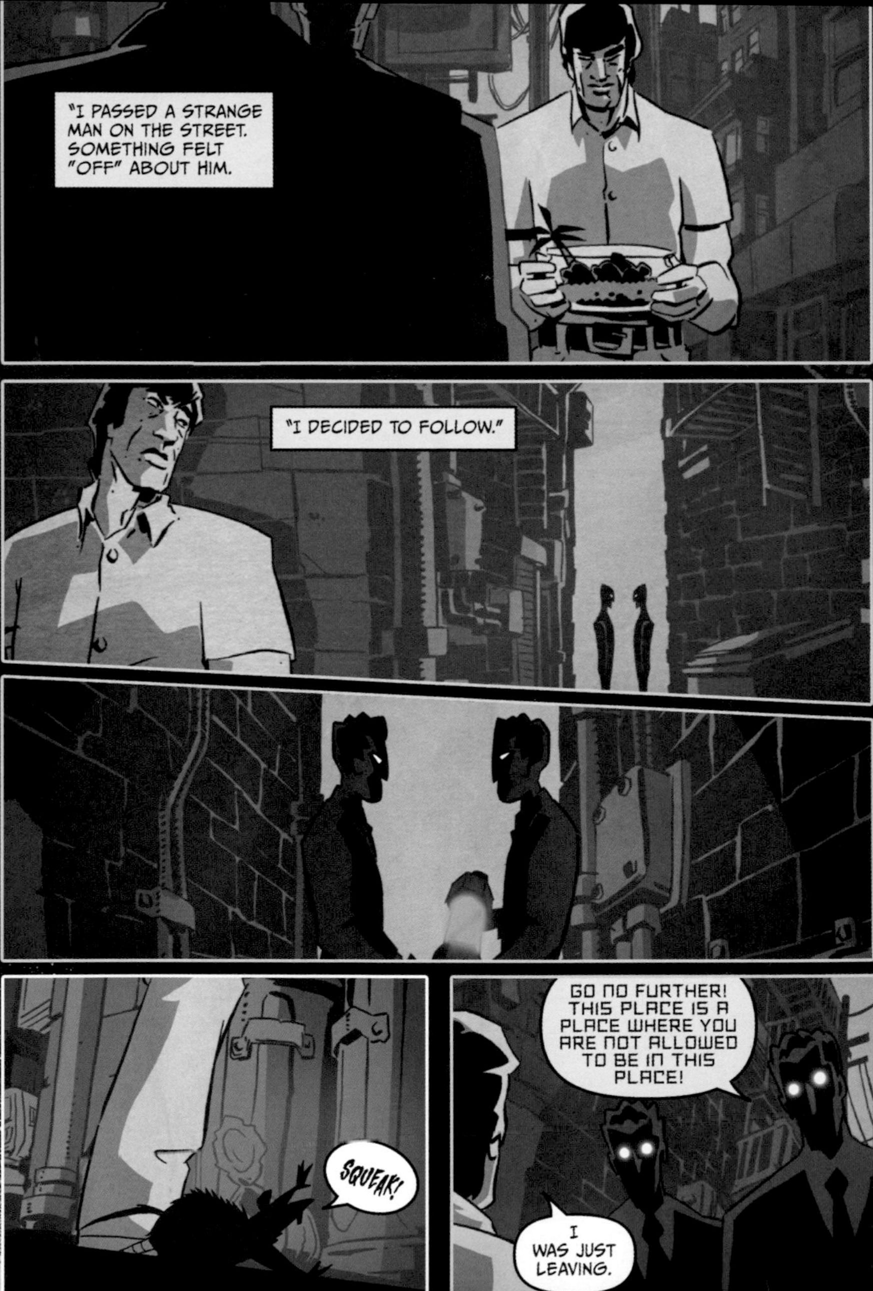
"I PASSED A STRANGE MAN ON THE STREET. SOMETHING FELT "OFF" ABOUT HIM.
"I DECIDED TO FOLLOW."
SQUEAK!
GO NO FURTHER! THIS PLACE IS A PLACE WHERE YOU ARE NOT ALLOWED TO BE IN THIS PLACE!
I WAS JUST LEAVING.

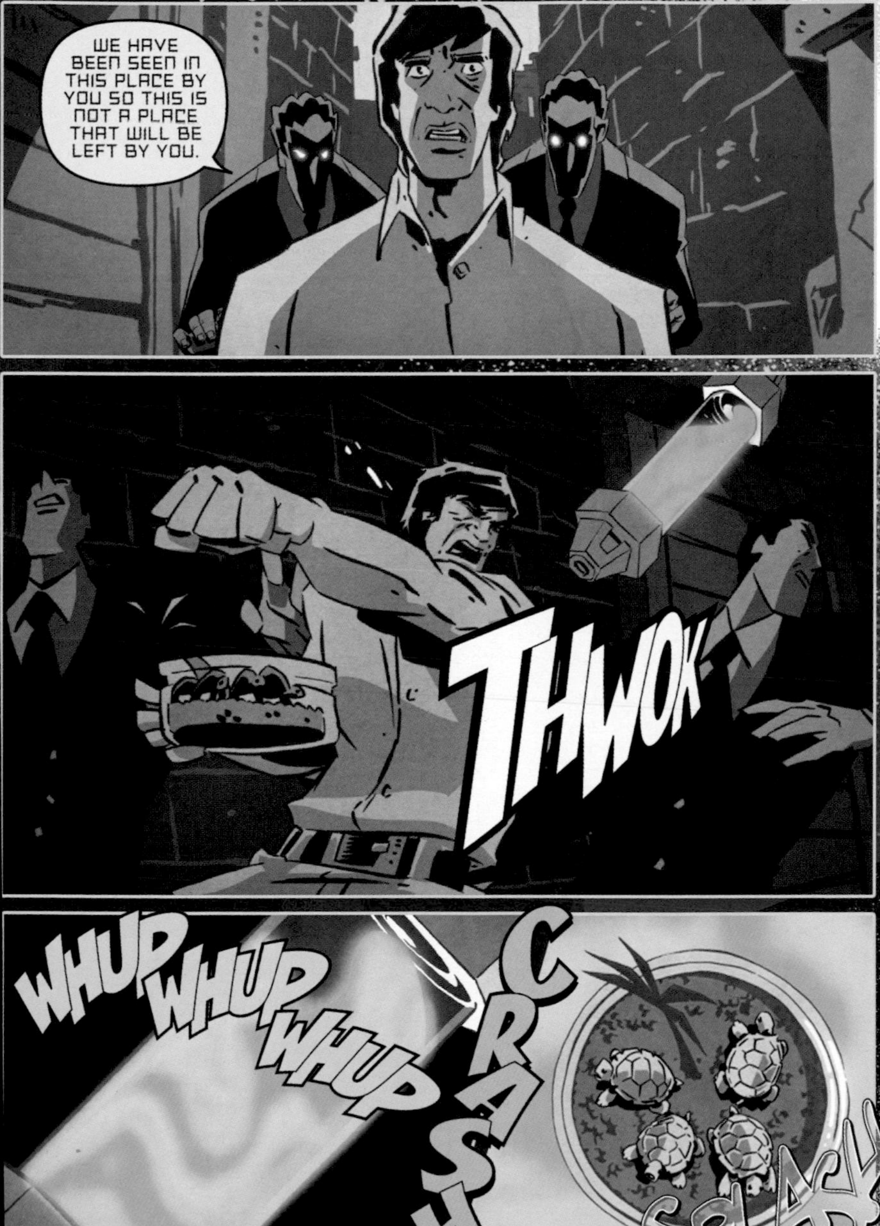

WE HAVE BEEN SEEN IN THIS PLACE BY YOU SO THIS IS NOT A PLACE THAT WILL BE LEFT BY YOU.
THWOK
WHUP WHUP WHUP
CRASH
SPLASH

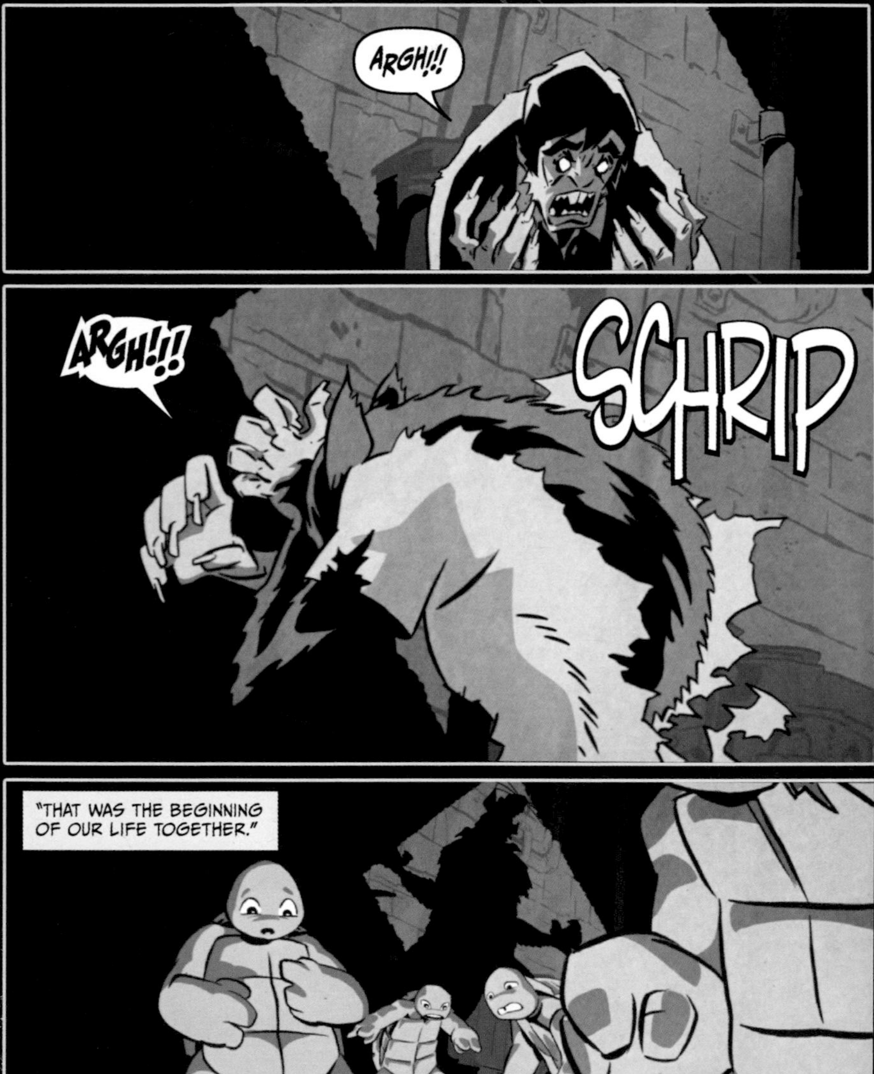
ARGH!!!
ARGH!!!
SCHRIP
"THAT WAS THE BEGINNING OF OUR LIFE TOGETHER."

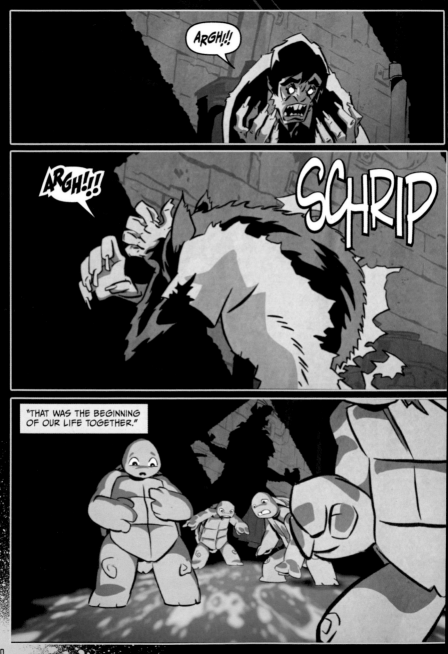

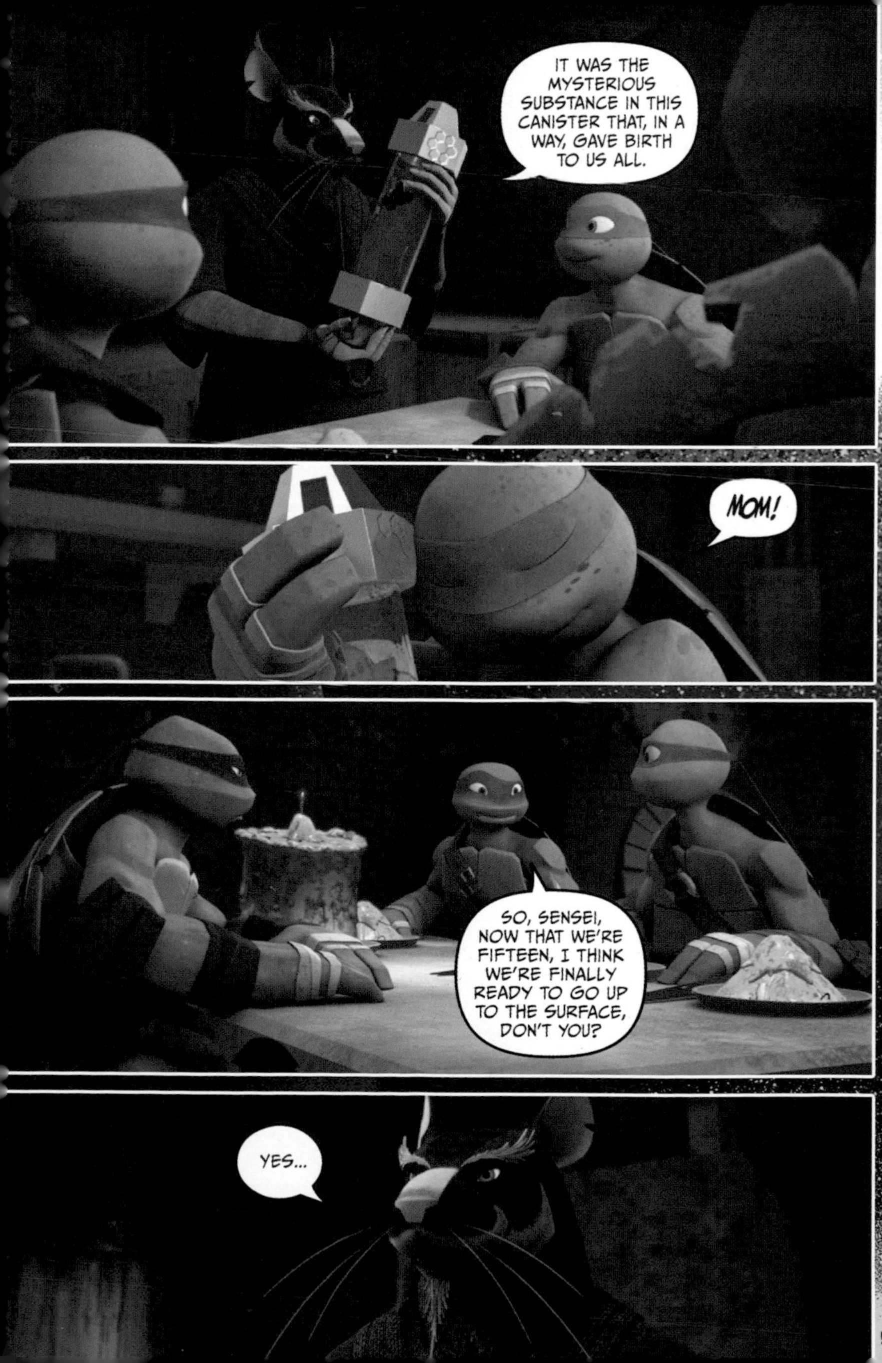
IT WAS THE MYSTERIOUS SUBSTANCE IN THIS CANISTER THAT, IN A WAY, GAVE BIRTH TO US ALL.
MOM!
SO, SENSEI, NOW THAT WE'RE FIFTEEN, I THINK WE'RE FINALLY READY TO GO UP TO THE SURFACE, DON'T YOU?
YES...

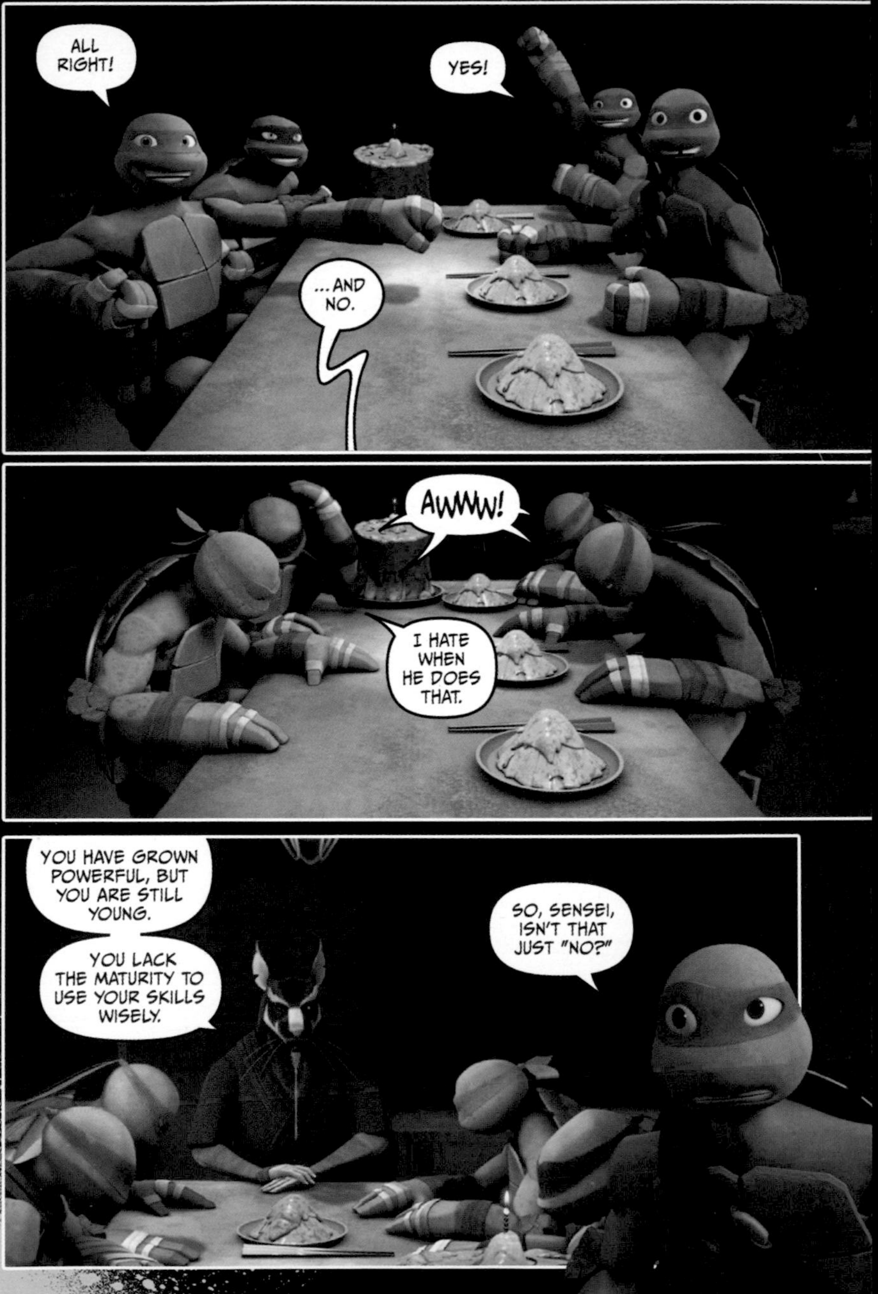
ALL RIGHT!
YES!
...AND NO.
AWWW!
I HATE WHEN HE DOES THAT.
YOU HAVE GROWN POWERFUL, BUT YOU ARE STILL YOUNG.
YOU LACK THE MATURITY TO USE YOUR SKILLS WISELY.
SO, SENSEI, ISN'T THAT JUST "NO?"

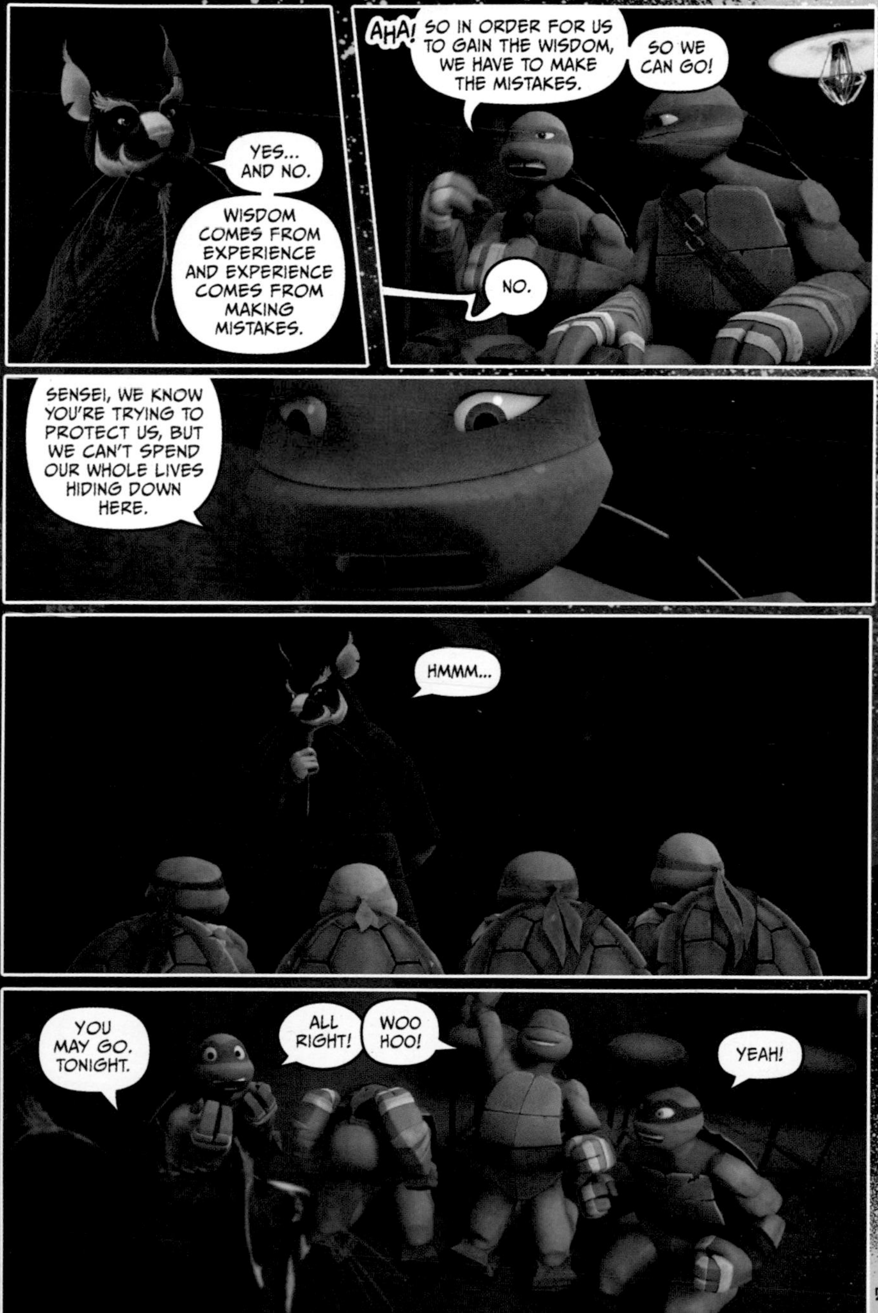
YES... AND NO.
WISDOM COMES FROM EXPERIENCE AND EXPERIENCE COMES FROM MAKING MISTAKES.
AHA!
SO IN ORDER FOR US TO GAIN THE WISDOM, WE HAVE TO MAKE THE MISTAKES.
SO WE CAN GO!
NO.
SENSEI, WE KNOW YOU'RE TRYING TO PROTECT US, BUT WE CAN'T SPEND OUR WHOLE LIVES HIDING DOWN HERE.
HMMM...
YOU MAY GO. TONIGHT.
ALL RIGHT!
WOO HOO!
YEAH!

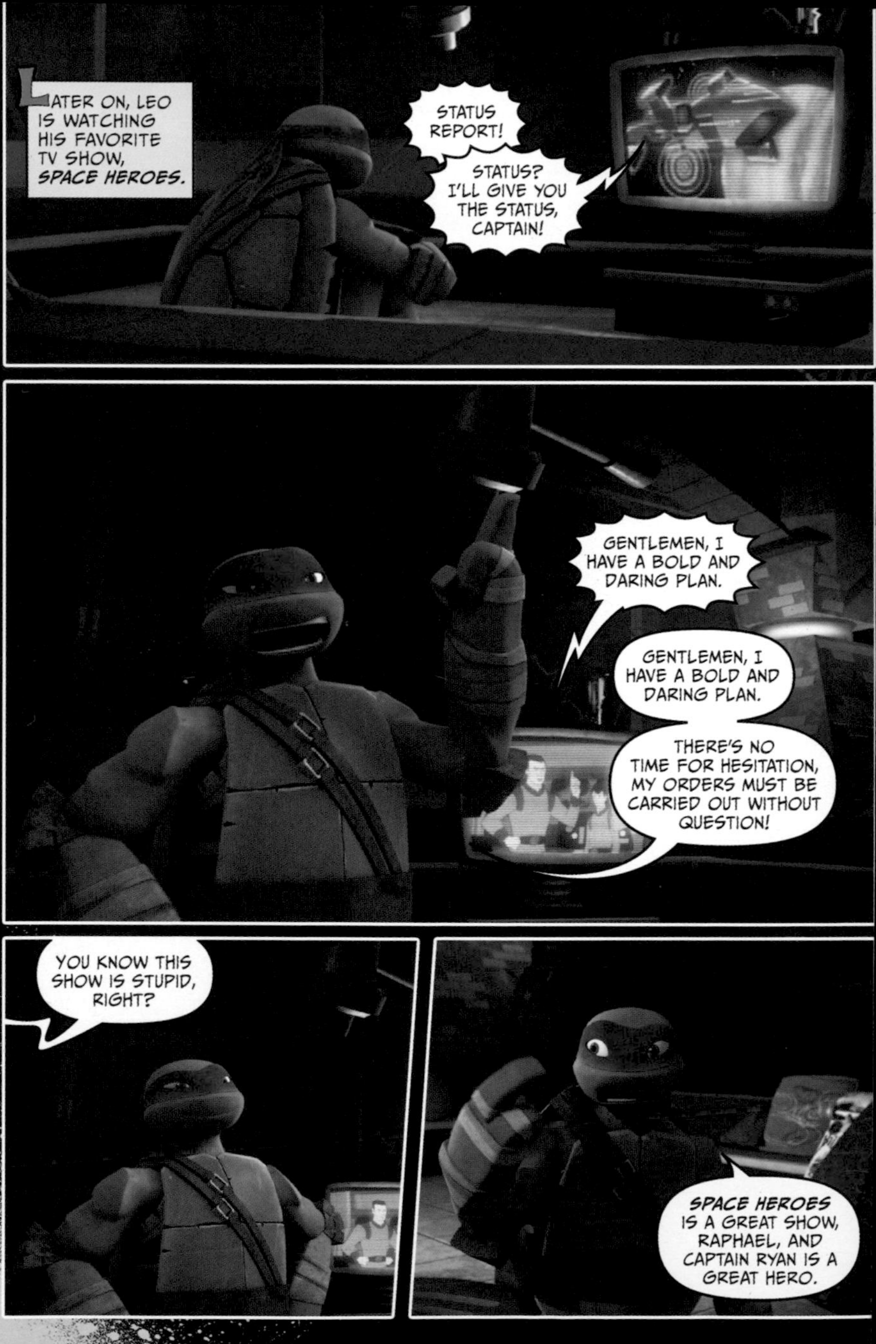
LATER ON, LEO IS WATCHING HIS FAVORITE TV SHOW, *SPACE HEROES.*
STATUS REPORT!
STATUS? I'LL GIVE YOU THE STATUS, CAPTAIN!
GENTLEMEN, I HAVE A BOLD AND DARING PLAN.
GENTLEMEN, I HAVE A BOLD AND DARING PLAN.
THERE'S NO TIME FOR HESITATION, MY ORDERS MUST BE CARRIED OUT WITHOUT QUESTION!
YOU KNOW THIS SHOW IS STUPID, RIGHT?
SPACE HEROES IS A GREAT SHOW, RAPHAEL, AND CAPTAIN RYAN IS A GREAT HERO.

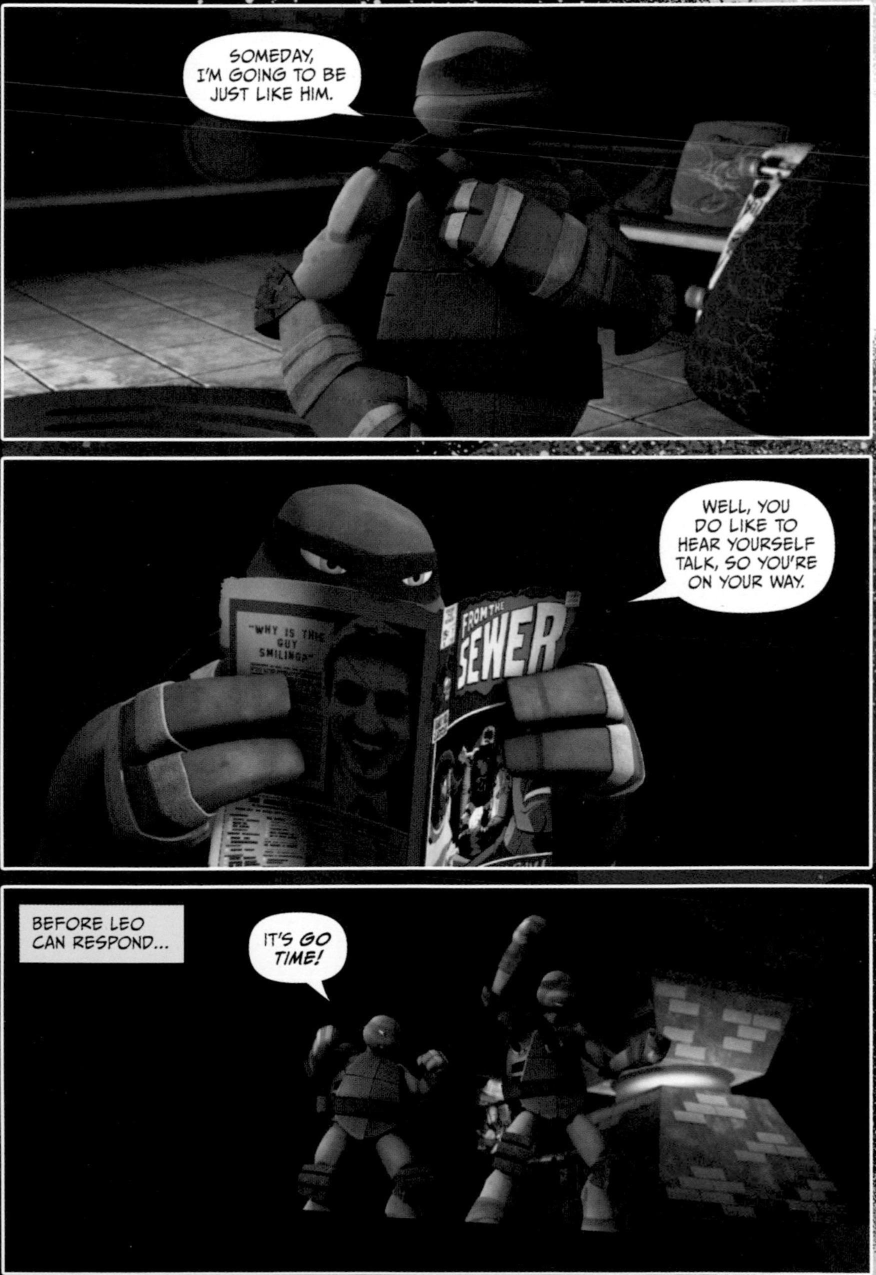
SOMEDAY, I'M GOING TO BE JUST LIKE HIM.
"WHY IS THIS GUY SMILING?"
FROM THE SEWER
WELL, YOU DO LIKE TO HEAR YOURSELF TALK, SO YOU'RE ON YOUR WAY.
BEFORE LEO CAN RESPOND...
IT'S GO TIME!

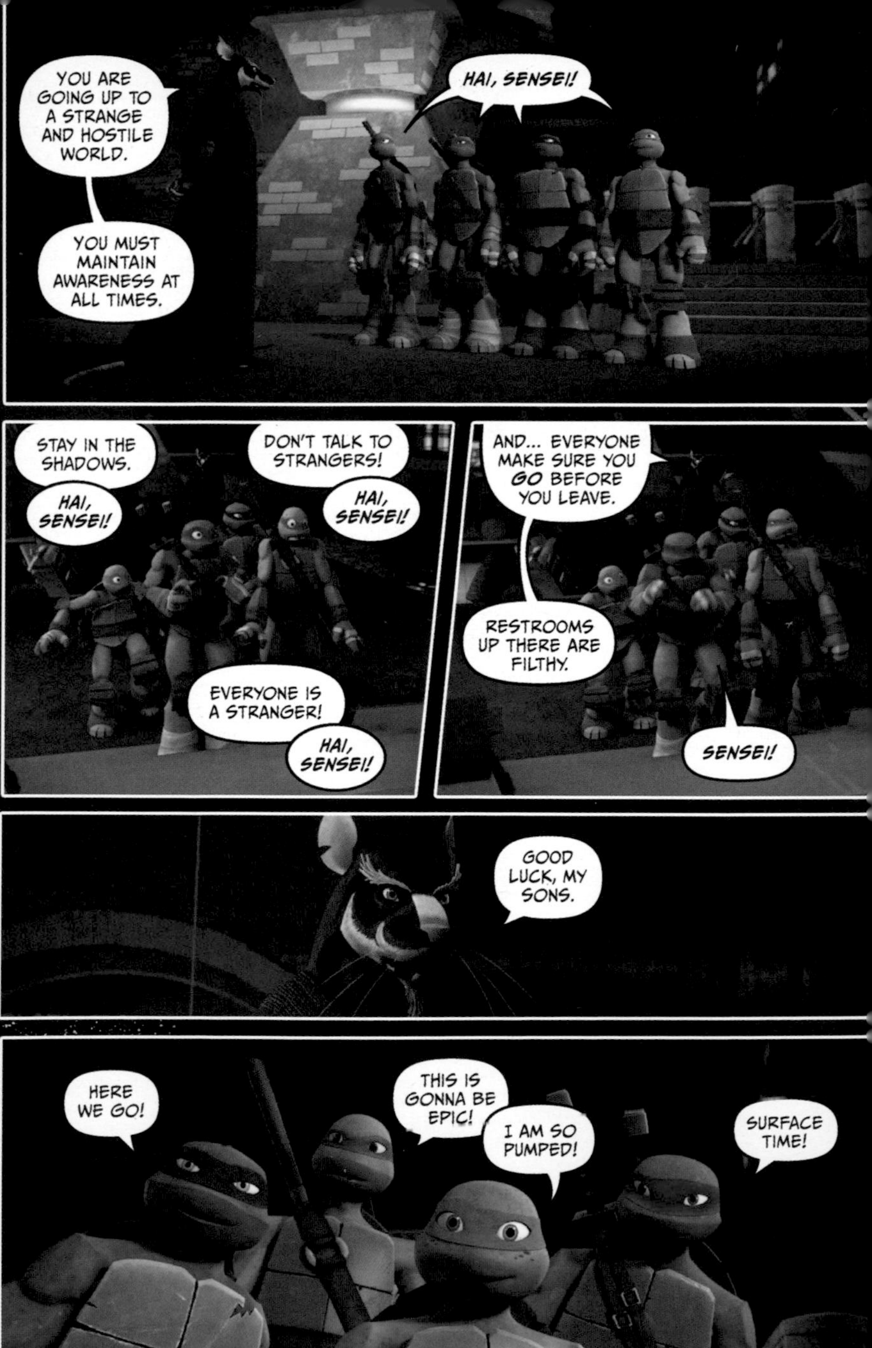
YOU ARE GOING UP TO A STRANGE AND HOSTILE WORLD.
YOU MUST MAINTAIN AWARENESS AT ALL TIMES.
HAI, SENSEI!
STAY IN THE SHADOWS.
HAI, SENSEI!
DON'T TALK TO STRANGERS!
HAI, SENSEI!
EVERYONE IS A STRANGER!
HAI, SENSEI!
AND... EVERYONE MAKE SURE YOU *GO* BEFORE YOU LEAVE.
RESTROOMS UP THERE ARE FILTHY.
SENSEI!
GOOD LUCK, MY SONS.
HERE WE GO!
THIS IS GONNA BE EPIC!
I AM SO PUMPED!
SURFACE TIME!

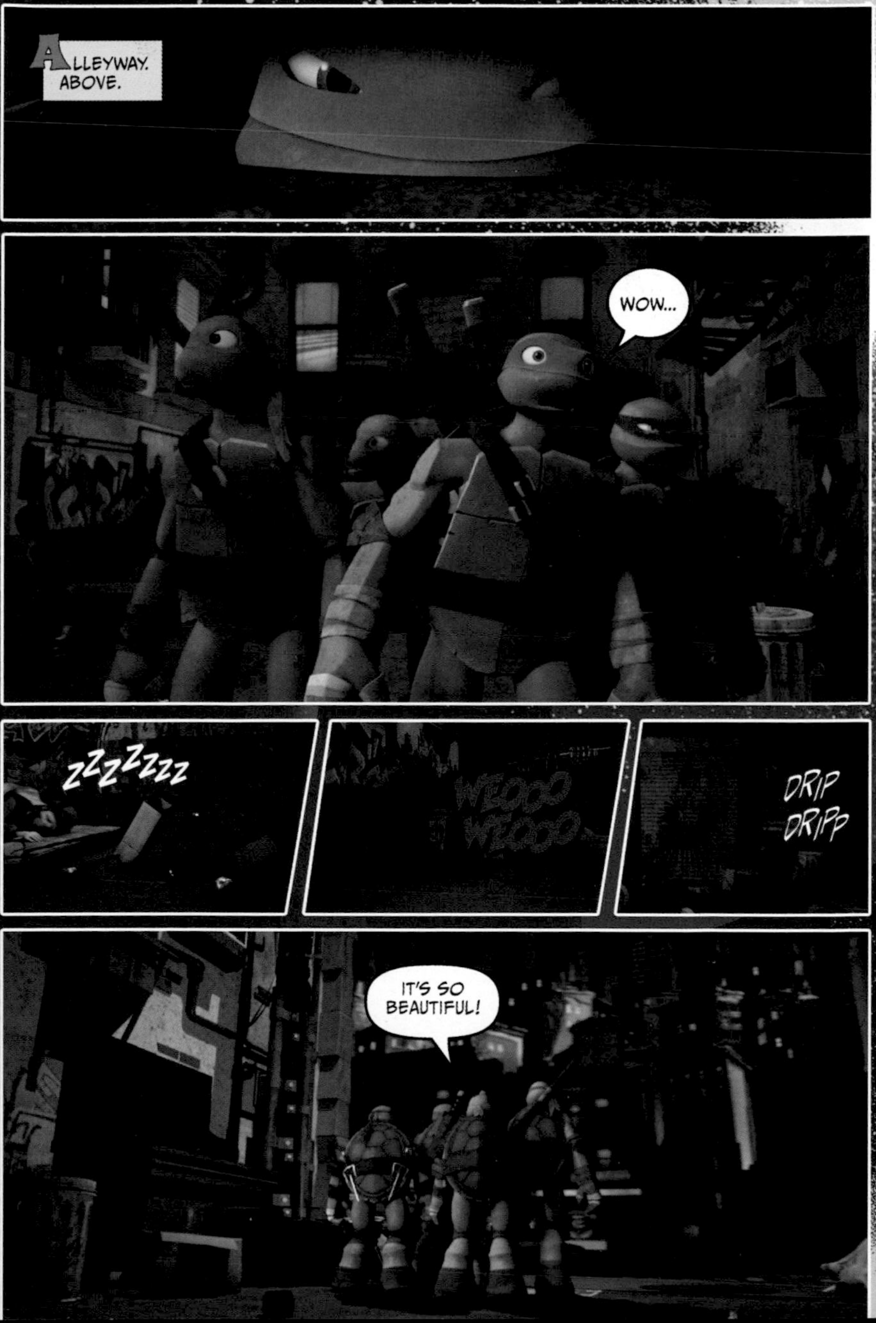
ALLEYWAY. ABOVE.
WOW...
ZZZZZZZ
WEOOO
WEOOO
DRIP
DRIPP
IT'S SO BEAUTIFUL!

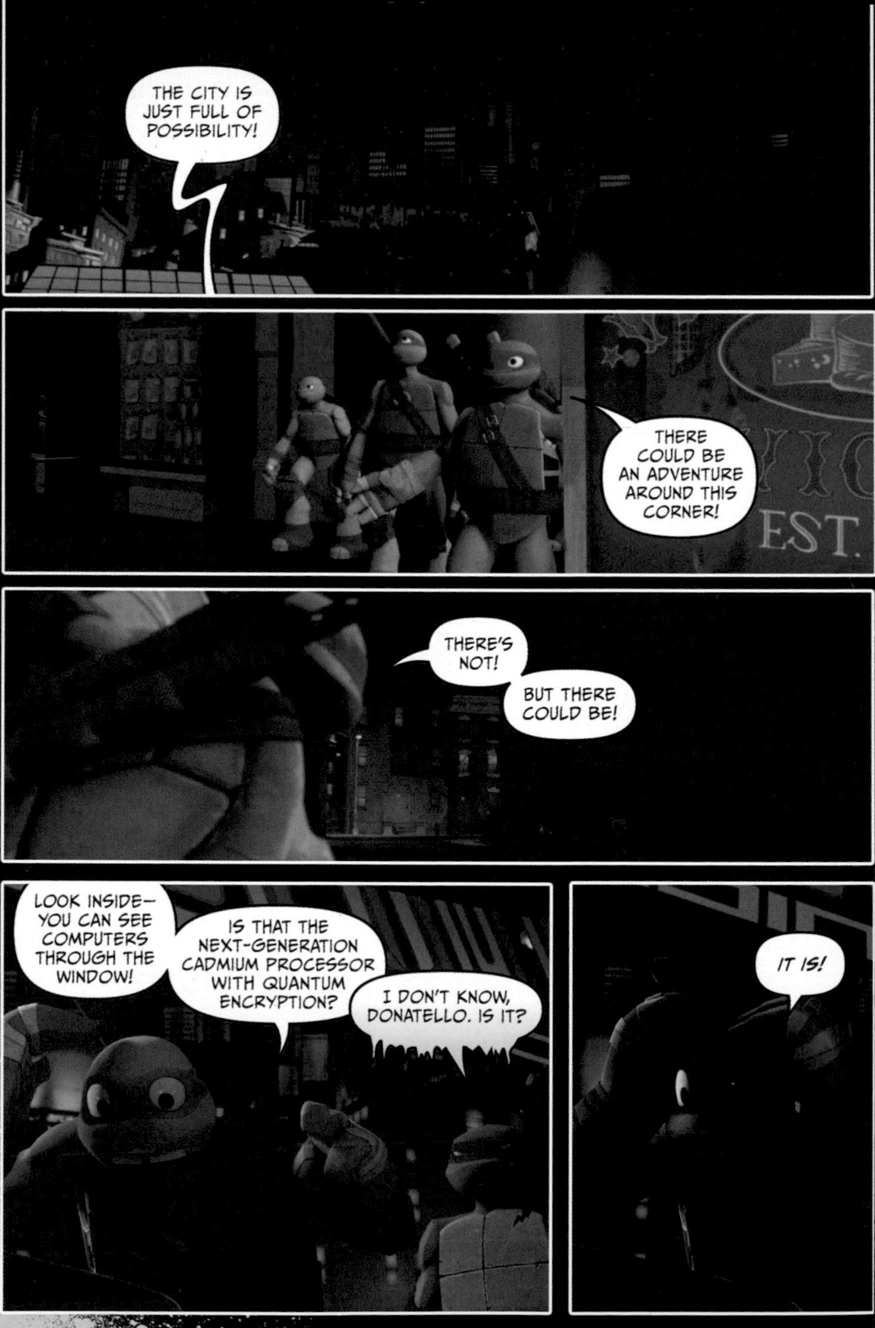
THE CITY IS JUST FULL OF POSSIBILITY!
THERE COULD BE AN ADVENTURE AROUND THIS CORNER!
EST.
THERE'S NOT!
BUT THERE COULD BE!
LOOK INSIDE—YOU CAN SEE COMPUTERS THROUGH THE WINDOW!
IS THAT THE NEXT-GENERATION CADMIUM PROCESSOR WITH QUANTUM ENCRYPTION?
I DON'T KNOW, DONATELLO. IS IT?
IT IS!

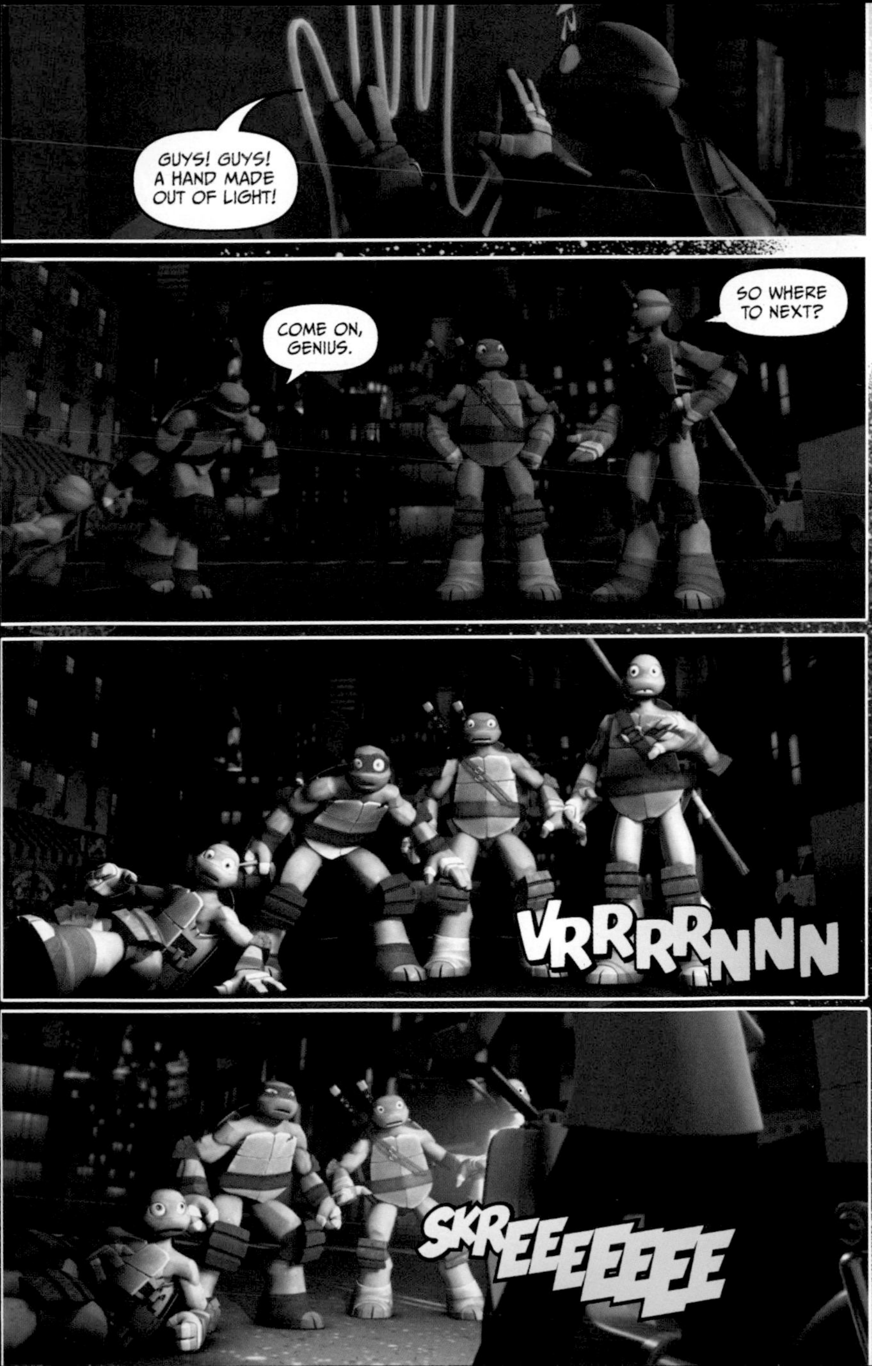
GUYS! GUYS! A HAND MADE OUT OF LIGHT!
COME ON, GENIUS.
SO WHERE TO NEXT?
VRRRRNNN
SKREEEEEEE

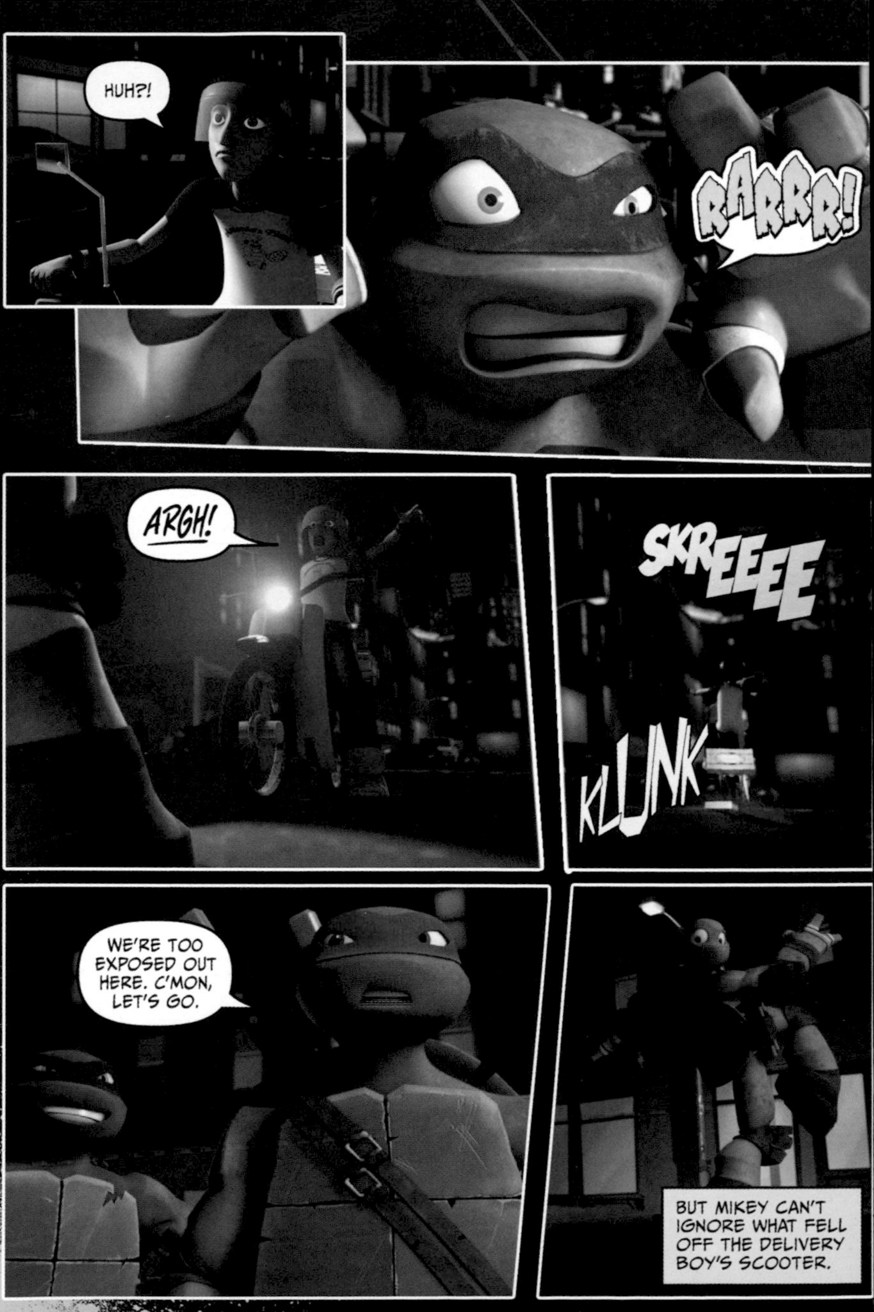

HUH?!
RARRR!
ARGH!
SKREEEE
KLUNK
WE'RE TOO EXPOSED OUT HERE. C'MON, LET'S GO.
BUT MIKEY CAN'T IGNORE WHAT FELL OFF THE DELIVERY BOY'S SCOOTER.

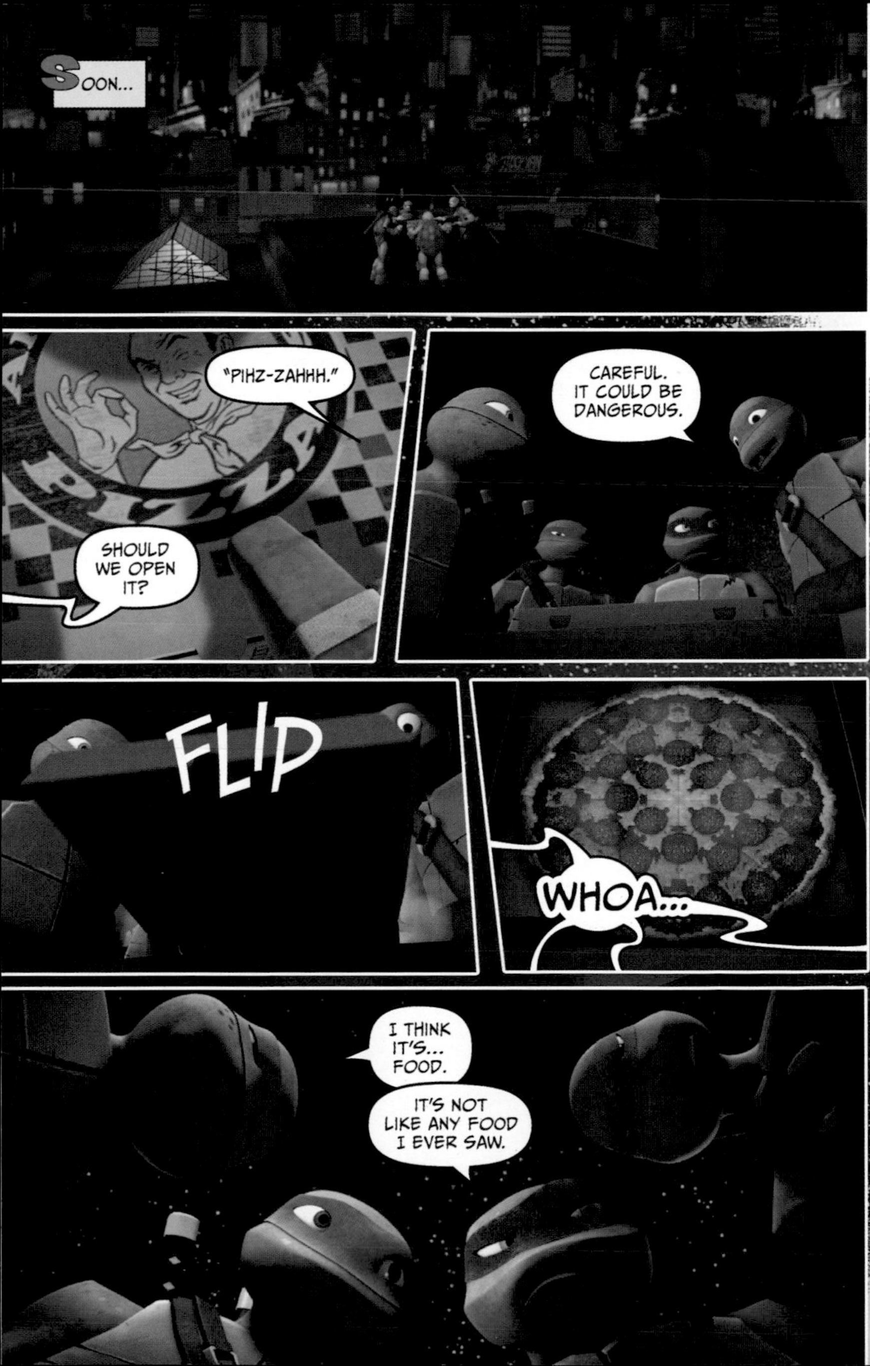
SOON...
"PIHZ-ZAHHH."
SHOULD WE OPEN IT?
CAREFUL. IT COULD BE DANGEROUS.
FLIP
WHOA...
I THINK IT'S... FOOD.
IT'S NOT LIKE ANY FOOD I EVER SAW.

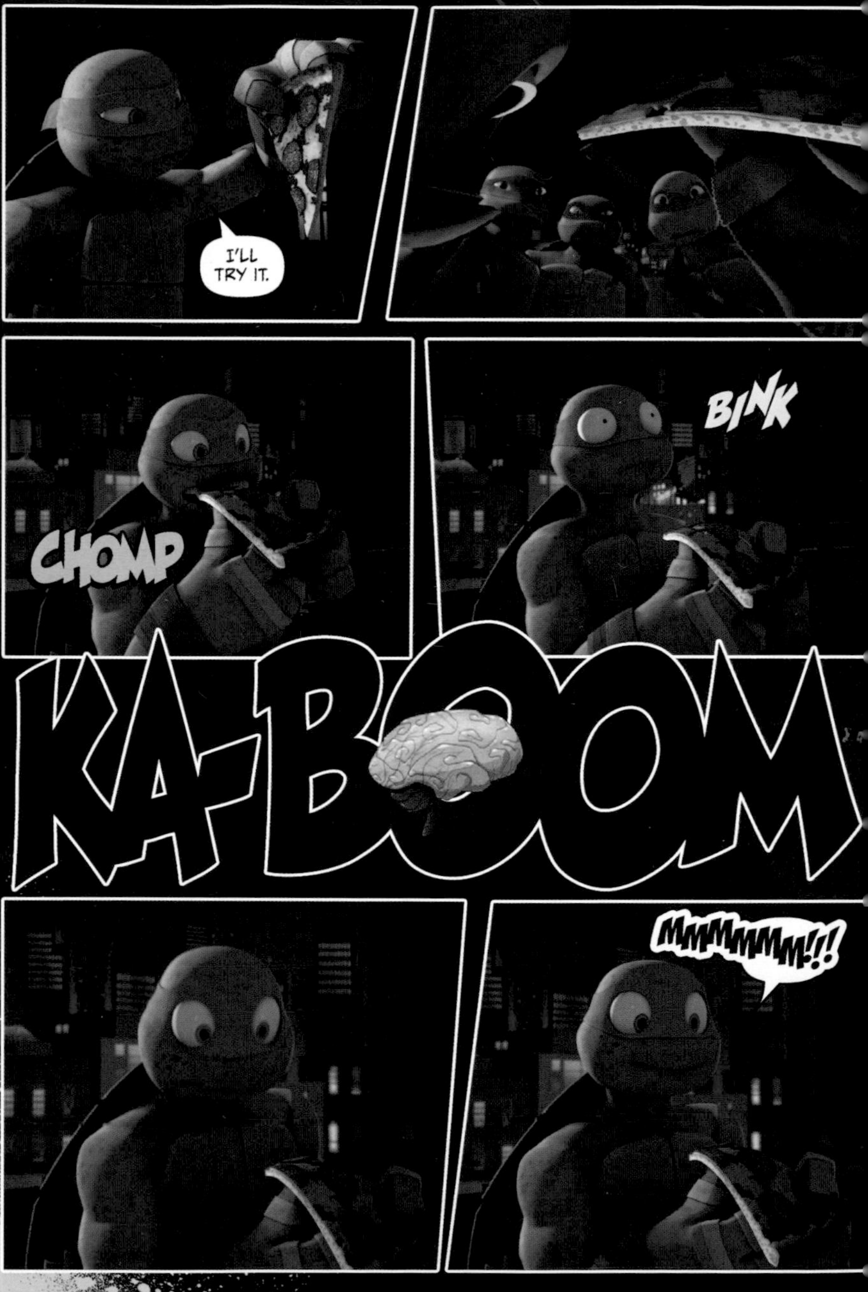
I'LL TRY IT.
CHOMP
BINK
KA-BOOM
MMMMMMM!?!

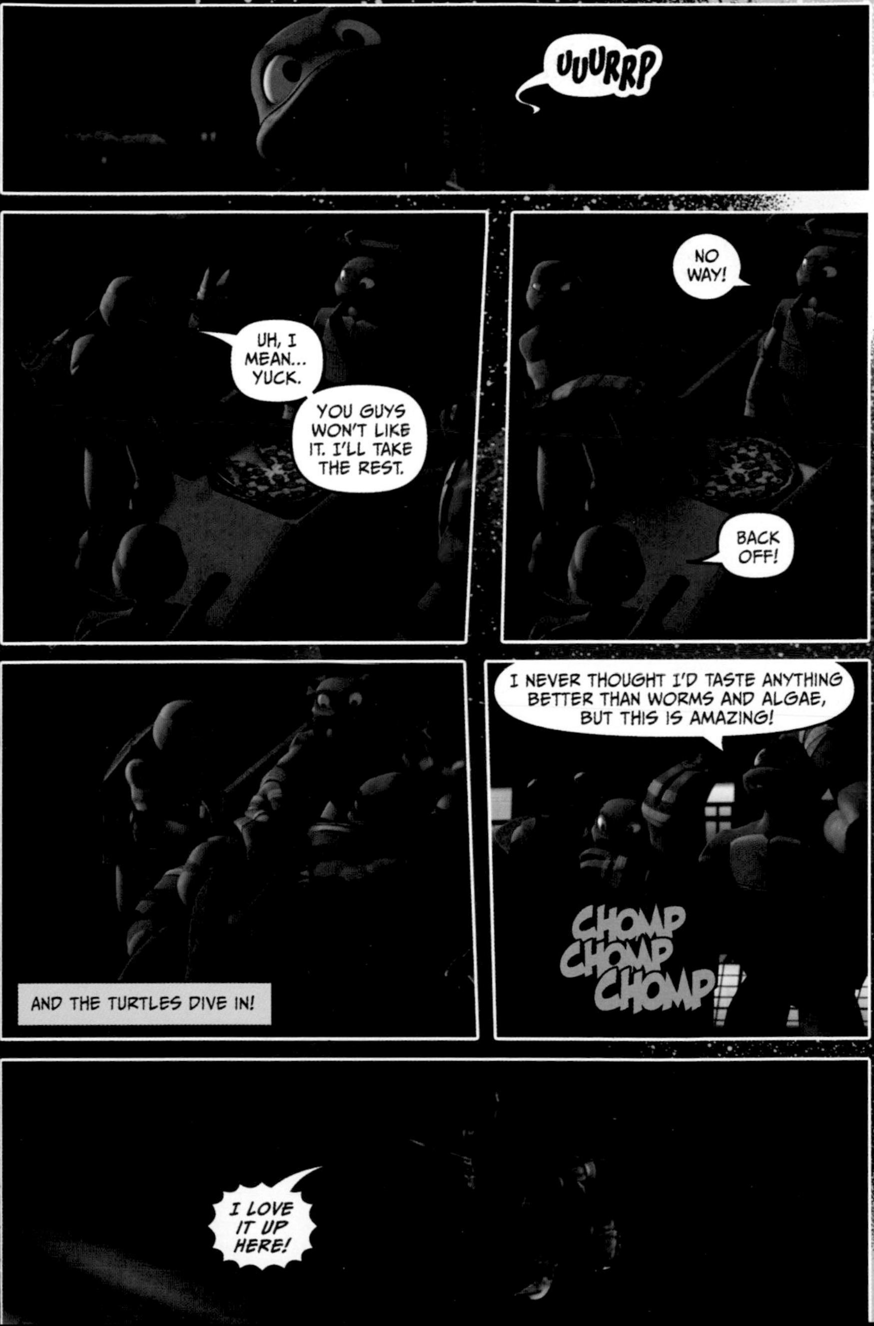
UUURRP
UH, I MEAN... YUCK.
YOU GUYS WON'T LIKE IT. I'LL TAKE THE REST.
NO WAY!
BACK OFF!
AND THE TURTLES DIVE IN!
I NEVER THOUGHT I'D TASTE ANYTHING BETTER THAN WORMS AND ALGAE, BUT THIS IS AMAZING!
CHOMP CHOMP CHOMP
I LOVE IT UP HERE!

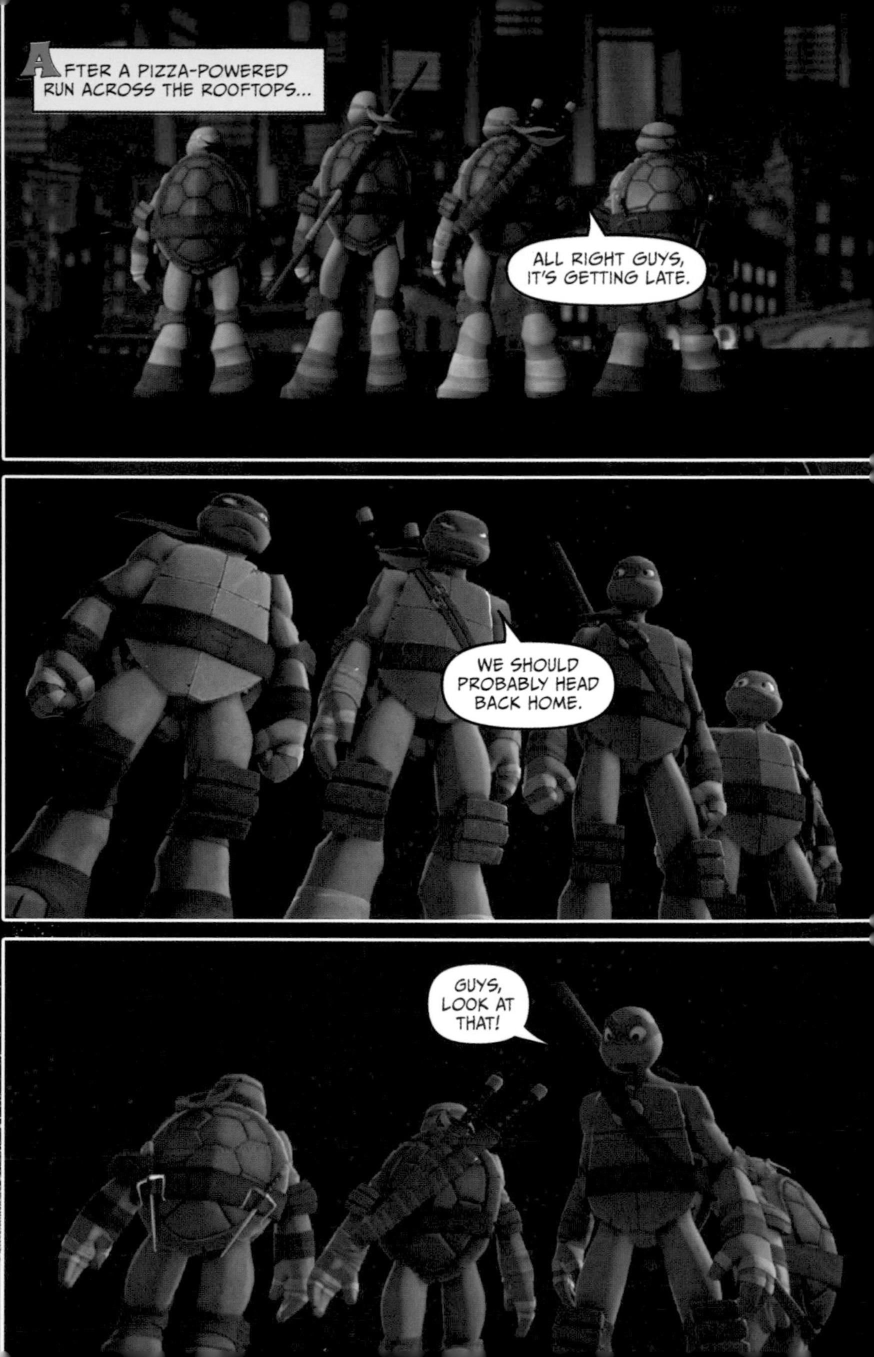
AFTER A PIZZA-POWERED RUN ACROSS THE ROOFTOPS...
ALL RIGHT GUYS, IT'S GETTING LATE.
WE SHOULD PROBABLY HEAD BACK HOME.
GUYS, LOOK AT THAT!

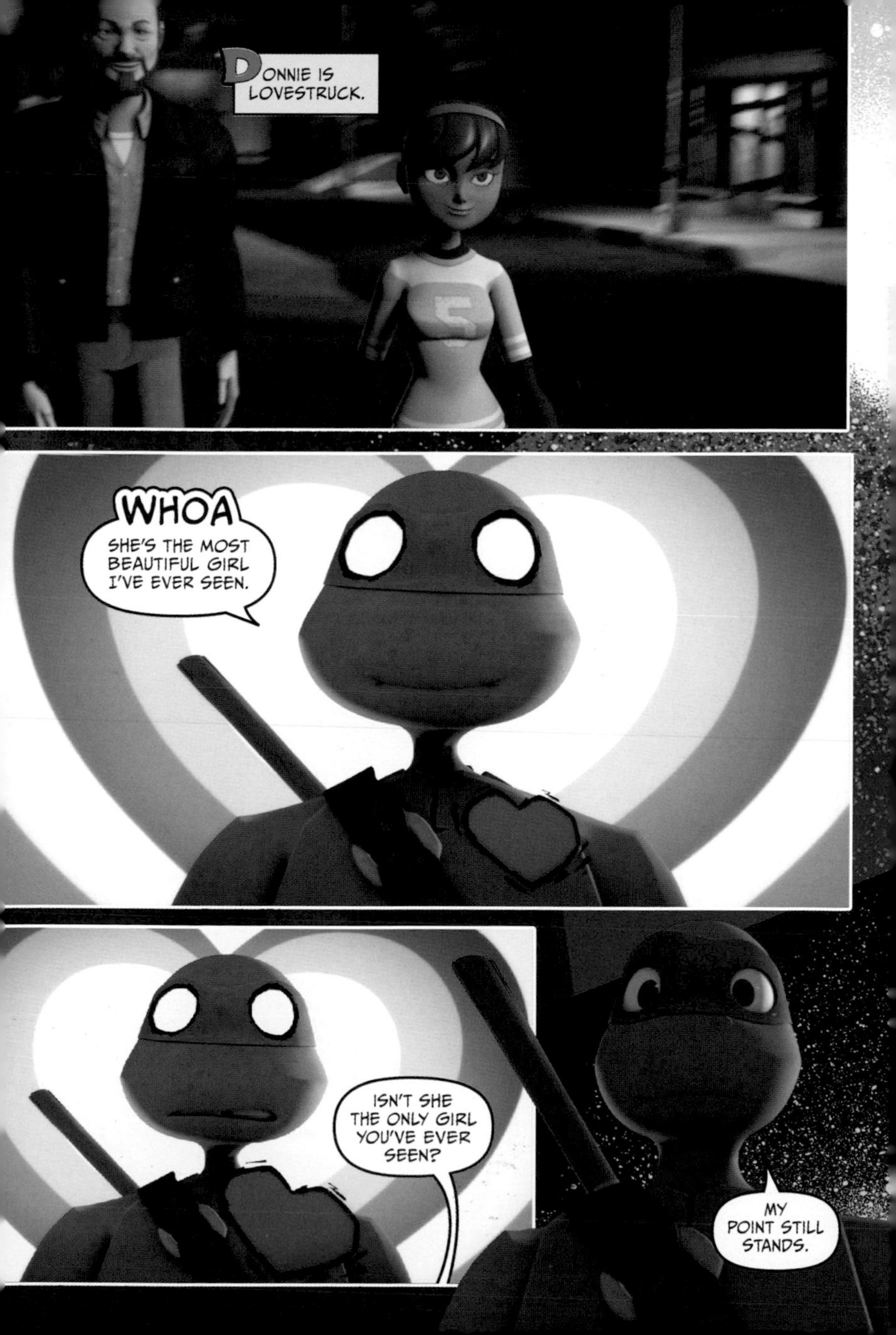
DONNIE IS LOVESTRUCK.
WHOA
SHE'S THE MOST BEAUTIFUL GIRL I'VE EVER SEEN.
ISN'T SHE THE ONLY GIRL YOU'VE EVER SEEN?
MY POINT STILL STANDS.

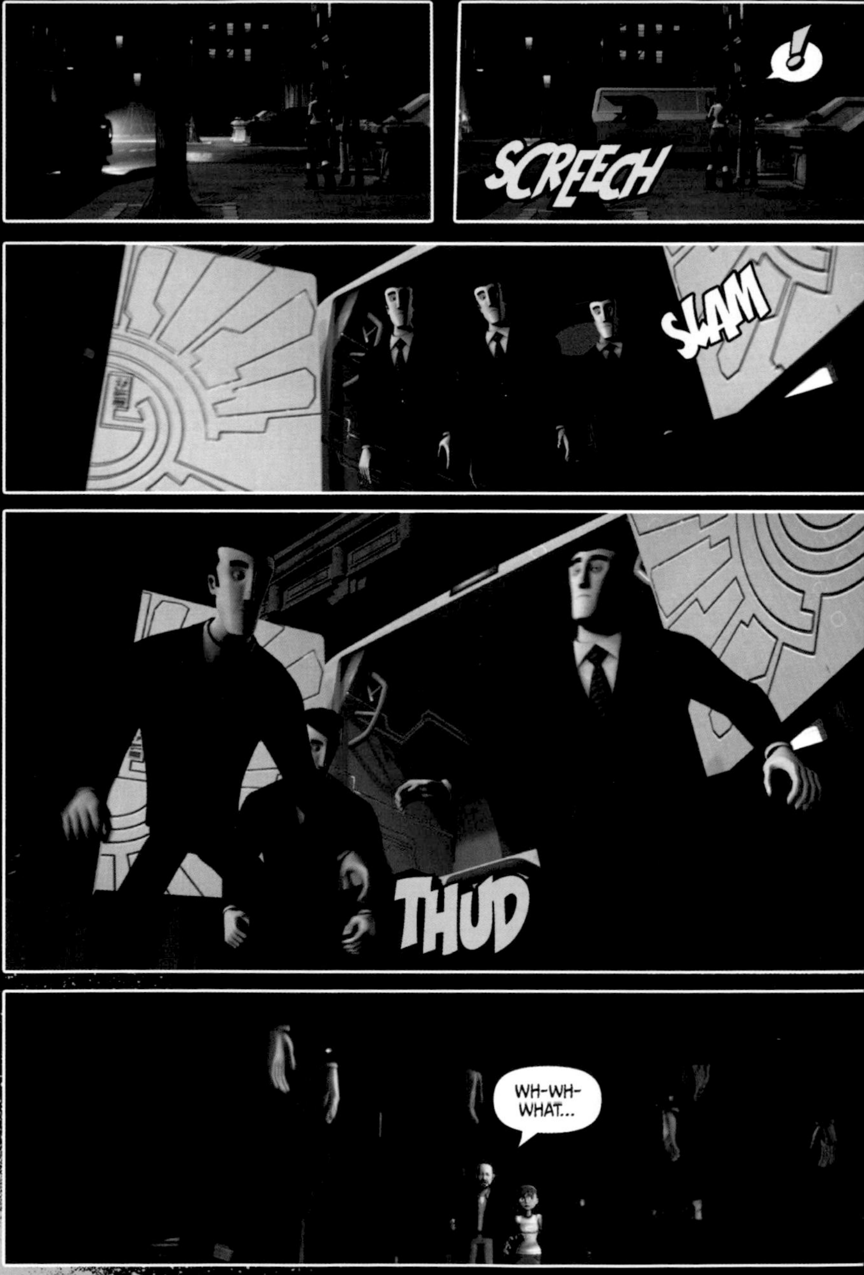
!
SCREECH
SLAM
THUD
WH-WH-
WHAT...

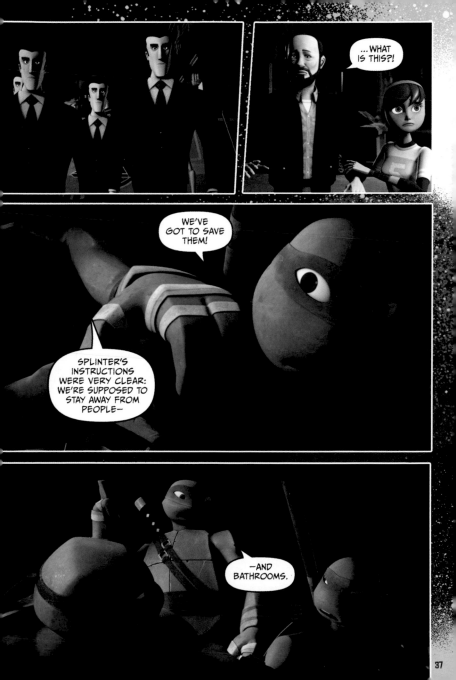

... WHAT IS THIS?!

WE'VE GOT TO SAVE THEM!

SPLINTER'S INSTRUCTIONS WERE VERY CLEAR: WE'RE SUPPOSED TO STAY AWAY FROM PEOPLE—

—AND BATHROOMS.

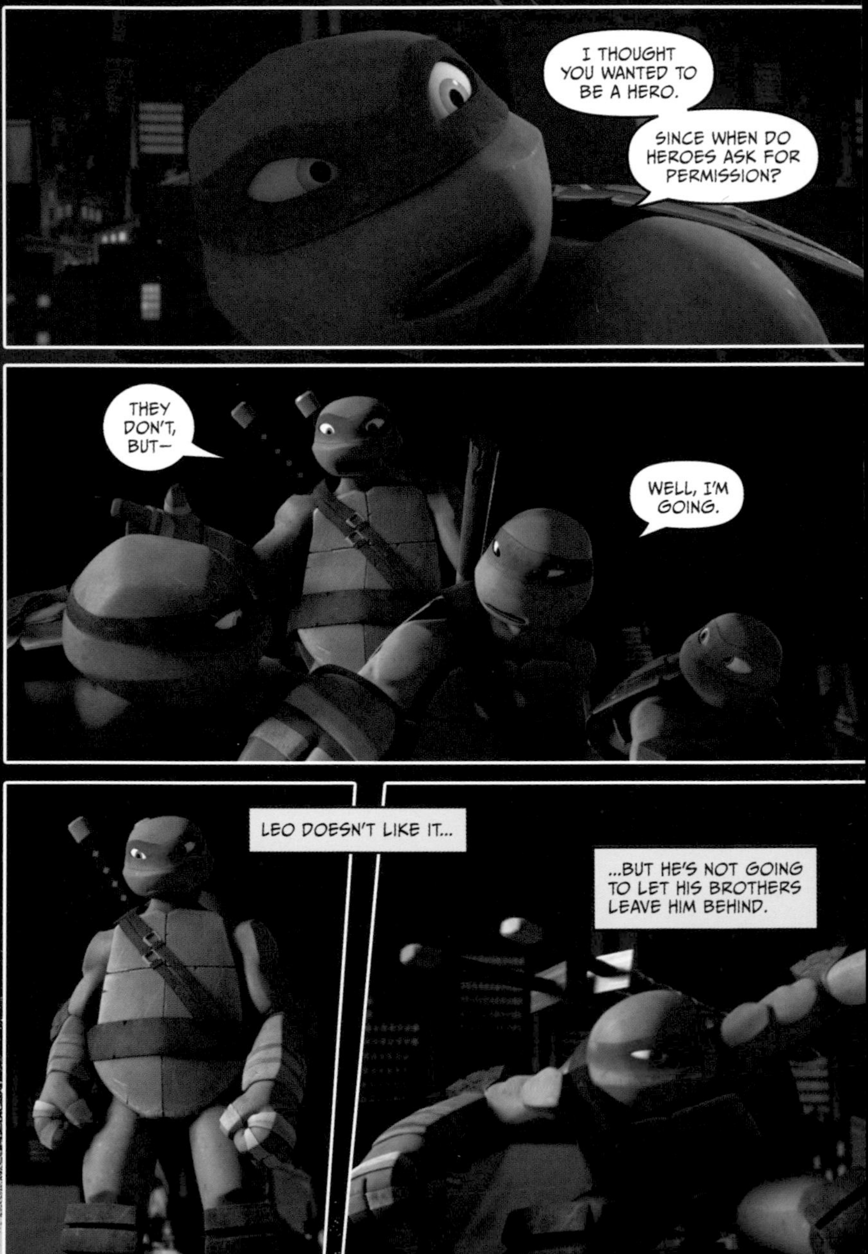
I THOUGHT YOU WANTED TO BE A HERO.
SINCE WHEN DO HEROES ASK FOR PERMISSION?
THEY DON'T, BUT—
WELL, I'M GOING.
LEO DOESN'T LIKE IT...
...BUT HE'S NOT GOING TO LET HIS BROTHERS LEAVE HIM BEHIND.

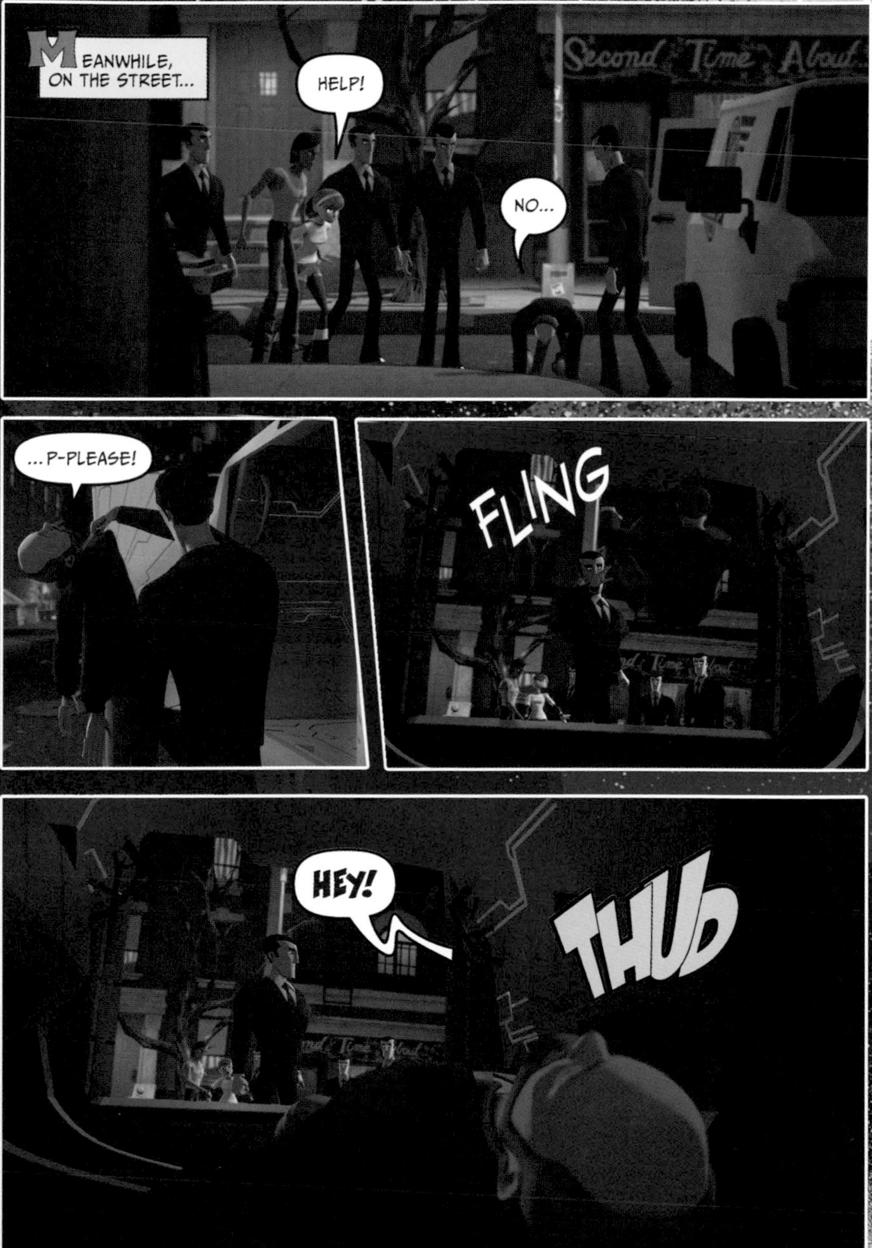
MEANWHILE, ON THE STREET...
Second Time Abou
HELP!
NO...
...P-PLEASE!
FLING
HEY!
THUD

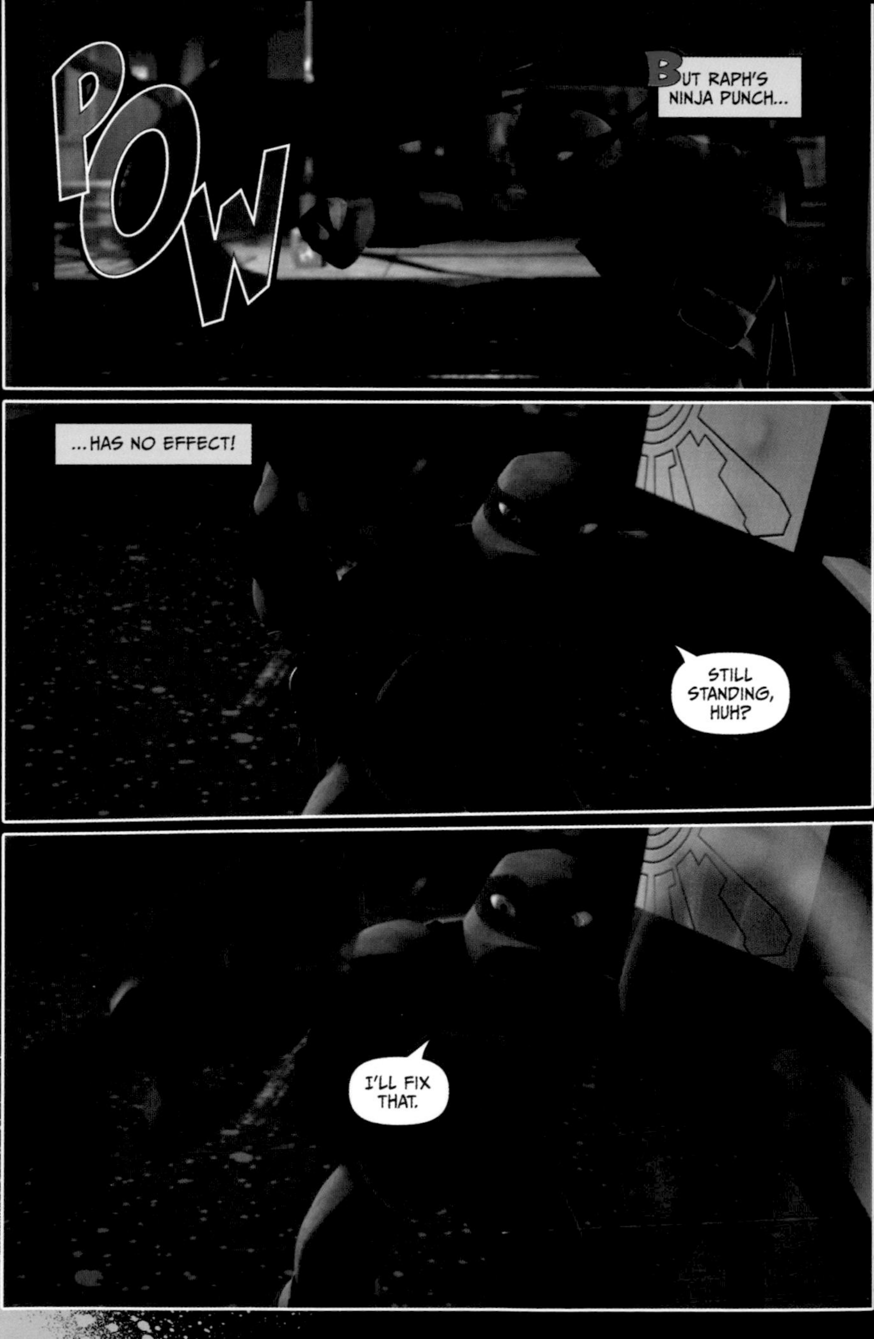
POW
BUT RAPH'S NINJA PUNCH...
...HAS NO EFFECT!
STILL STANDING, HUH?
I'LL FIX THAT.

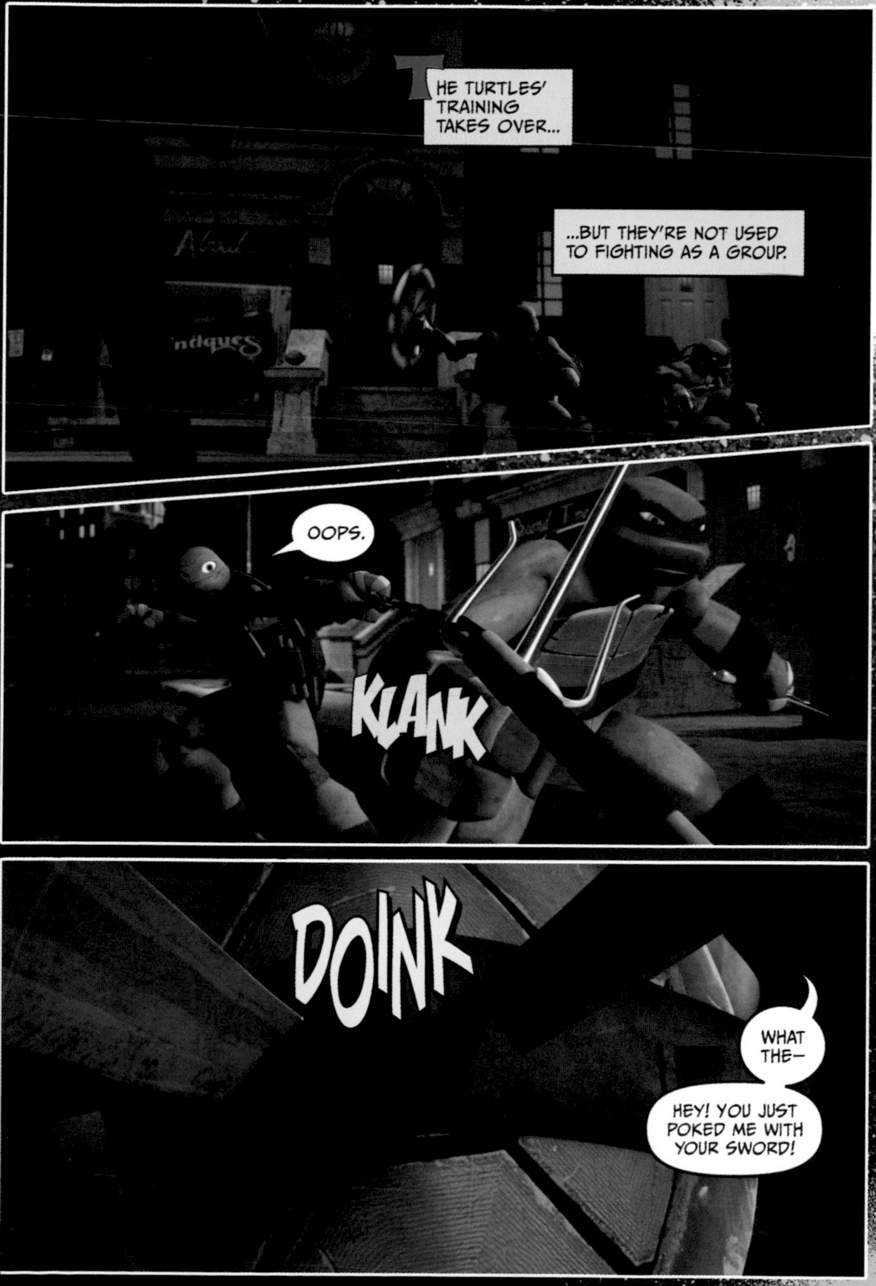
THE TURTLES' TRAINING TAKES OVER...
...BUT THEY'RE NOT USED TO FIGHTING AS A GROUP.
OOPS.
KLANK
DOINK
WHAT THE—
HEY! YOU JUST POKED ME WITH YOUR SWORD!

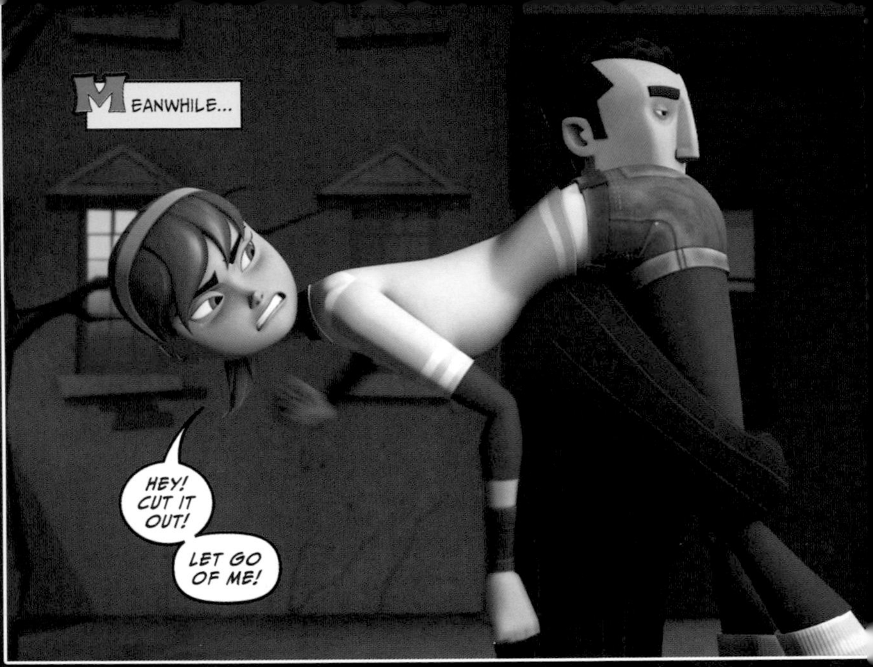
MEANWHILE...
HEY! CUT IT OUT!
LET GO OF ME!

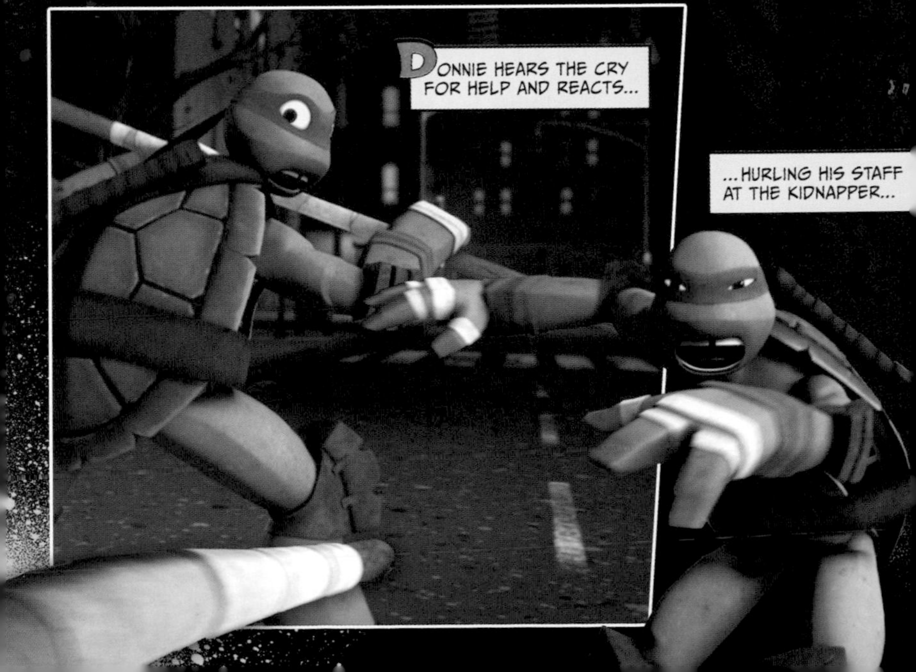
DONNIE HEARS THE CRY FOR HELP AND REACTS...
...HURLING HIS STAFF AT THE KIDNAPPER...

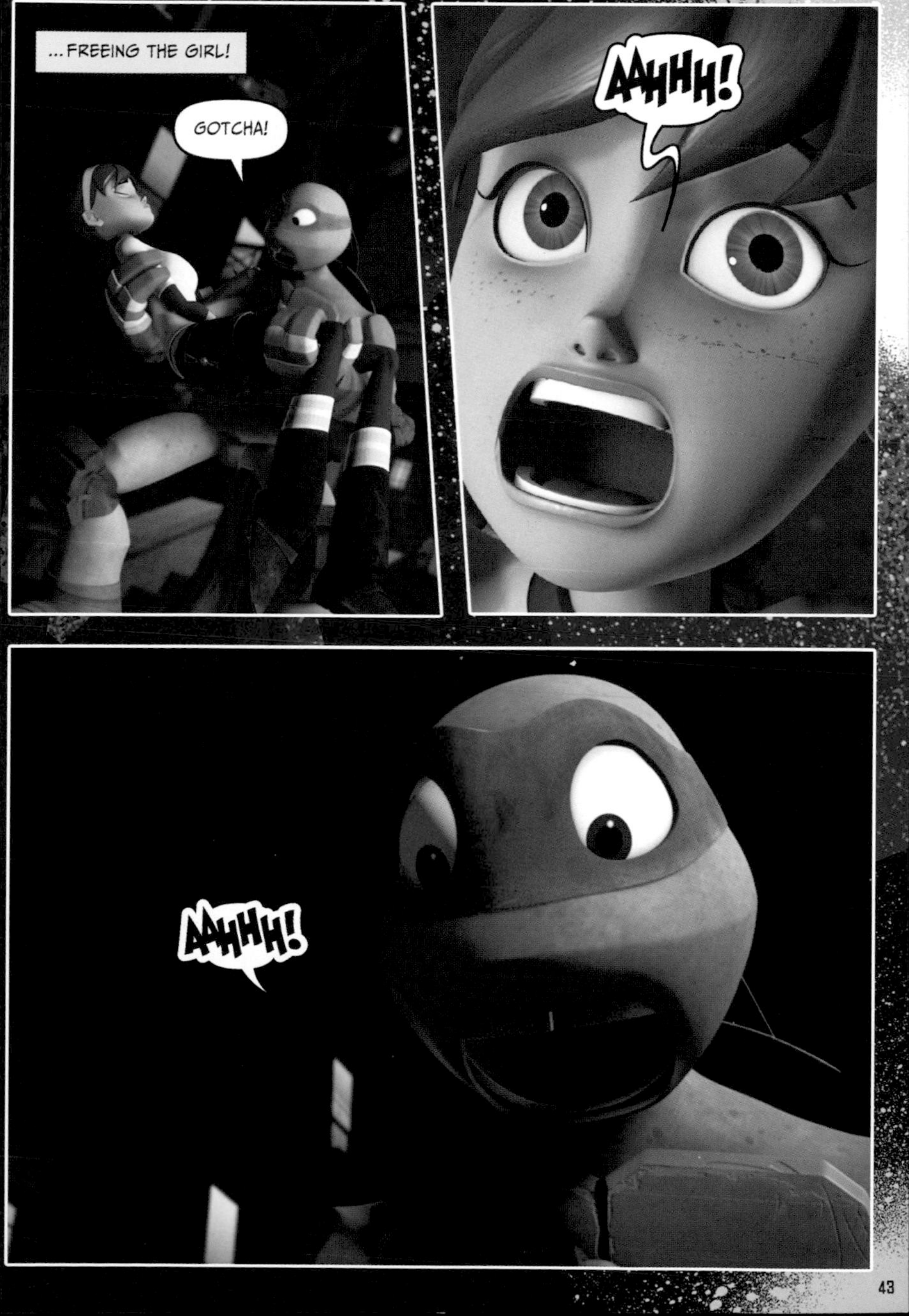
...FREEING THE GIRL!
GOTCHA!
AAHHH!
AAHHH!

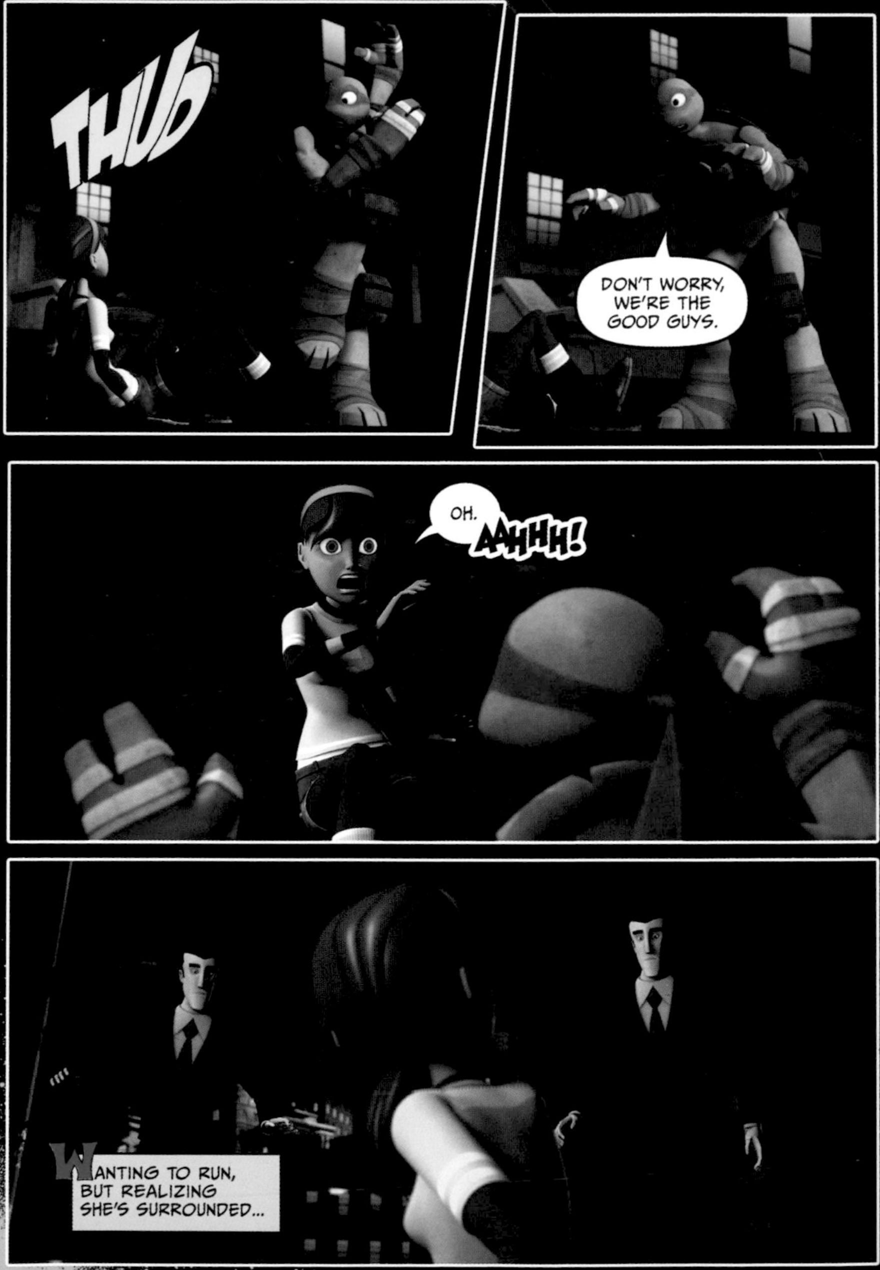
THUD
DON'T WORRY, WE'RE THE GOOD GUYS.
OH. AAHHH!
WANTING TO RUN, BUT REALIZING SHE'S SURROUNDED...

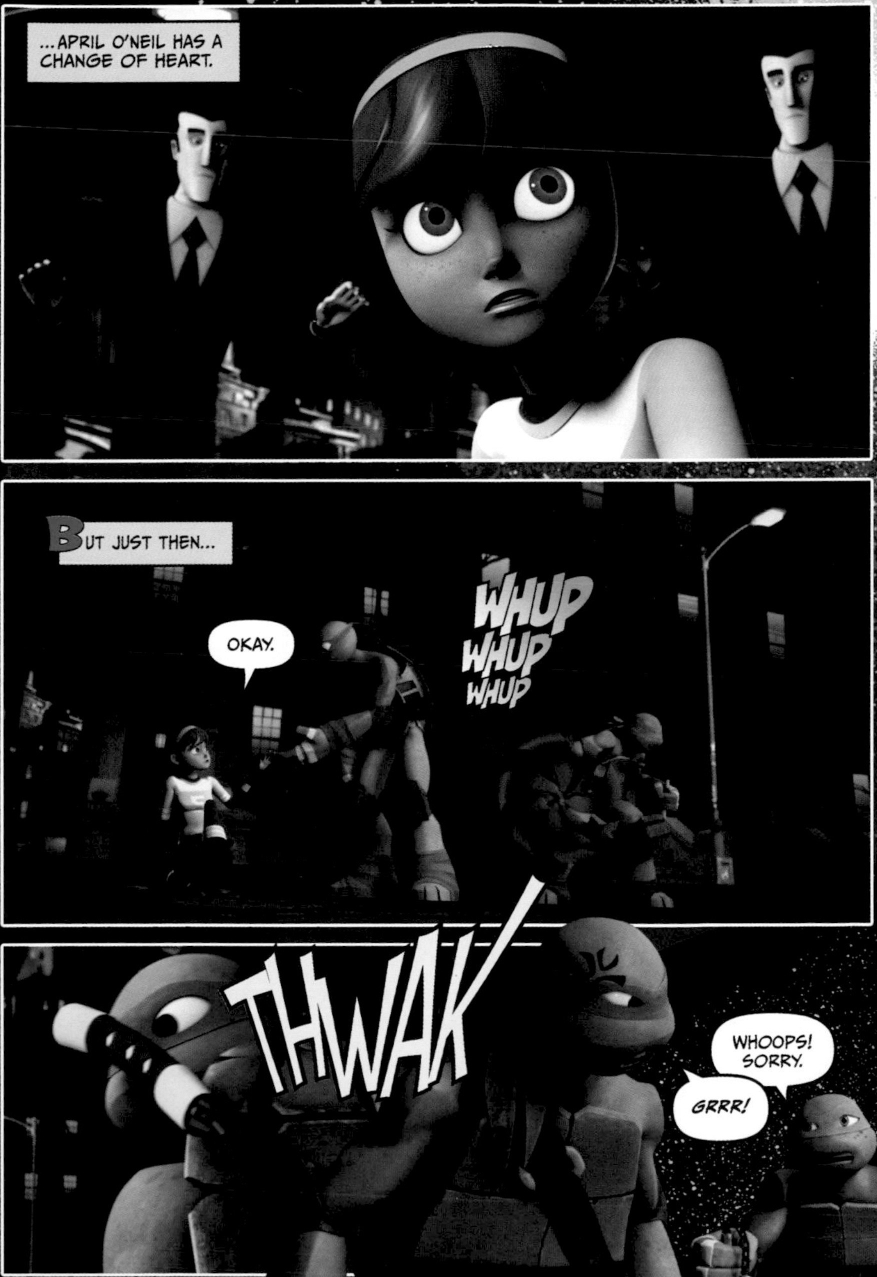
...APRIL O'NEIL HAS A CHANGE OF HEART.
BUT JUST THEN...
WHUP WHUP WHUP
OKAY.
THWAK
GRRR!
WHOOPS! SORRY.

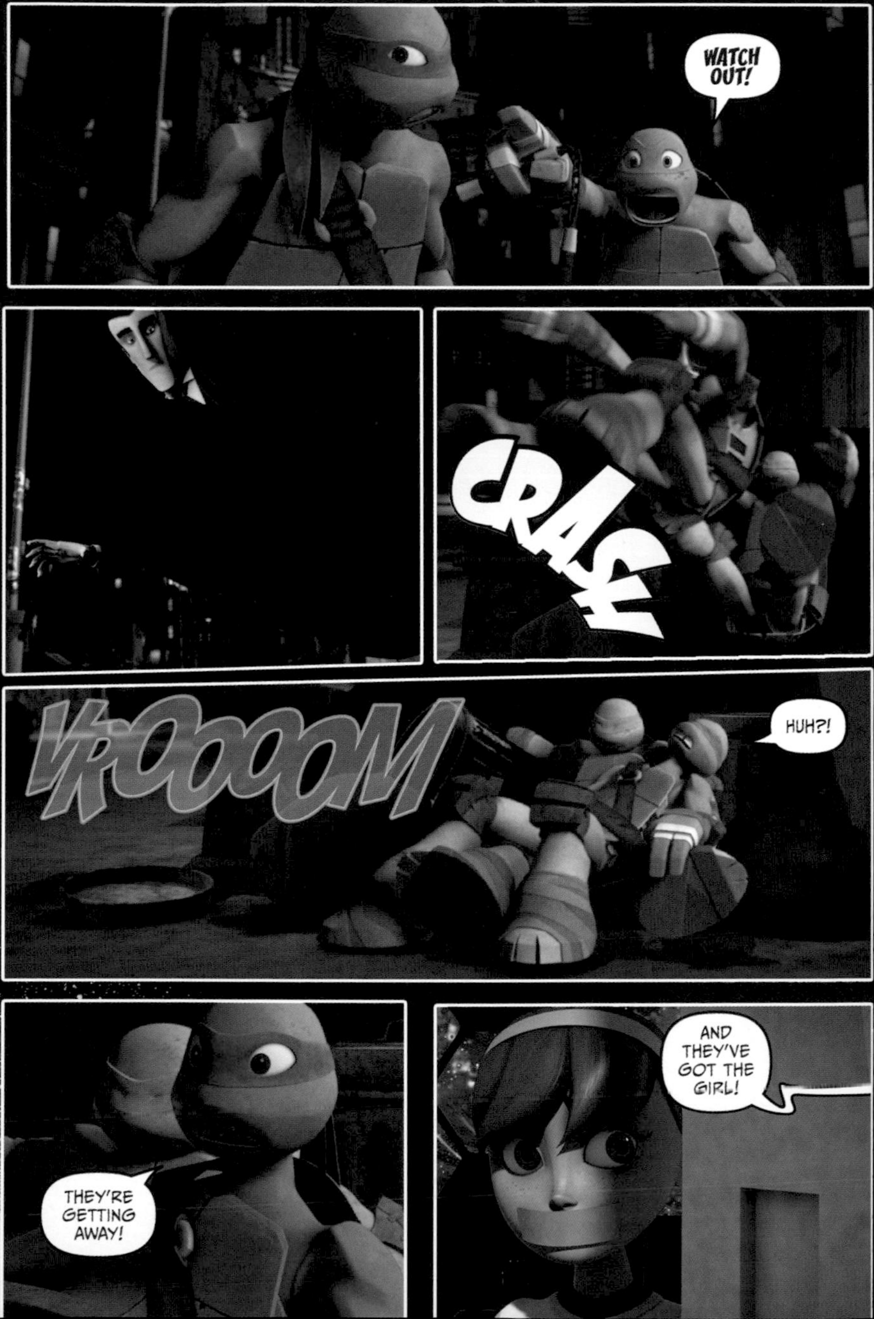
WATCH OUT!
CRASH
VROOOOM
HUH?!
THEY'RE GETTING AWAY!
AND THEY'VE GOT THE GIRL!

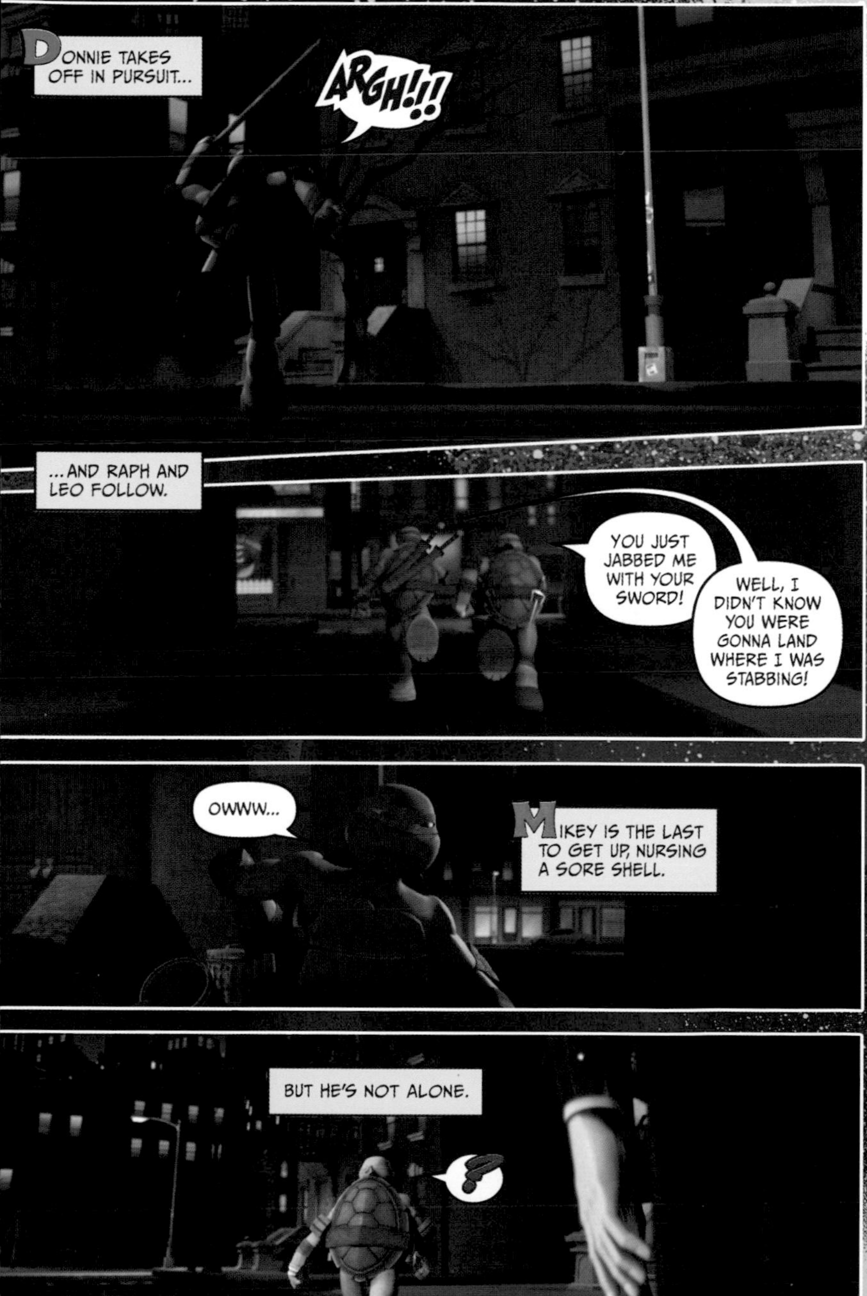
DONNIE TAKES OFF IN PURSUIT...
ARGH!!!
...AND RAPH AND LEO FOLLOW.
YOU JUST JABBED ME WITH YOUR SWORD!
WELL, I DIDN'T KNOW YOU WERE GONNA LAND WHERE I WAS STABBING!
OWWW...
MIKEY IS THE LAST TO GET UP, NURSING A SORE SHELL.
BUT HE'S NOT ALONE.
?

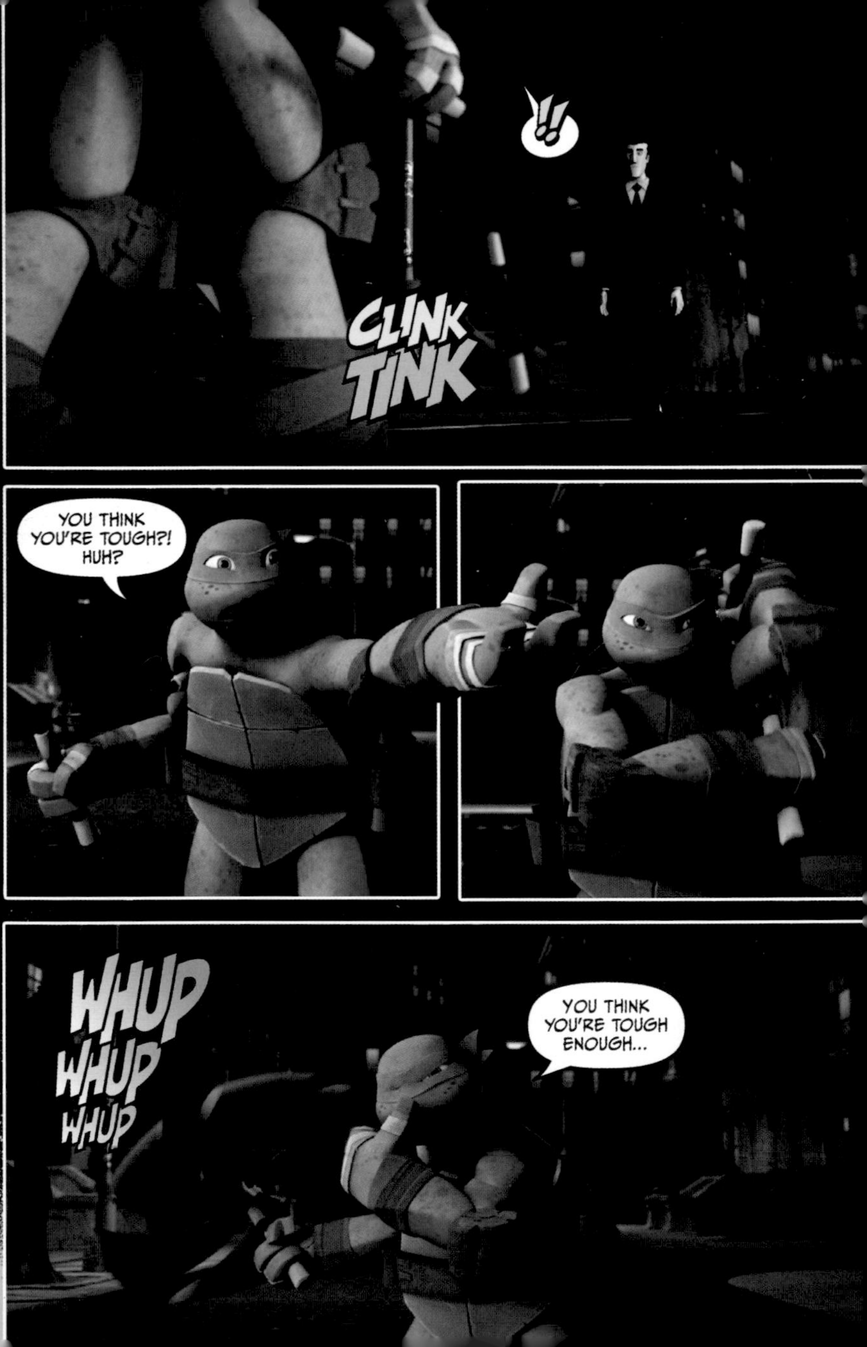
!!
CLINK
TINK
YOU THINK YOU'RE TOUGH?! HUH?
WHUP
WHUP
WHUP
YOU THINK YOU'RE TOUGH ENOUGH...

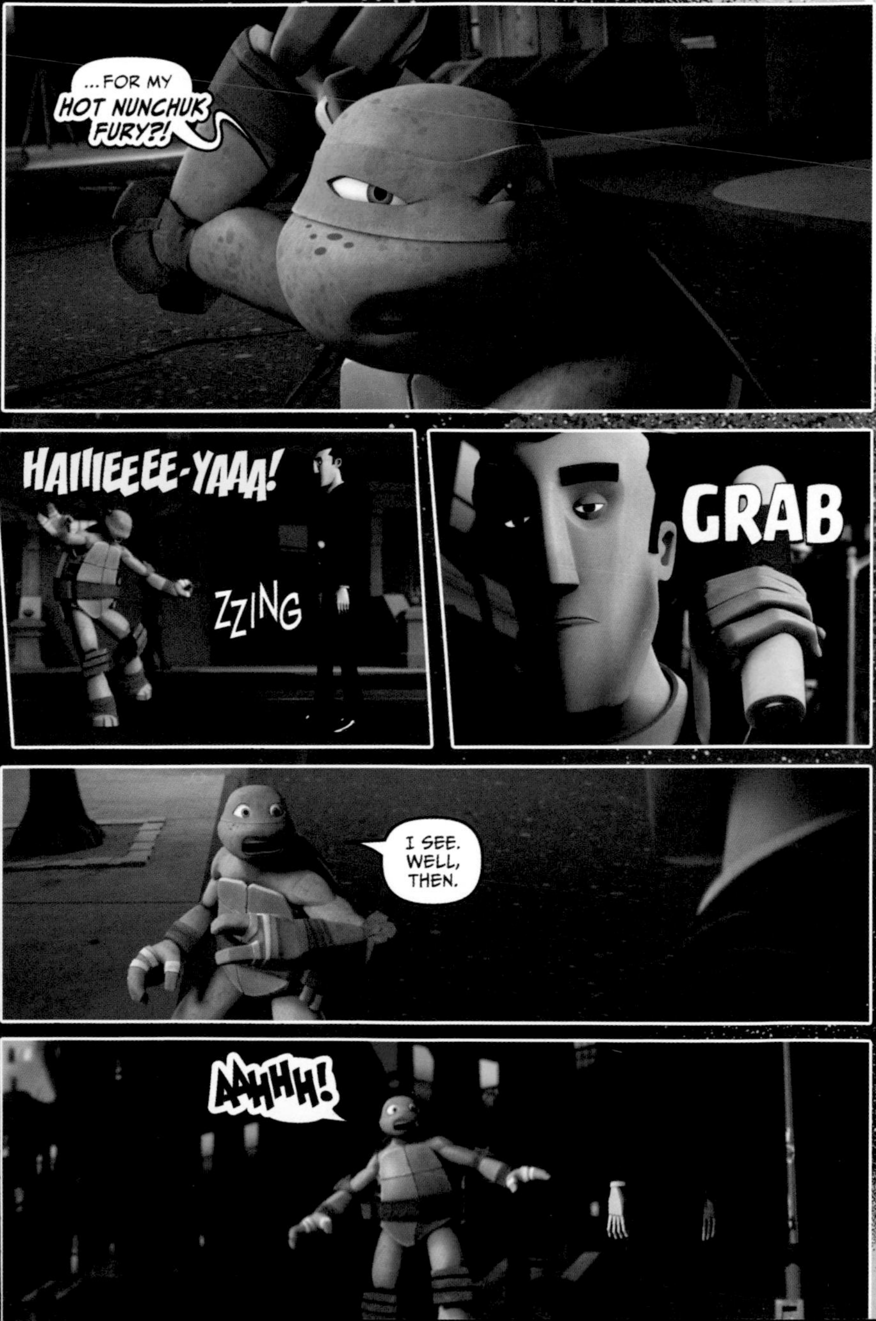
...FOR MY HOT NUNCHUK FURY?!
HAIIIEEEE-YAAA!
ZZING
GRAB
I SEE. WELL, THEN.
AAHHH!

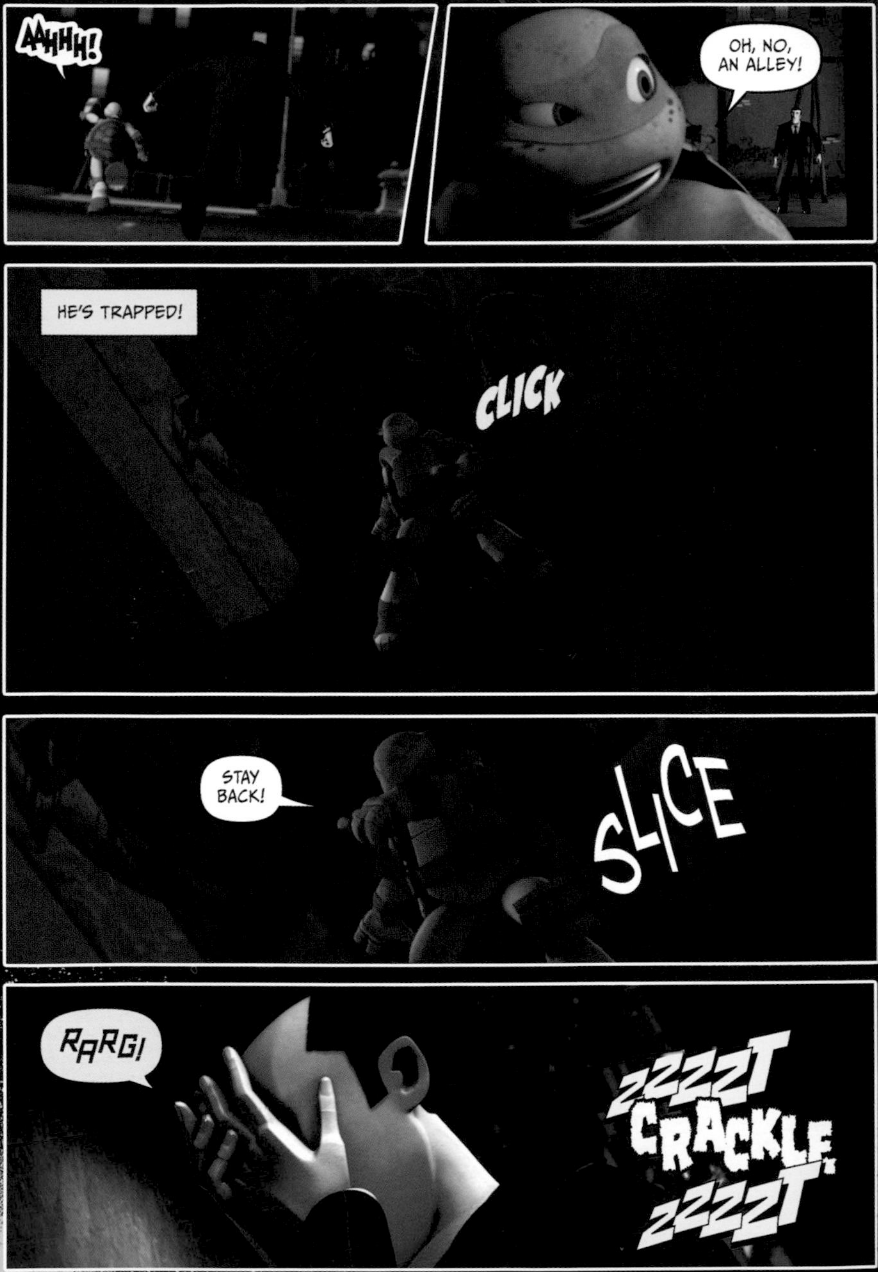
AAHHH!
OH, NO, AN ALLEY!
HE'S TRAPPED!
CLICK
STAY BACK!
SLICE
RARG!
ZZZZT
CRACKLE
ZZZZT

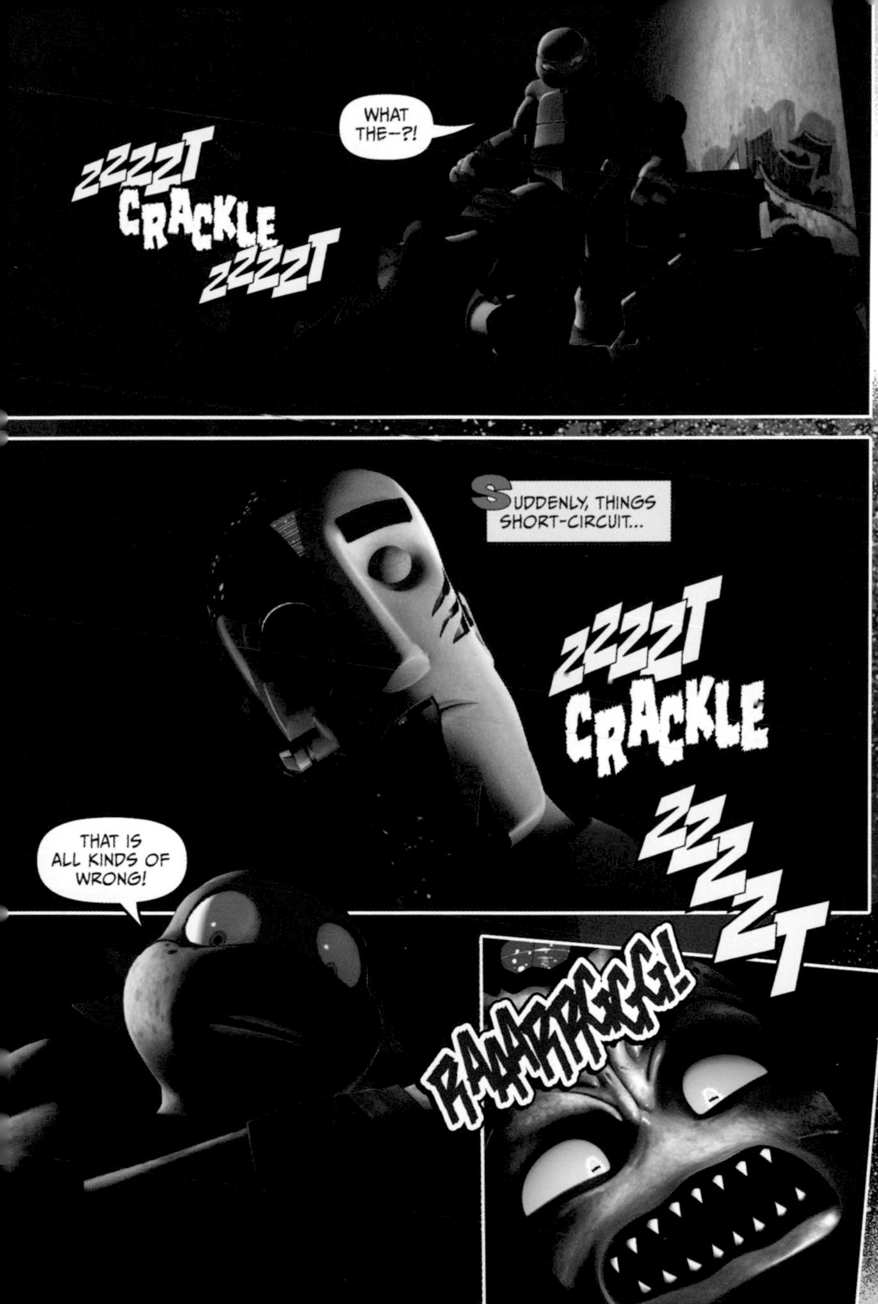

WHAT THE—?!
ZZZZT
CRACKLE
ZZZZT
SUDDENLY, THINGS SHORT-CIRCUIT...
ZZZZT
CRACKLE
ZZZZZT
THAT IS ALL KINDS OF WRONG!
RAAARRGG!

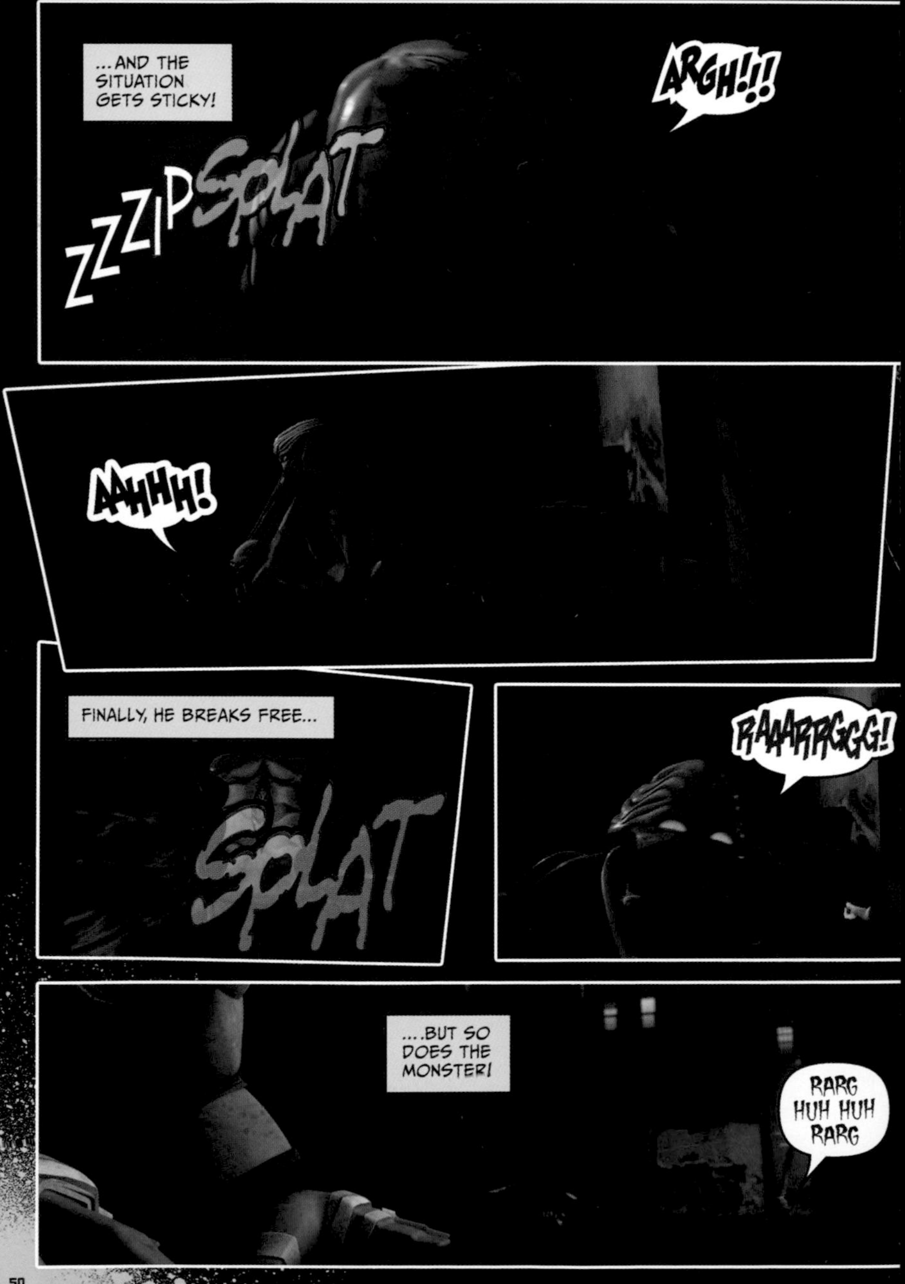

...AND THE SITUATION GETS STICKY!
ARGH!!!
ZZZIP
SPLAT
AAHHH!
FINALLY, HE BREAKS FREE...
SPLAT
RAAARRGGG!
....BUT SO DOES THE MONSTER!
RARG HUH HUH RARG

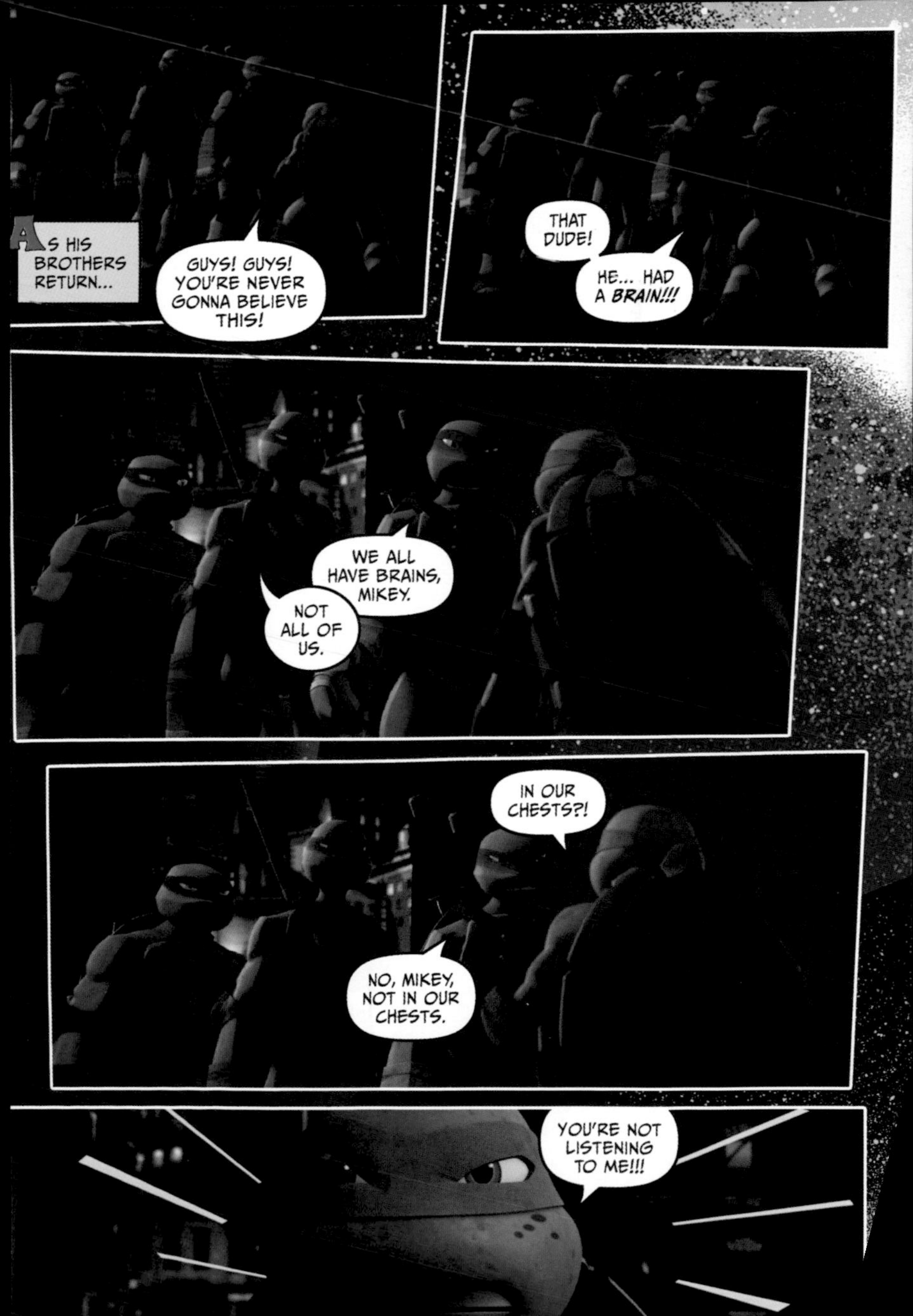
AS HIS BROTHERS RETURN...
GUYS! GUYS! YOU'RE NEVER GONNA BELIEVE THIS!
THAT DUDE!
HE... HAD A *BRAIN!!!*
WE ALL HAVE BRAINS, MIKEY.
NOT ALL OF US.
IN OUR CHESTS?!
NO, MIKEY, NOT IN OUR CHESTS.
YOU'RE NOT LISTENING TO ME!!!

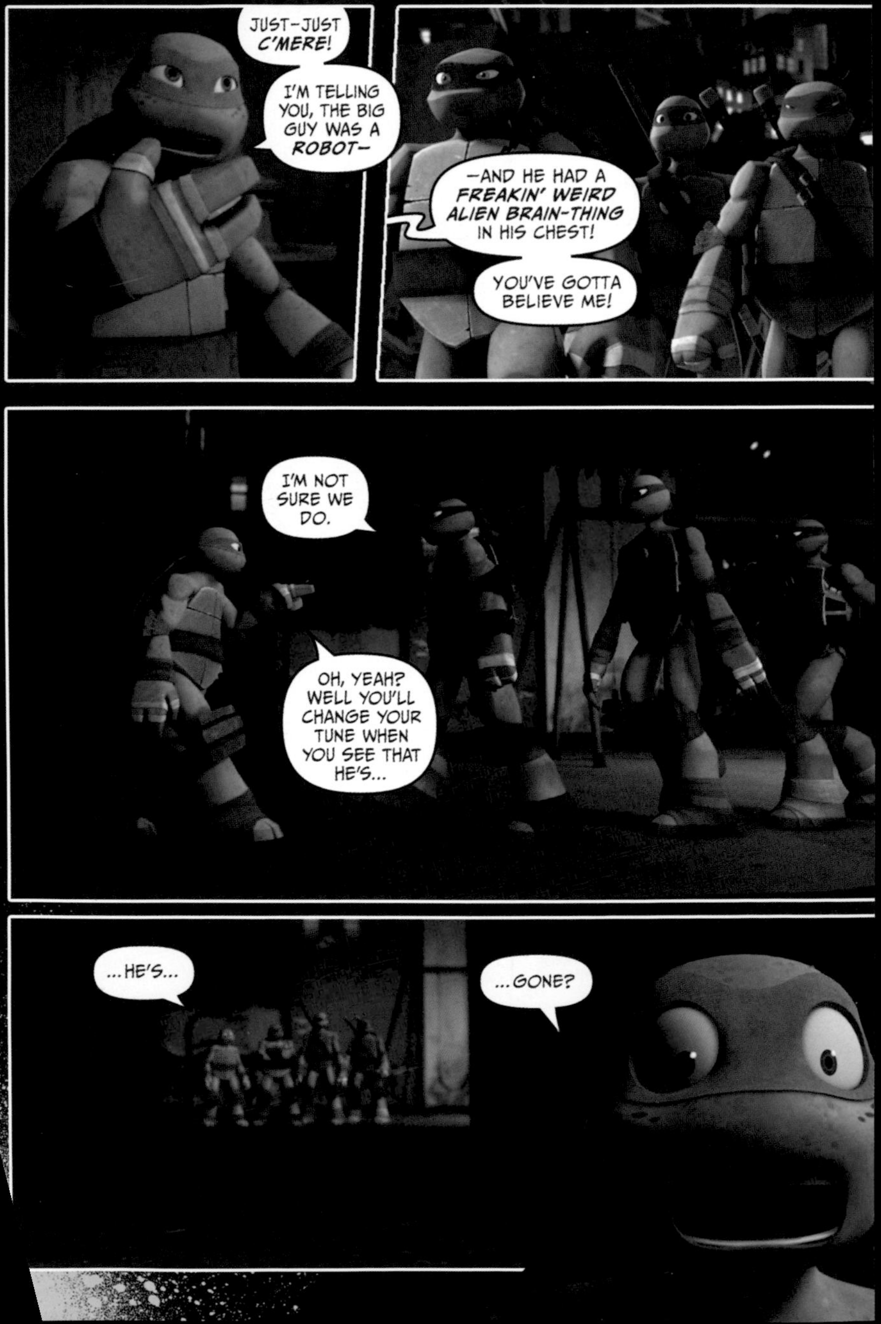
JUST–JUST *C'MERE!*
I'M TELLING YOU, THE BIG GUY WAS A *ROBOT*–
–AND HE HAD A *FREAKIN' WEIRD ALIEN BRAIN-THING* IN HIS CHEST!
YOU'VE GOTTA BELIEVE ME!
I'M NOT SURE WE DO.
OH, YEAH? WELL YOU'LL CHANGE YOUR TUNE WHEN YOU SEE THAT HE'S...
...HE'S...
...GONE?

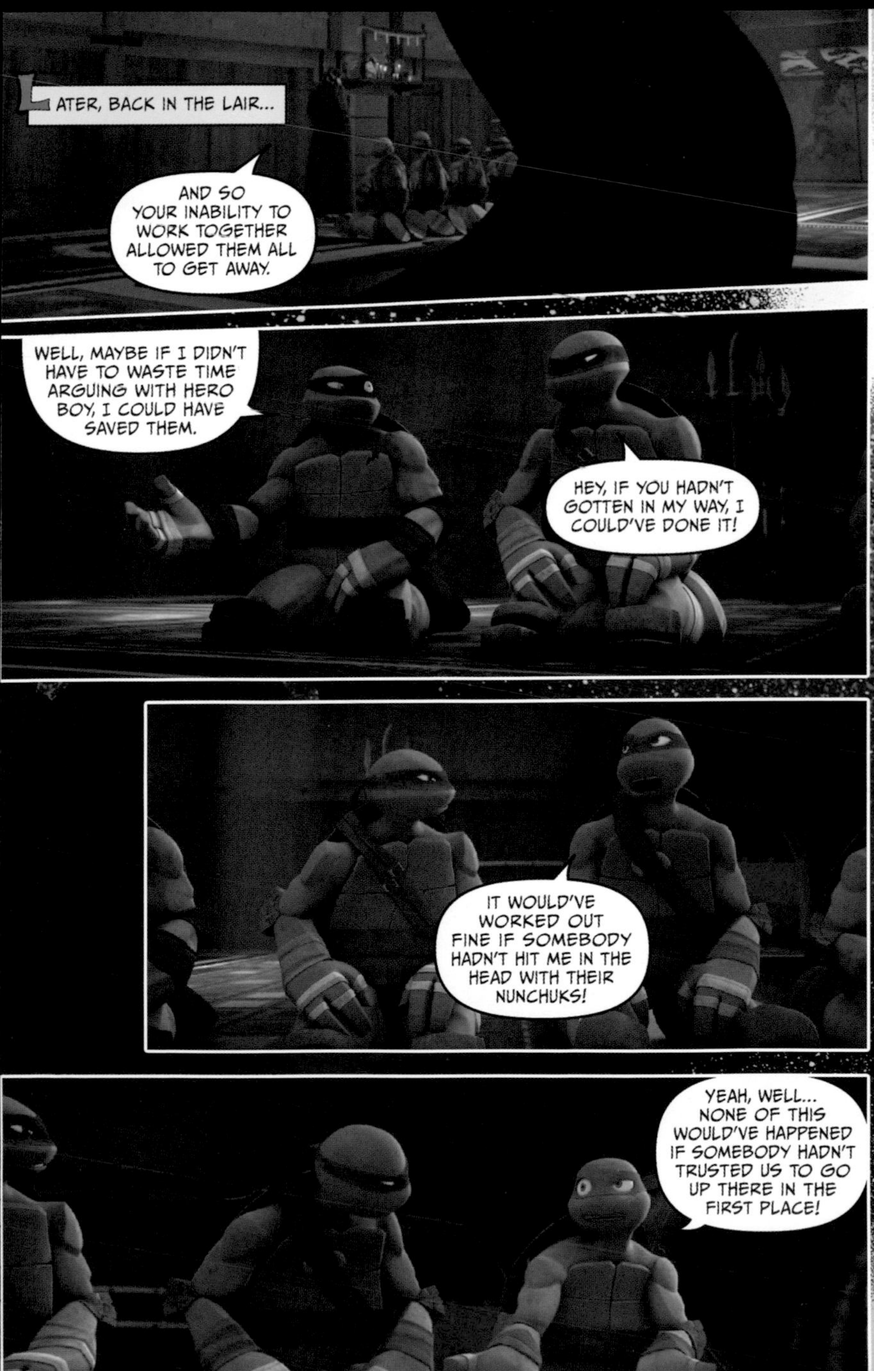

LATER, BACK IN THE LAIR...
AND SO YOUR INABILITY TO WORK TOGETHER ALLOWED THEM ALL TO GET AWAY.
WELL, MAYBE IF I DIDN'T HAVE TO WASTE TIME ARGUING WITH HERO BOY, I COULD HAVE SAVED THEM.
HEY, IF YOU HADN'T GOTTEN IN MY WAY, I COULD'VE DONE IT!
IT WOULD'VE WORKED OUT FINE IF SOMEBODY HADN'T HIT ME IN THE HEAD WITH THEIR NUNCHUKS!
YEAH, WELL... NONE OF THIS WOULD'VE HAPPENED IF SOMEBODY HADN'T TRUSTED US TO GO UP THERE IN THE FIRST PLACE!

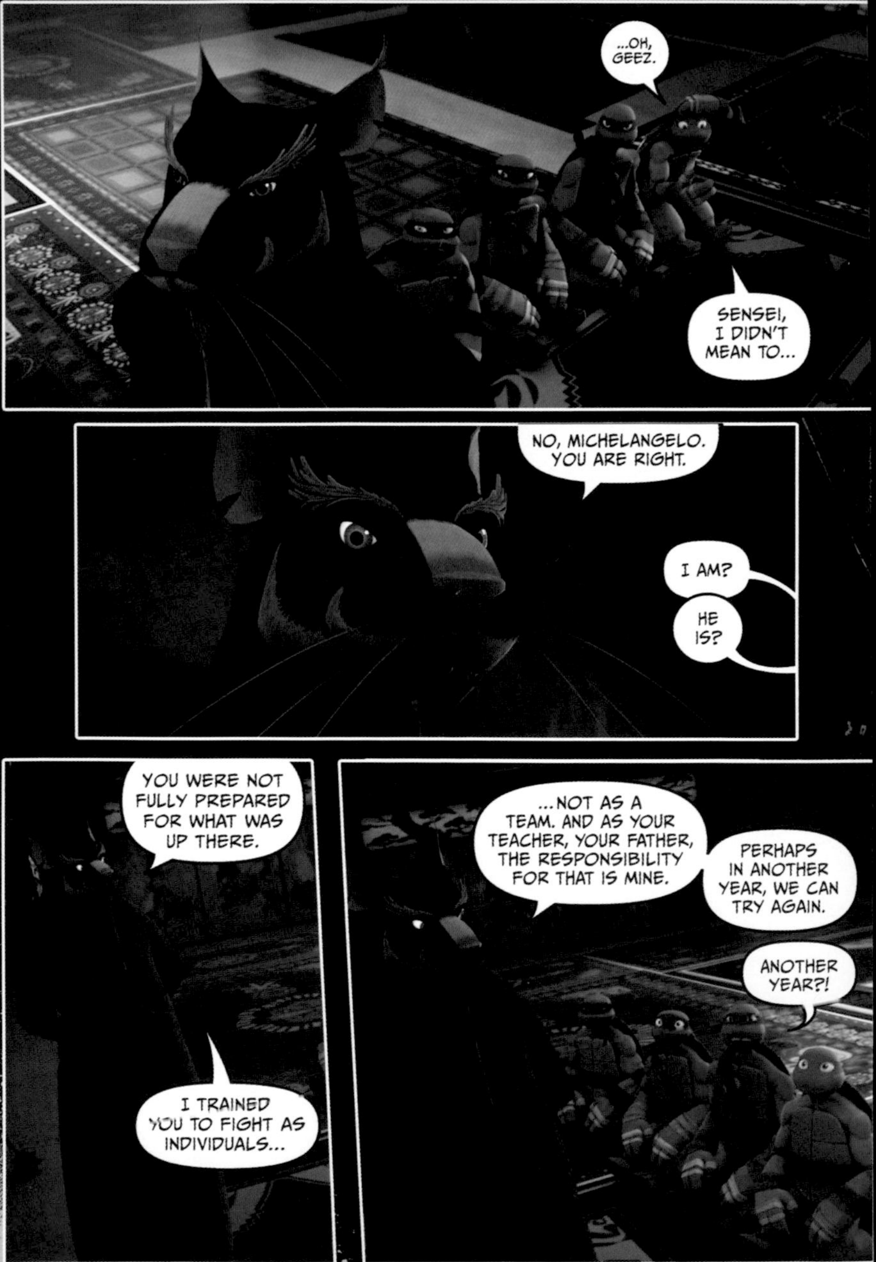

...OH, GEEZ.
SENSEI, I DIDN'T MEAN TO...
NO, MICHELANGELO. YOU ARE RIGHT.
I AM?
HE IS?
YOU WERE NOT FULLY PREPARED FOR WHAT WAS UP THERE.
I TRAINED YOU TO FIGHT AS INDIVIDUALS...
...NOT AS A TEAM. AND AS YOUR TEACHER, YOUR FATHER, THE RESPONSIBILITY FOR THAT IS MINE.
PERHAPS IN ANOTHER YEAR, WE CAN TRY AGAIN.
ANOTHER YEAR?!

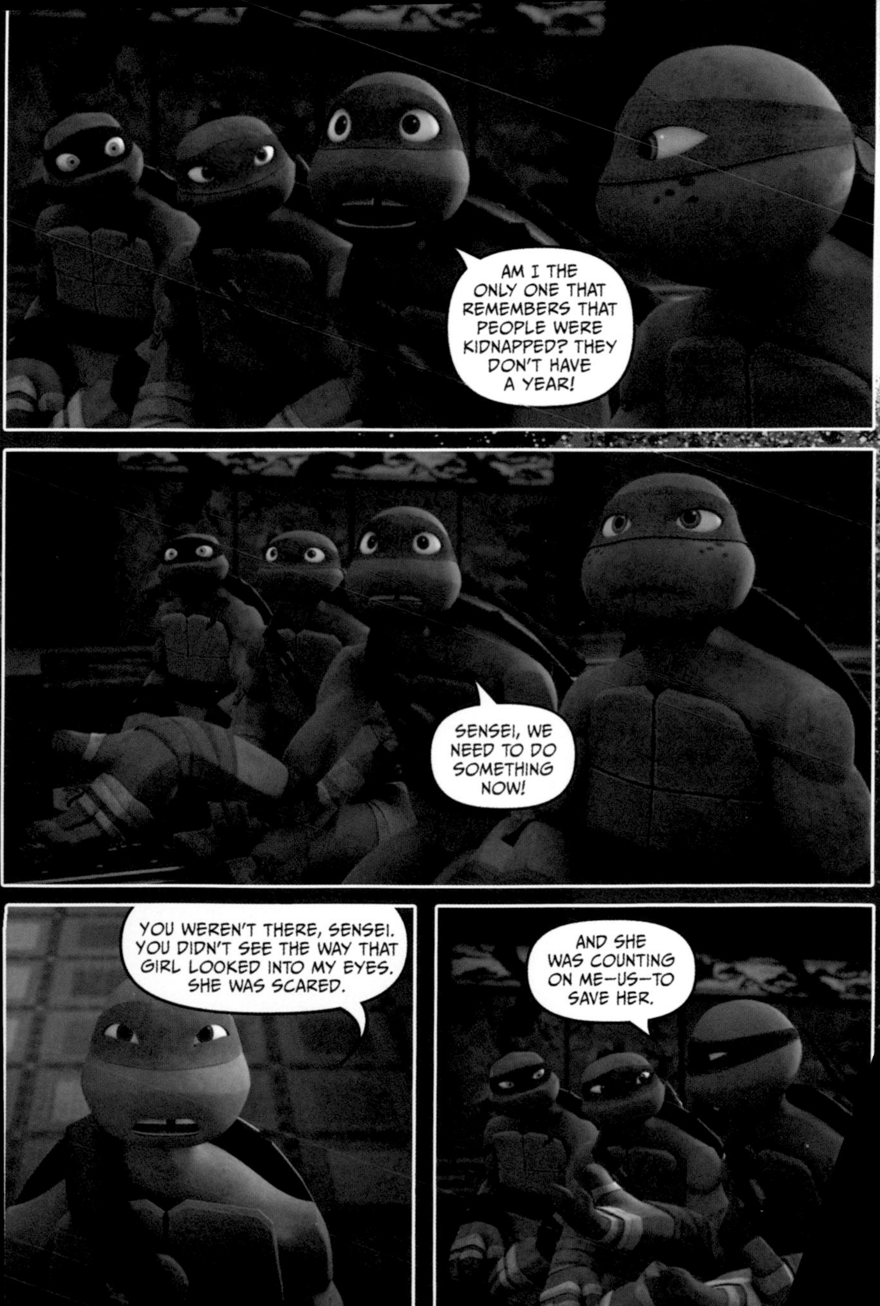
AM I THE ONLY ONE THAT REMEMBERS THAT PEOPLE WERE KIDNAPPED? THEY DON'T HAVE A YEAR!
SENSEI, WE NEED TO DO SOMETHING NOW!
YOU WEREN'T THERE, SENSEI. YOU DIDN'T SEE THE WAY THAT GIRL LOOKED INTO MY EYES. SHE WAS SCARED.
AND SHE WAS COUNTING ON ME—US—TO SAVE HER.

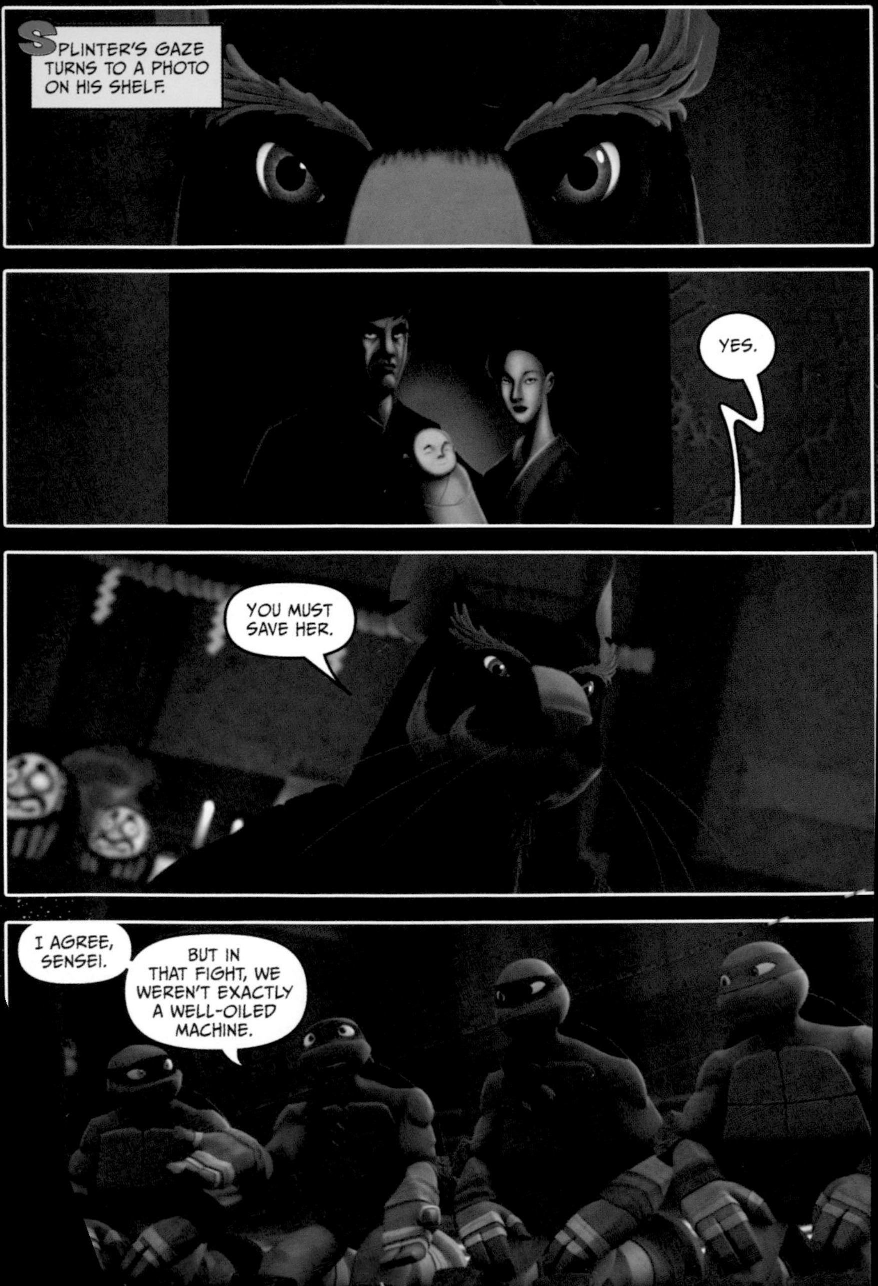
SPLINTER'S GAZE TURNS TO A PHOTO ON HIS SHELF.
YES.
YOU MUST SAVE HER.
I AGREE, SENSEI.
BUT IN THAT FIGHT, WE WEREN'T EXACTLY A WELL-OILED MACHINE.

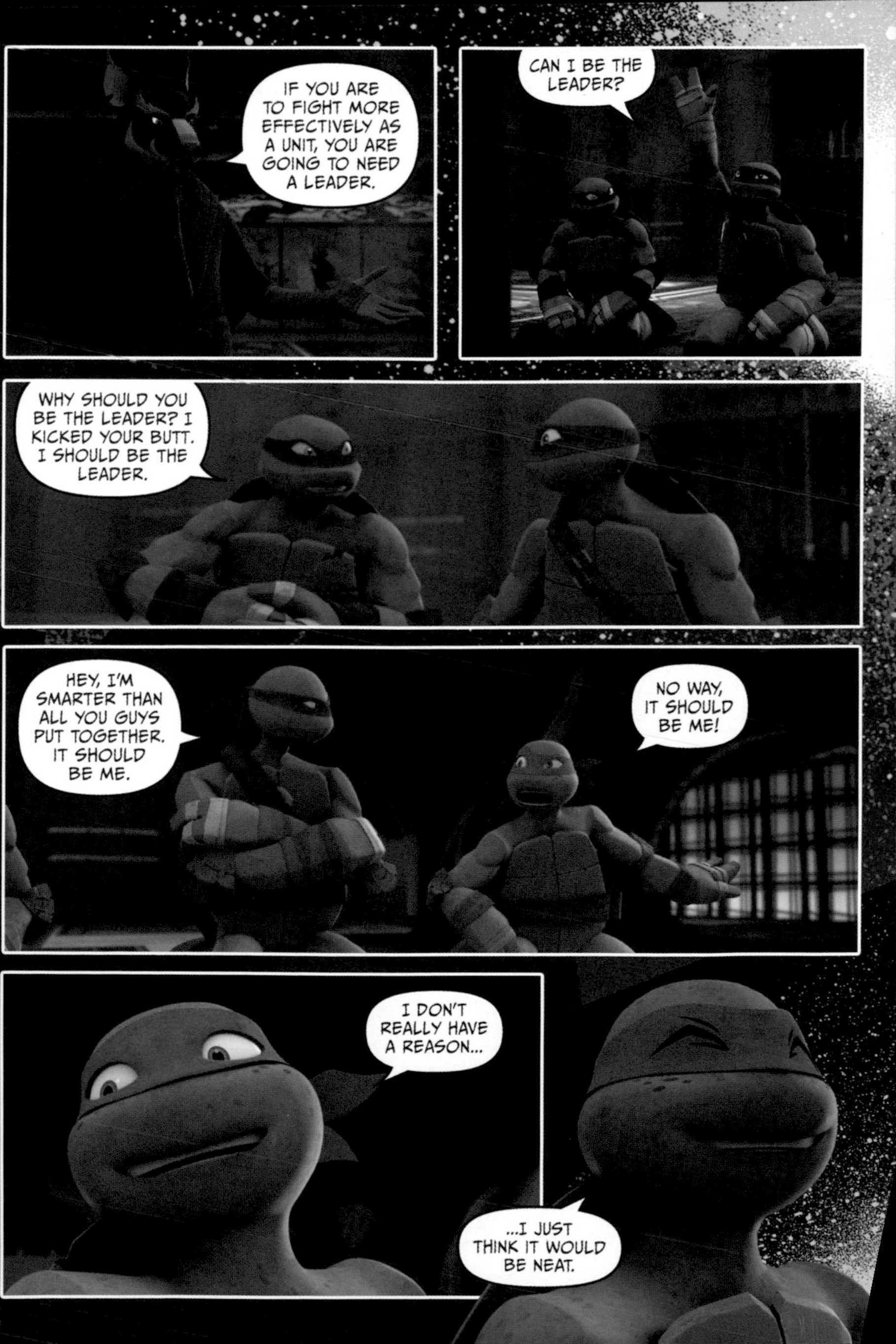
IF YOU ARE TO FIGHT MORE EFFECTIVELY AS A UNIT, YOU ARE GOING TO NEED A LEADER.
CAN I BE THE LEADER?
WHY SHOULD YOU BE THE LEADER? I KICKED YOUR BUTT. I SHOULD BE THE LEADER.
HEY, I'M SMARTER THAN ALL YOU GUYS PUT TOGETHER. IT SHOULD BE ME.
NO WAY, IT SHOULD BE ME!
I DON'T REALLY HAVE A REASON...
...I JUST THINK IT WOULD BE NEAT.

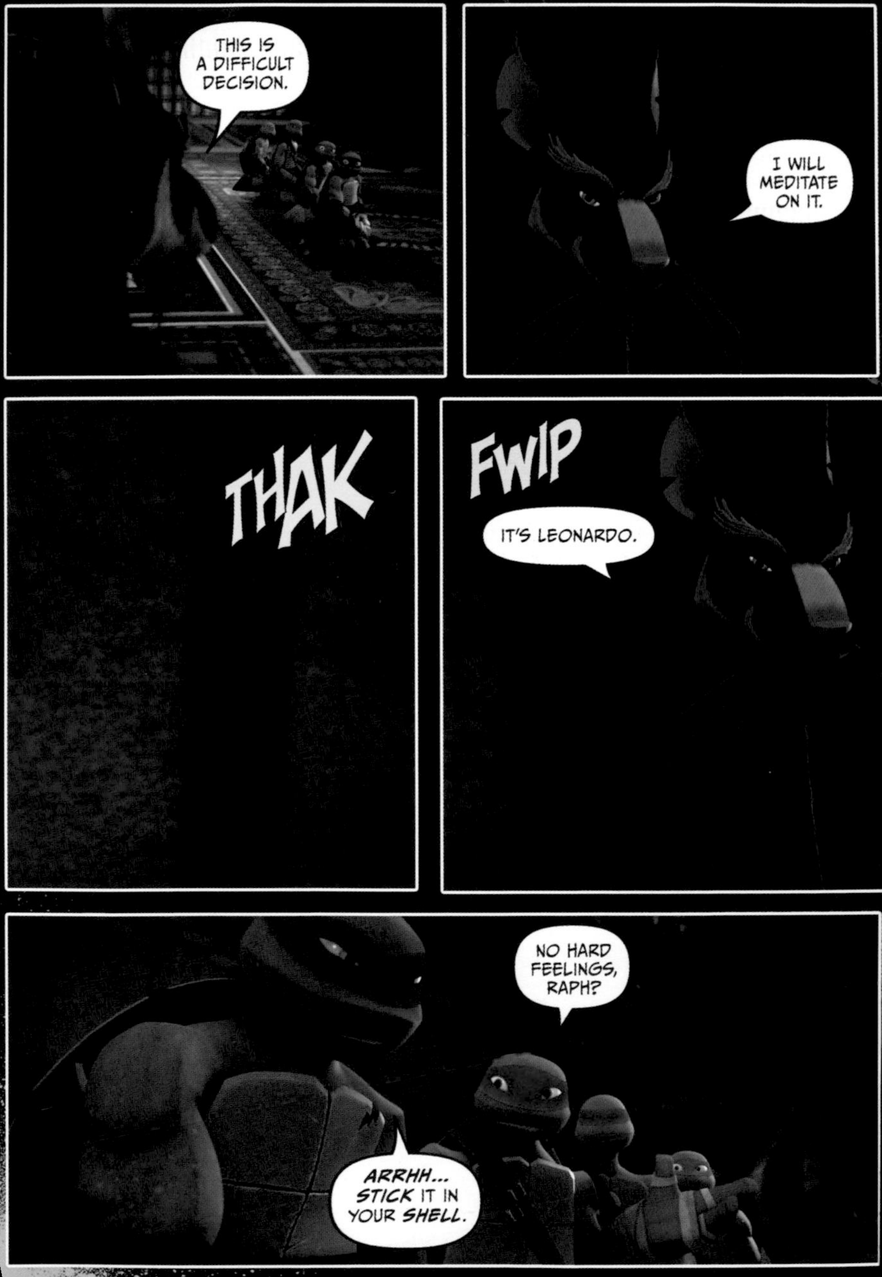
THIS IS A DIFFICULT DECISION.
I WILL MEDITATE ON IT.
THAK
FWIP
IT'S LEONARDO.
NO HARD FEELINGS, RAPH?
ARRHH... STICK IT IN YOUR SHELL.

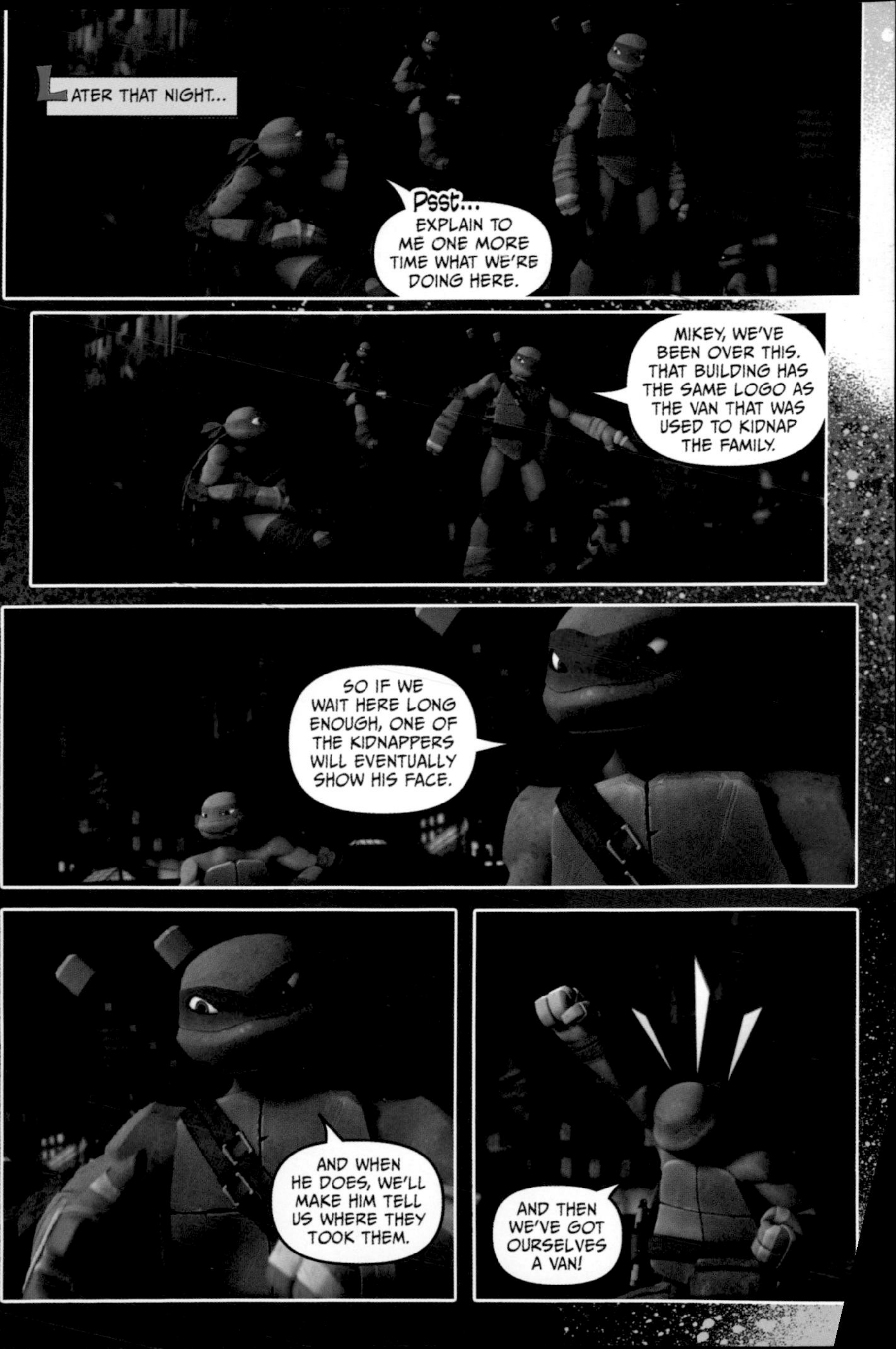

LATER THAT NIGHT...
Psst... EXPLAIN TO ME ONE MORE TIME WHAT WE'RE DOING HERE.
MIKEY, WE'VE BEEN OVER THIS. THAT BUILDING HAS THE SAME LOGO AS THE VAN THAT WAS USED TO KIDNAP THE FAMILY.
SO IF WE WAIT HERE LONG ENOUGH, ONE OF THE KIDNAPPERS WILL EVENTUALLY SHOW HIS FACE.
AND WHEN HE DOES, WE'LL MAKE HIM TELL US WHERE THEY TOOK THEM.
AND THEN WE'VE GOT OURSELVES A VAN!

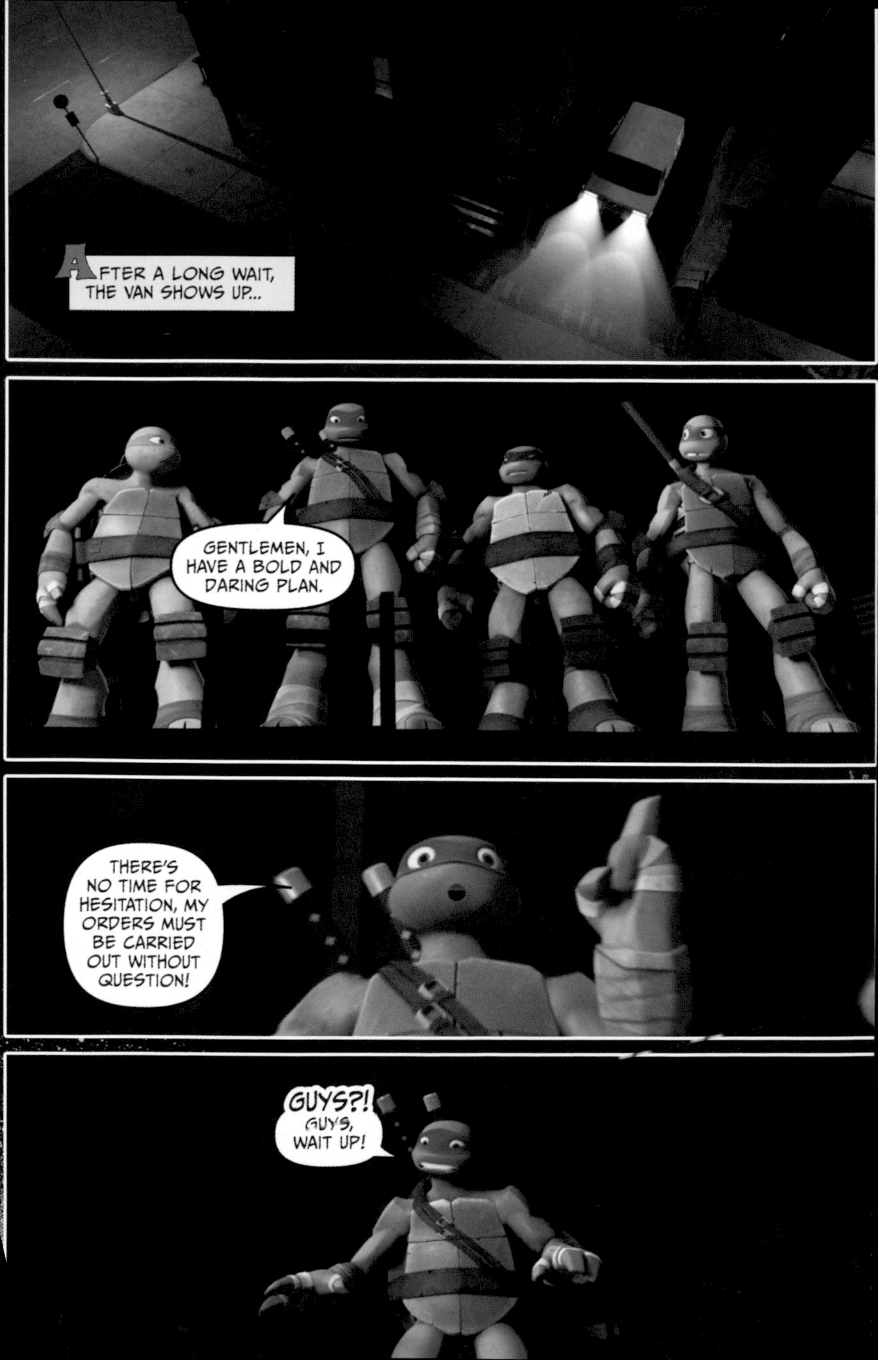
AFTER A LONG WAIT, THE VAN SHOWS UP...
GENTLEMEN, I HAVE A BOLD AND DARING PLAN.
THERE'S NO TIME FOR HESITATION, MY ORDERS MUST BE CARRIED OUT WITHOUT QUESTION!
GUYS?! GUYS, WAIT UP!

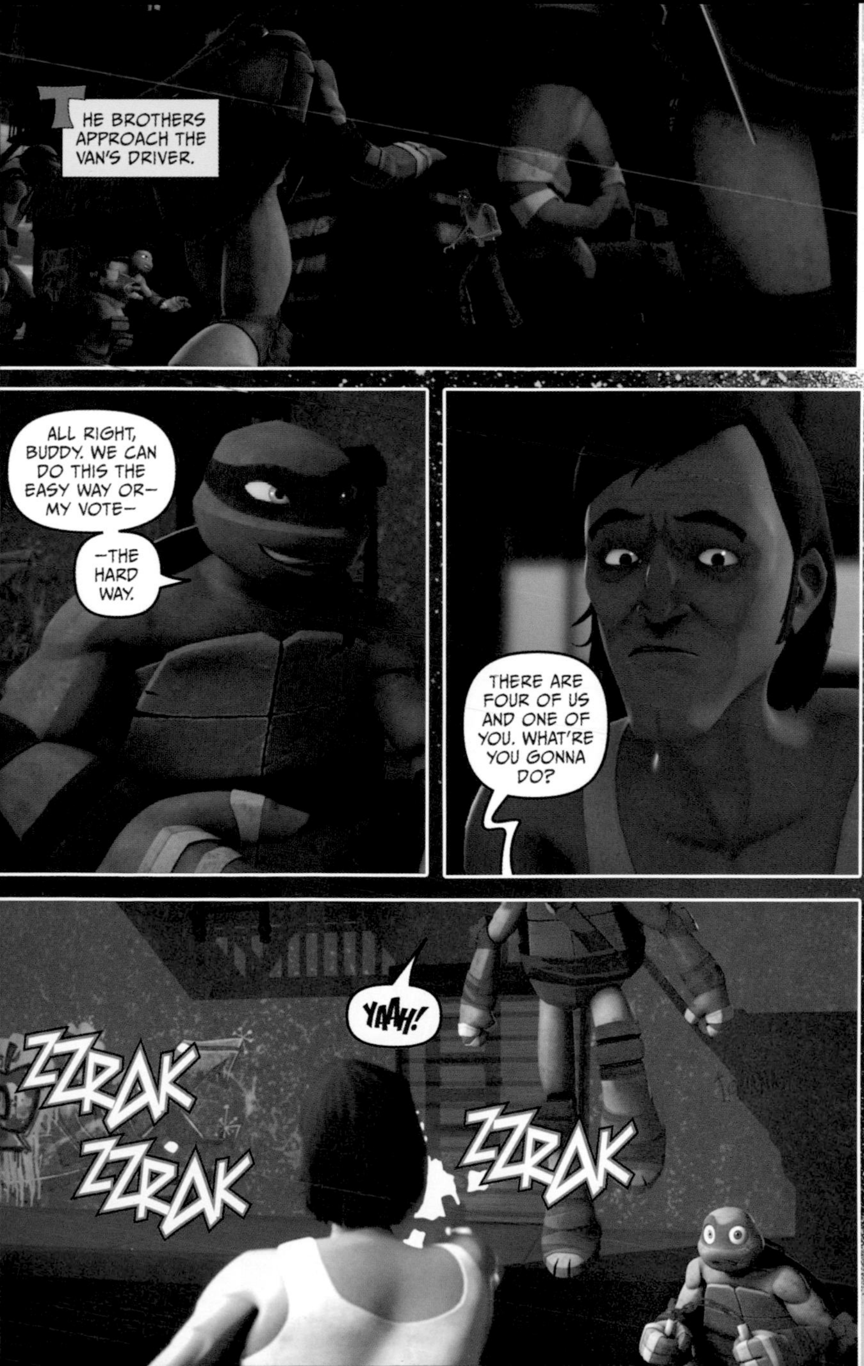
THE BROTHERS APPROACH THE VAN'S DRIVER.
ALL RIGHT, BUDDY. WE CAN DO THIS THE EASY WAY OR-- MY VOTE--
--THE HARD WAY.
THERE ARE FOUR OF US AND ONE OF YOU. WHAT'RE YOU GONNA DO?
YAAH!
ZZRAK
ZZRAK
ZZRAK

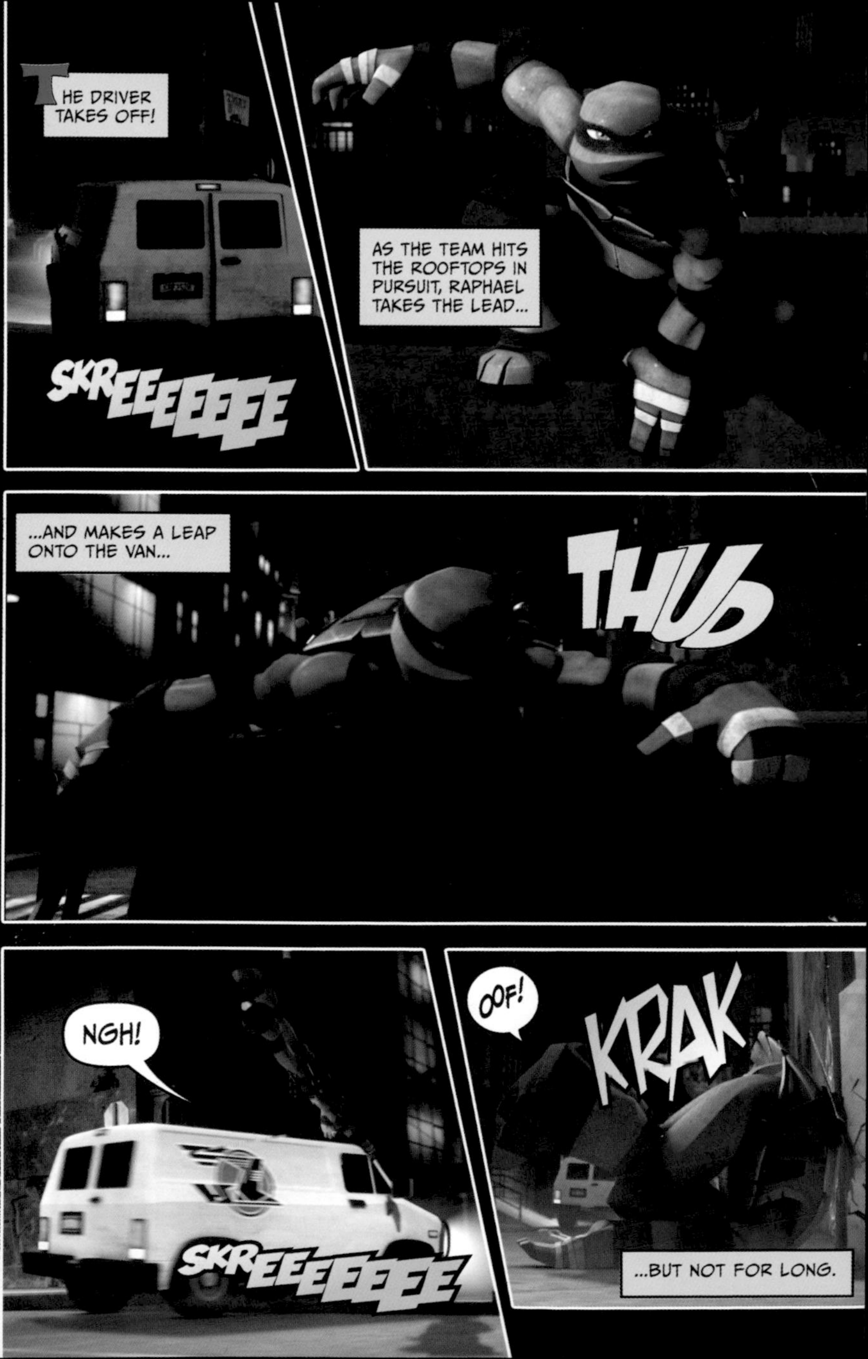
THE DRIVER TAKES OFF!
SKREEEEEEEE
AS THE TEAM HITS THE ROOFTOPS IN PURSUIT, RAPHAEL TAKES THE LEAD...
...AND MAKES A LEAP ONTO THE VAN...
THUD
NGH!
SKREEEEEEEE
OOF!
KRAK
...BUT NOT FOR LONG.

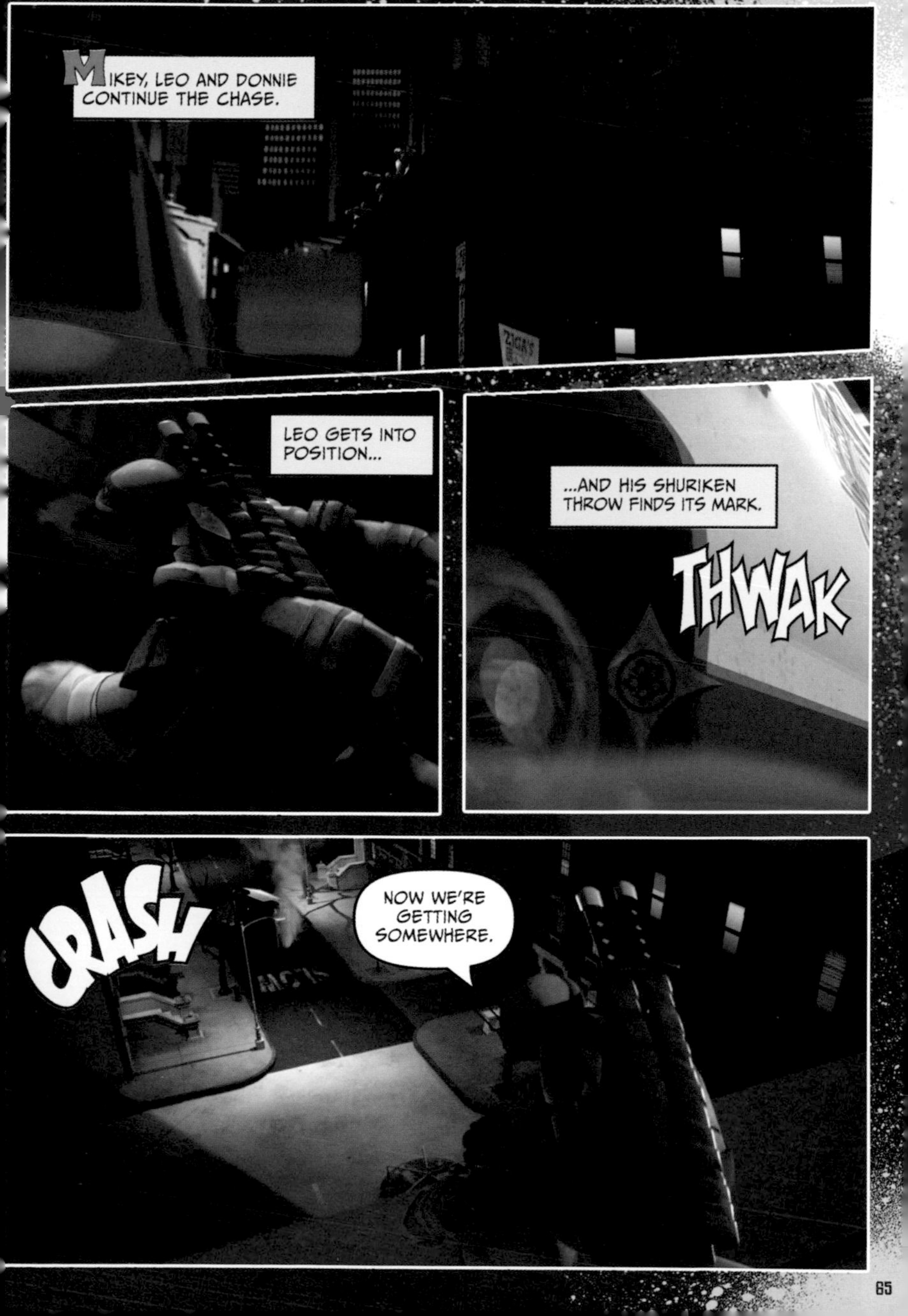
MIKEY, LEO AND DONNIE CONTINUE THE CHASE.
LEO GETS INTO POSITION...
...AND HIS SHURIKEN THROW FINDS ITS MARK.
THWAK
CRASH
NOW WE'RE GETTING SOMEWHERE.

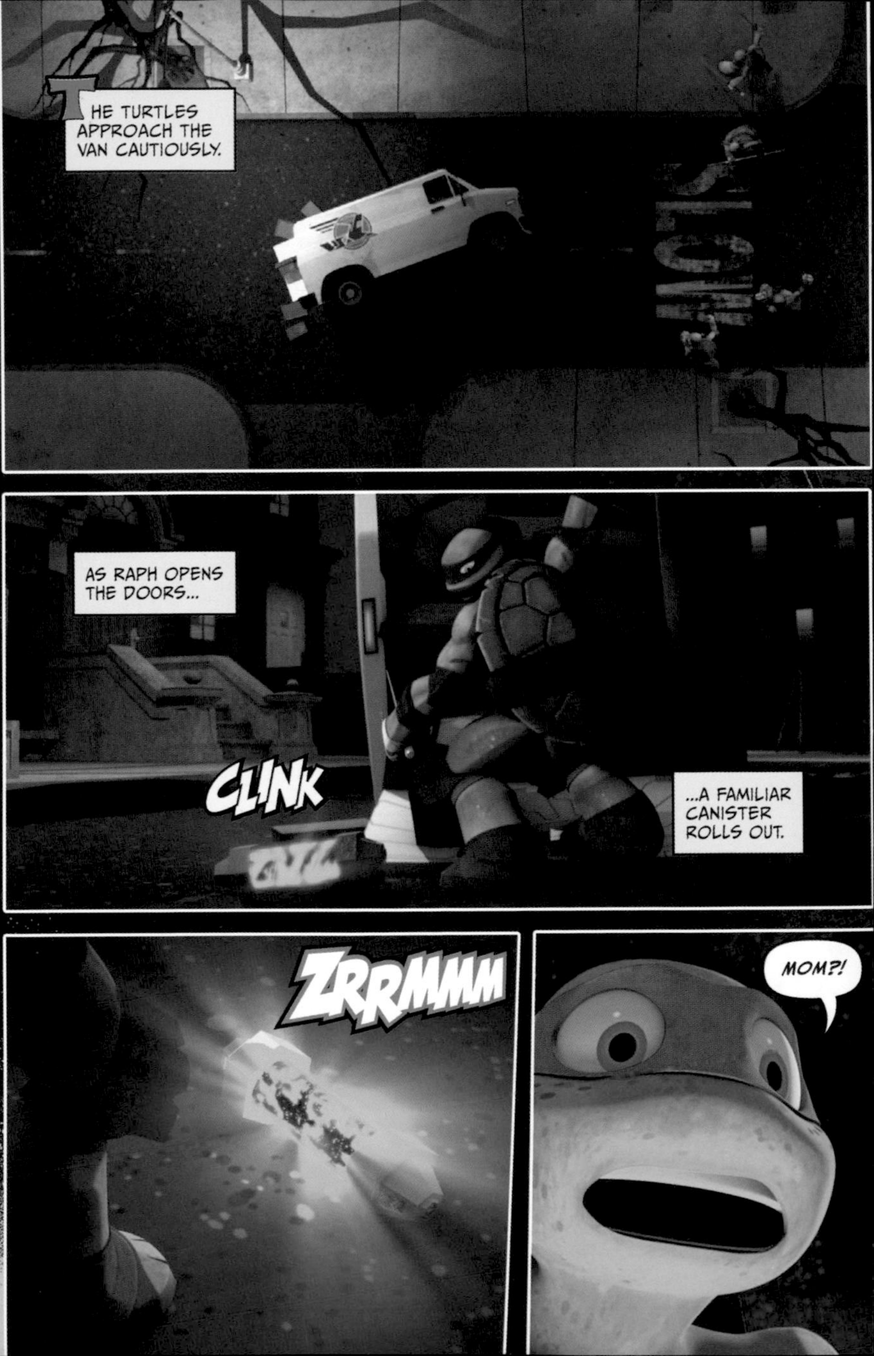
THE TURTLES APPROACH THE VAN CAUTIOUSLY.
AS RAPH OPENS THE DOORS...
CLINK
...A FAMILIAR CANISTER ROLLS OUT.
ZRRMMM
MOM?!

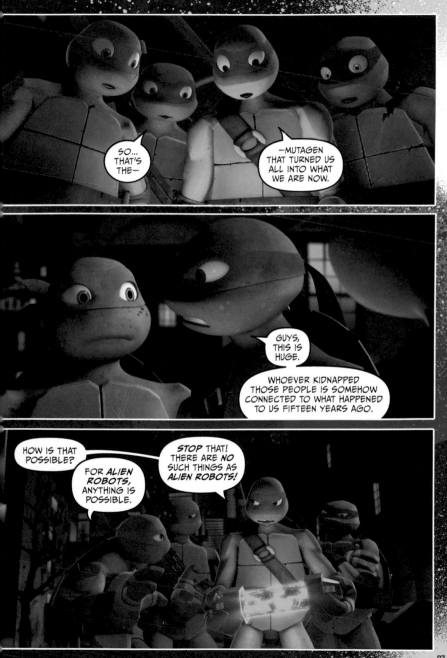

SO... THAT'S THE—

—MUTAGEN THAT TURNED US ALL INTO WHAT WE ARE NOW.

GUYS, THIS IS HUGE.

WHOEVER KIDNAPPED THOSE PEOPLE IS SOMEHOW CONNECTED TO WHAT HAPPENED TO US FIFTEEN YEARS AGO.

HOW IS THAT POSSIBLE?

FOR *ALIEN ROBOTS*, ANYTHING IS POSSIBLE.

STOP THAT! THERE ARE *NO* SUCH THINGS AS *ALIEN ROBOTS!*

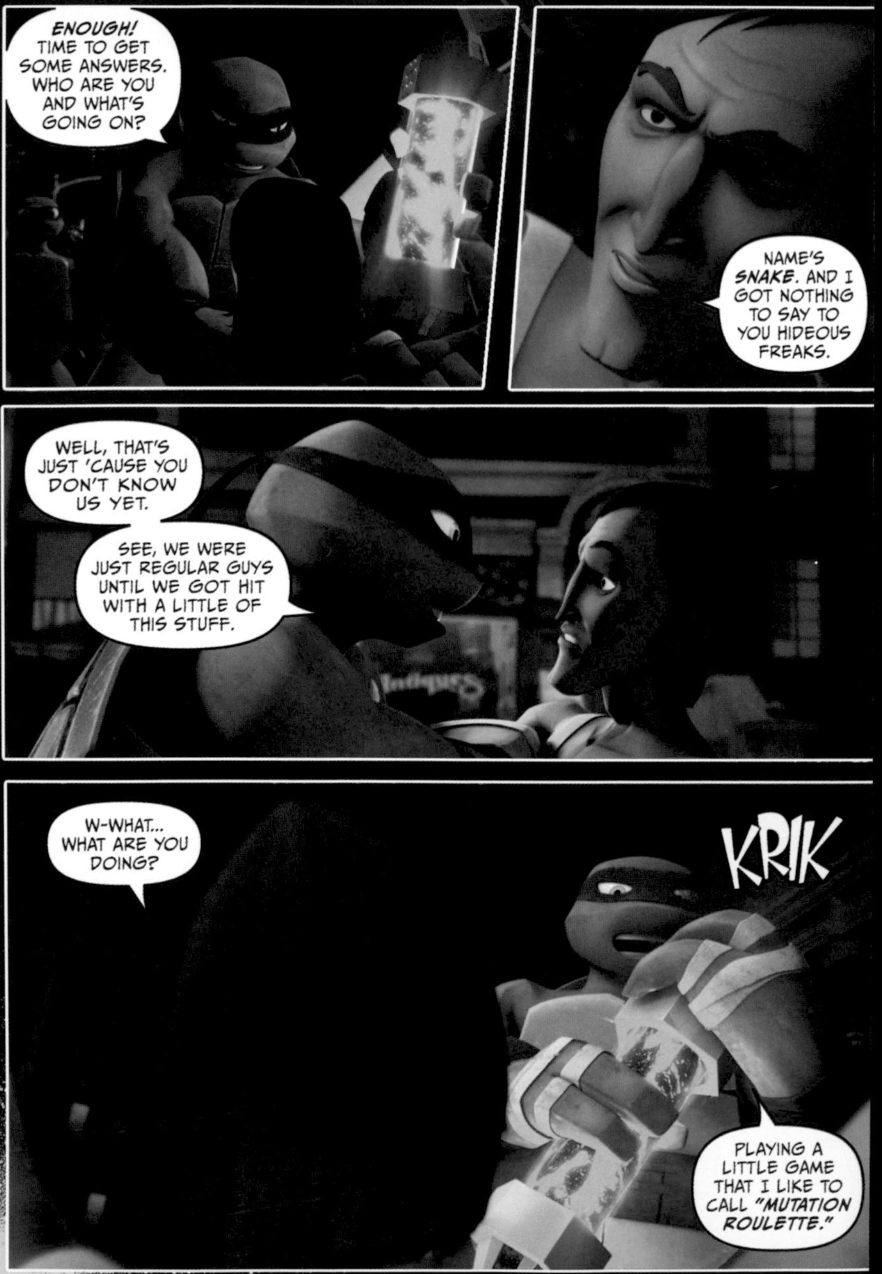
ENOUGH! TIME TO GET SOME ANSWERS. WHO ARE YOU AND WHAT'S GOING ON?
NAME'S SNAKE. AND I GOT NOTHING TO SAY TO YOU HIDEOUS FREAKS.
WELL, THAT'S JUST 'CAUSE YOU DON'T KNOW US YET.
SEE, WE WERE JUST REGULAR GUYS UNTIL WE GOT HIT WITH A LITTLE OF THIS STUFF.
W-WHAT... WHAT ARE YOU DOING?
KRIK
PLAYING A LITTLE GAME THAT I LIKE TO CALL "MUTATION ROULETTE."

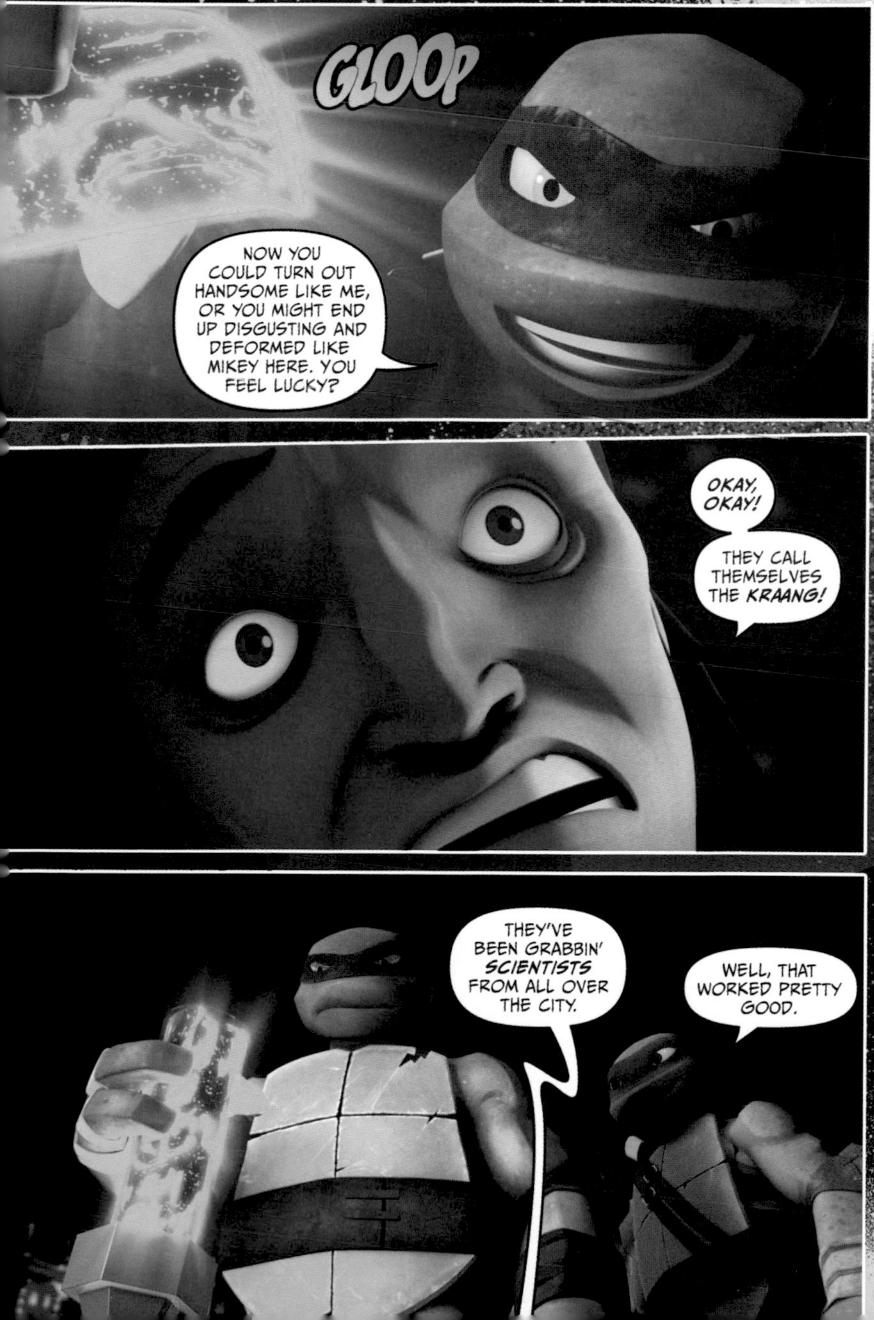
GLOOP
NOW YOU COULD TURN OUT HANDSOME LIKE ME, OR YOU MIGHT END UP DISGUSTING AND DEFORMED LIKE MIKEY HERE. YOU FEEL LUCKY?
OKAY, OKAY!
THEY CALL THEMSELVES THE KRAANG!
THEY'VE BEEN GRABBIN' SCIENTISTS FROM ALL OVER THE CITY.
WELL, THAT WORKED PRETTY GOOD.

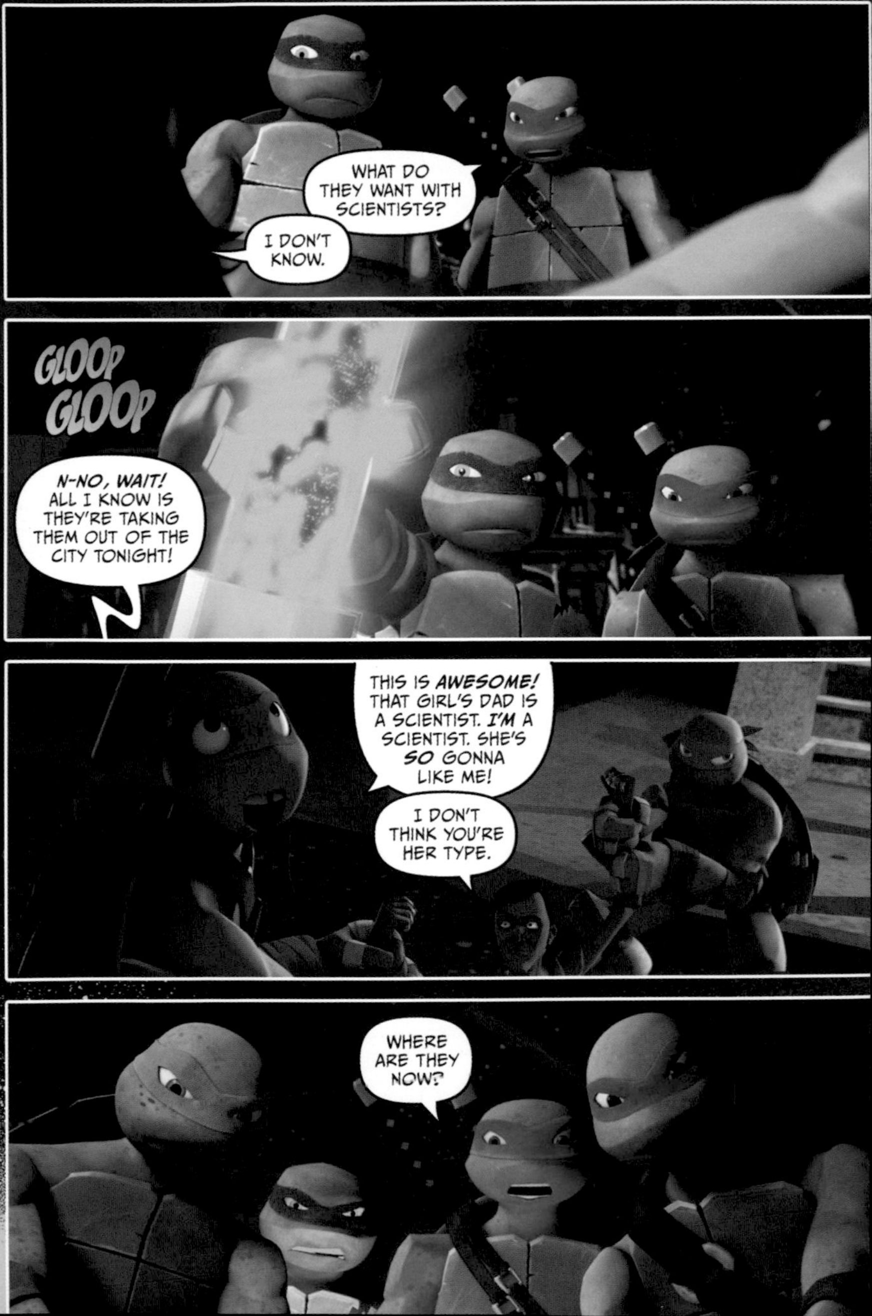
WHAT DO THEY WANT WITH SCIENTISTS?
I DON'T KNOW.
GLOOP GLOOP
N-NO, WAIT! ALL I KNOW IS THEY'RE TAKING THEM OUT OF THE CITY TONIGHT!
THIS IS AWESOME! THAT GIRL'S DAD IS A SCIENTIST. I'M A SCIENTIST. SHE'S SO GONNA LIKE ME!
I DON'T THINK YOU'RE HER TYPE.
WHERE ARE THEY NOW?

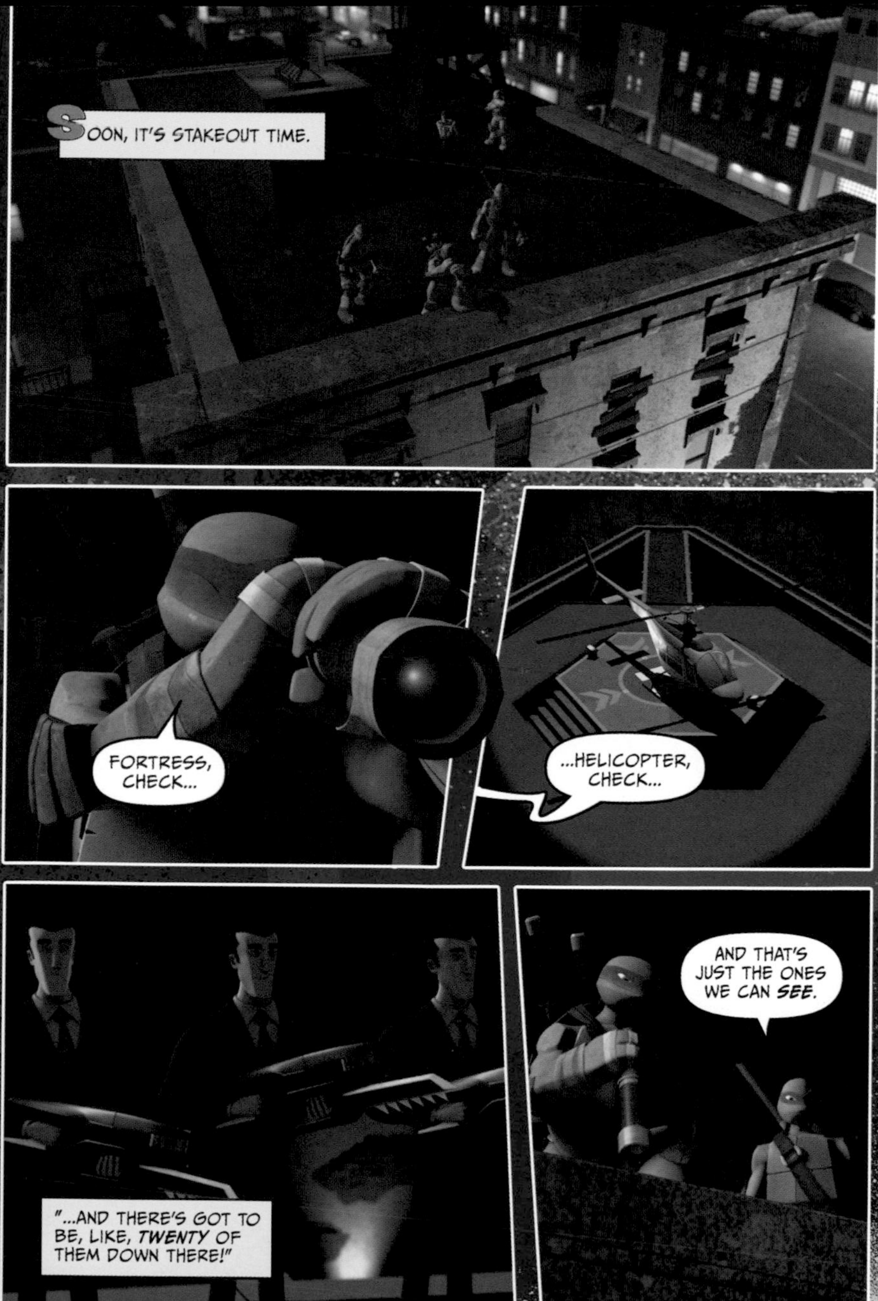
SOON, IT'S STAKEOUT TIME.
FORTRESS, CHECK...
...HELICOPTER, CHECK...
"...AND THERE'S GOT TO BE, LIKE, *TWENTY* OF THEM DOWN THERE!"
AND THAT'S JUST THE ONES WE CAN *SEE*.

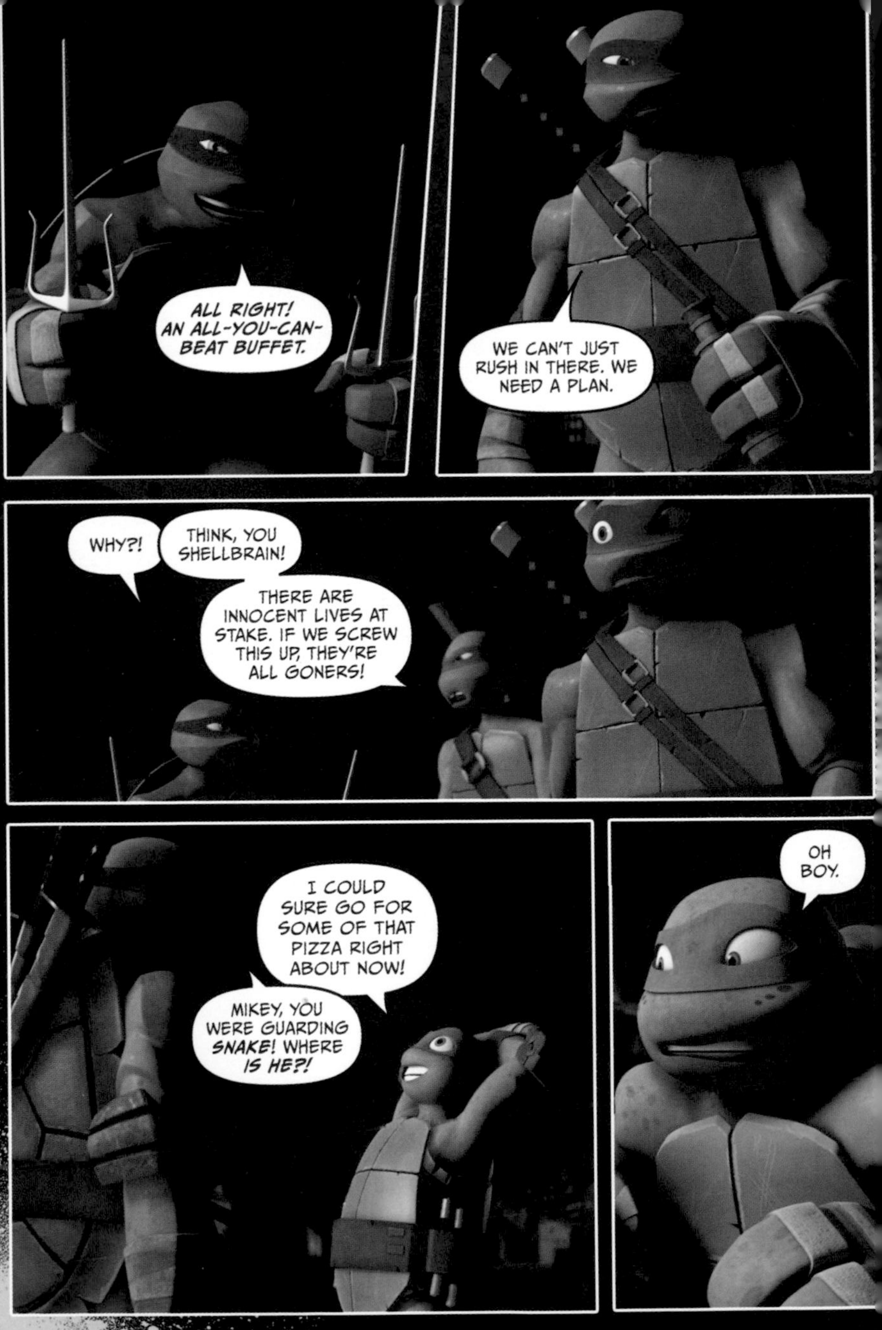
ALL RIGHT! AN ALL-YOU-CAN-BEAT BUFFET.
WE CAN'T JUST RUSH IN THERE. WE NEED A PLAN.
WHY?!
THINK, YOU SHELLBRAIN!
THERE ARE INNOCENT LIVES AT STAKE. IF WE SCREW THIS UP, THEY'RE ALL GONERS!
I COULD SURE GO FOR SOME OF THAT PIZZA RIGHT ABOUT NOW!
MIKEY, YOU WERE GUARDING SNAKE! WHERE IS HE?!
OH BOY.

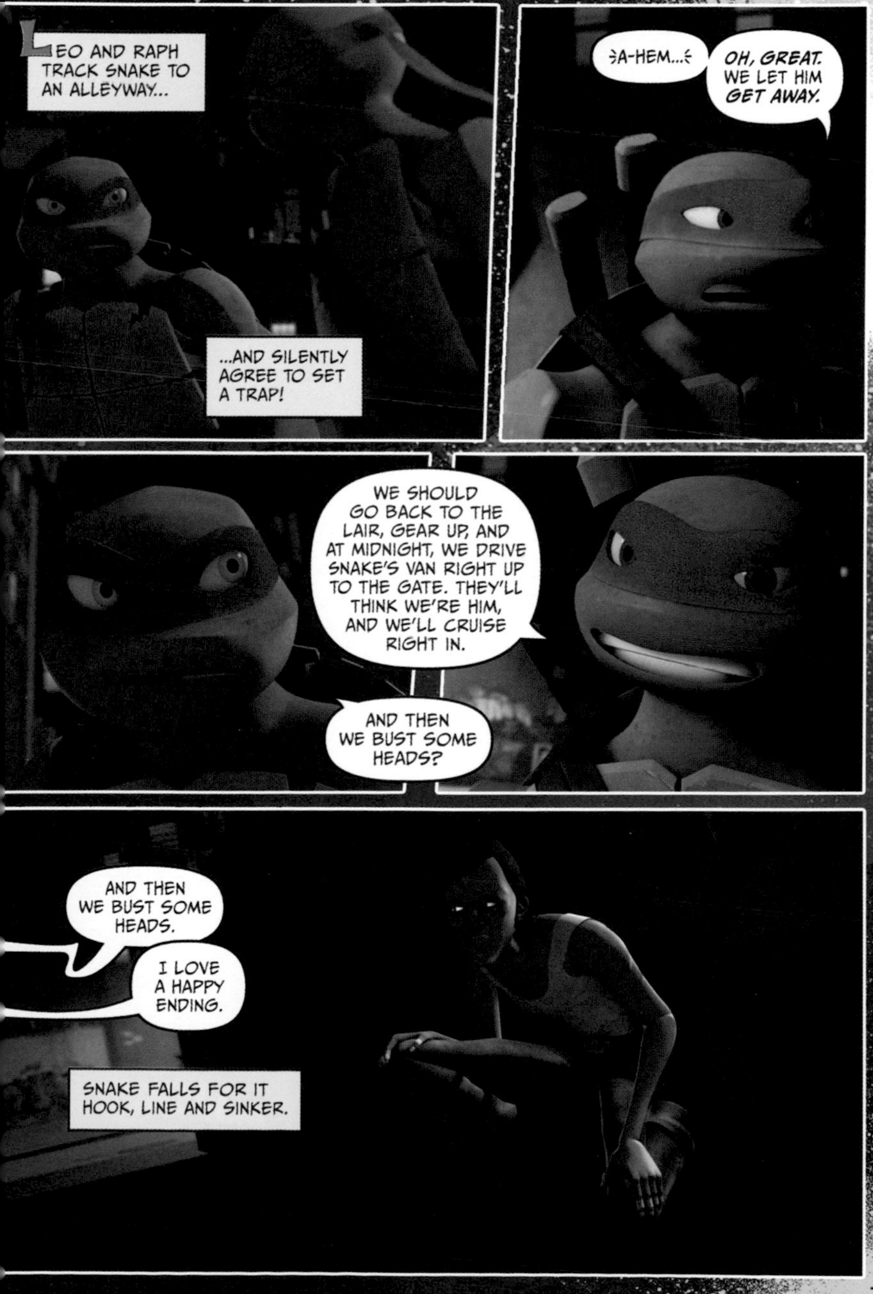
LEO AND RAPH TRACK SNAKE TO AN ALLEYWAY...
...AND SILENTLY AGREE TO SET A TRAP!
A-HEM...
OH, GREAT. WE LET HIM GET AWAY.
WE SHOULD GO BACK TO THE LAIR, GEAR UP, AND AT MIDNIGHT, WE DRIVE SNAKE'S VAN RIGHT UP TO THE GATE. THEY'LL THINK WE'RE HIM, AND WE'LL CRUISE RIGHT IN.
AND THEN WE BUST SOME HEADS?
AND THEN WE BUST SOME HEADS.
I LOVE A HAPPY ENDING.
SNAKE FALLS FOR IT HOOK, LINE AND SINKER.

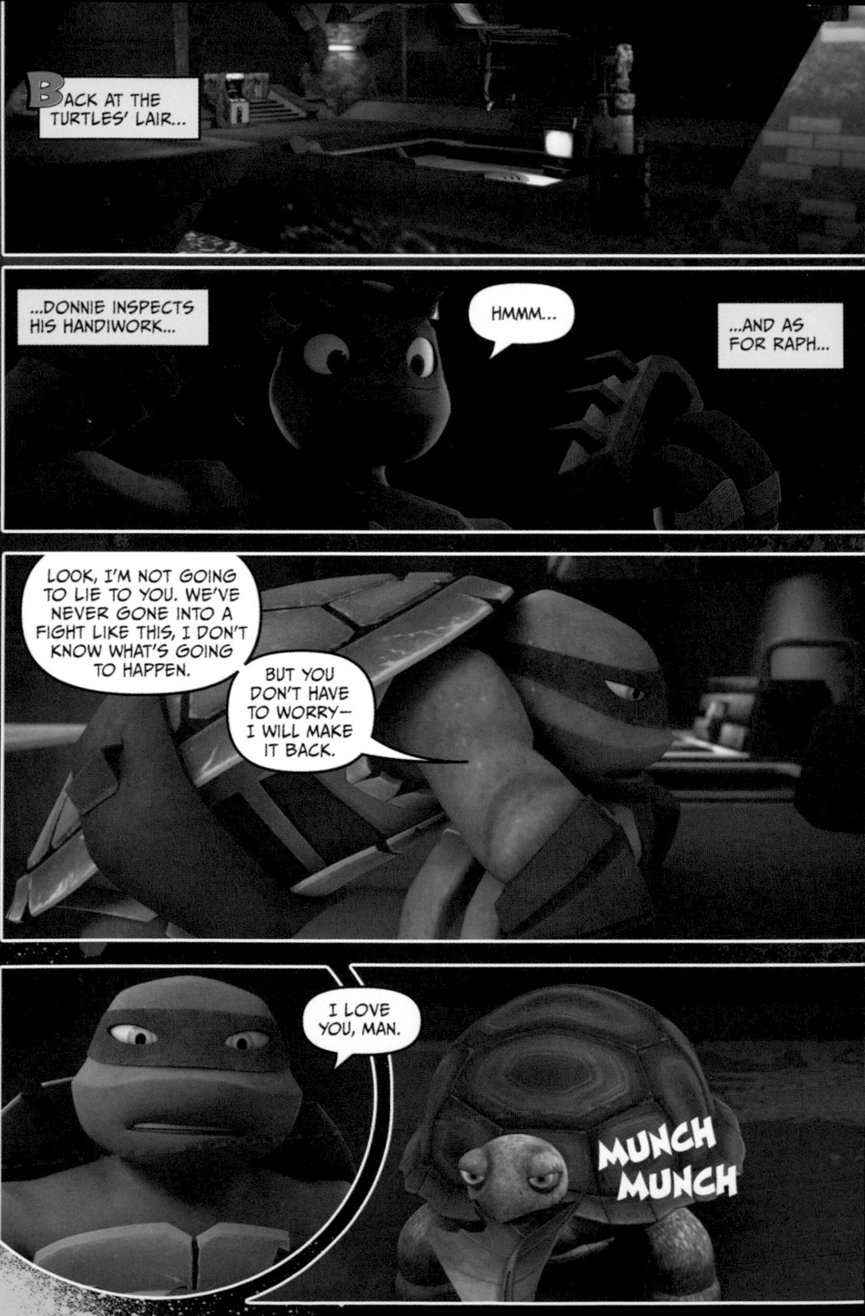
BACK AT THE TURTLES' LAIR...
...DONNIE INSPECTS HIS HANDIWORK...
HMMM...
...AND AS FOR RAPH...
LOOK, I'M NOT GOING TO LIE TO YOU. WE'VE NEVER GONE INTO A FIGHT LIKE THIS, I DON'T KNOW WHAT'S GOING TO HAPPEN.
BUT YOU DON'T HAVE TO WORRY— I WILL MAKE IT BACK.
I LOVE YOU, MAN.
MUNCH MUNCH

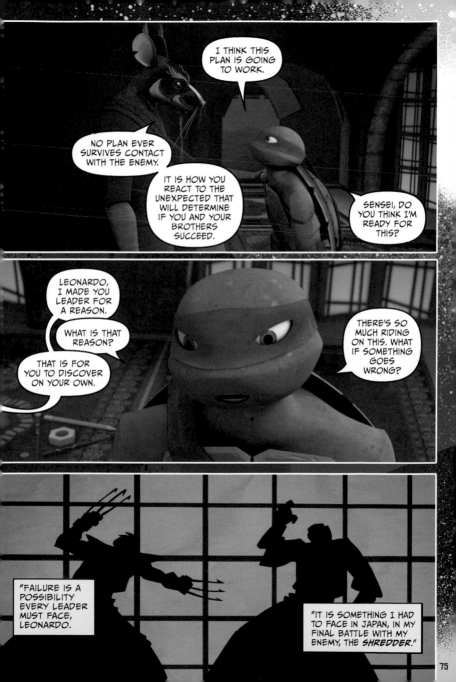

I THINK THIS PLAN IS GOING TO WORK.

NO PLAN EVER SURVIVES CONTACT WITH THE ENEMY.

IT IS HOW YOU REACT TO THE UNEXPECTED THAT WILL DETERMINE IF YOU AND YOUR BROTHERS SUCCEED.

SENSEI, DO YOU THINK I'M READY FOR THIS?

LEONARDO, I MADE YOU LEADER FOR A REASON.

WHAT IS THAT REASON?

THAT IS FOR YOU TO DISCOVER ON YOUR OWN.

THERE'S SO MUCH RIDING ON THIS. WHAT IF SOMETHING GOES WRONG?

"FAILURE IS A POSSIBILITY EVERY LEADER MUST FACE, LEONARDO.

"IT IS SOMETHING I HAD TO FACE IN JAPAN, IN MY FINAL BATTLE WITH MY ENEMY, THE *SHREDDER*."

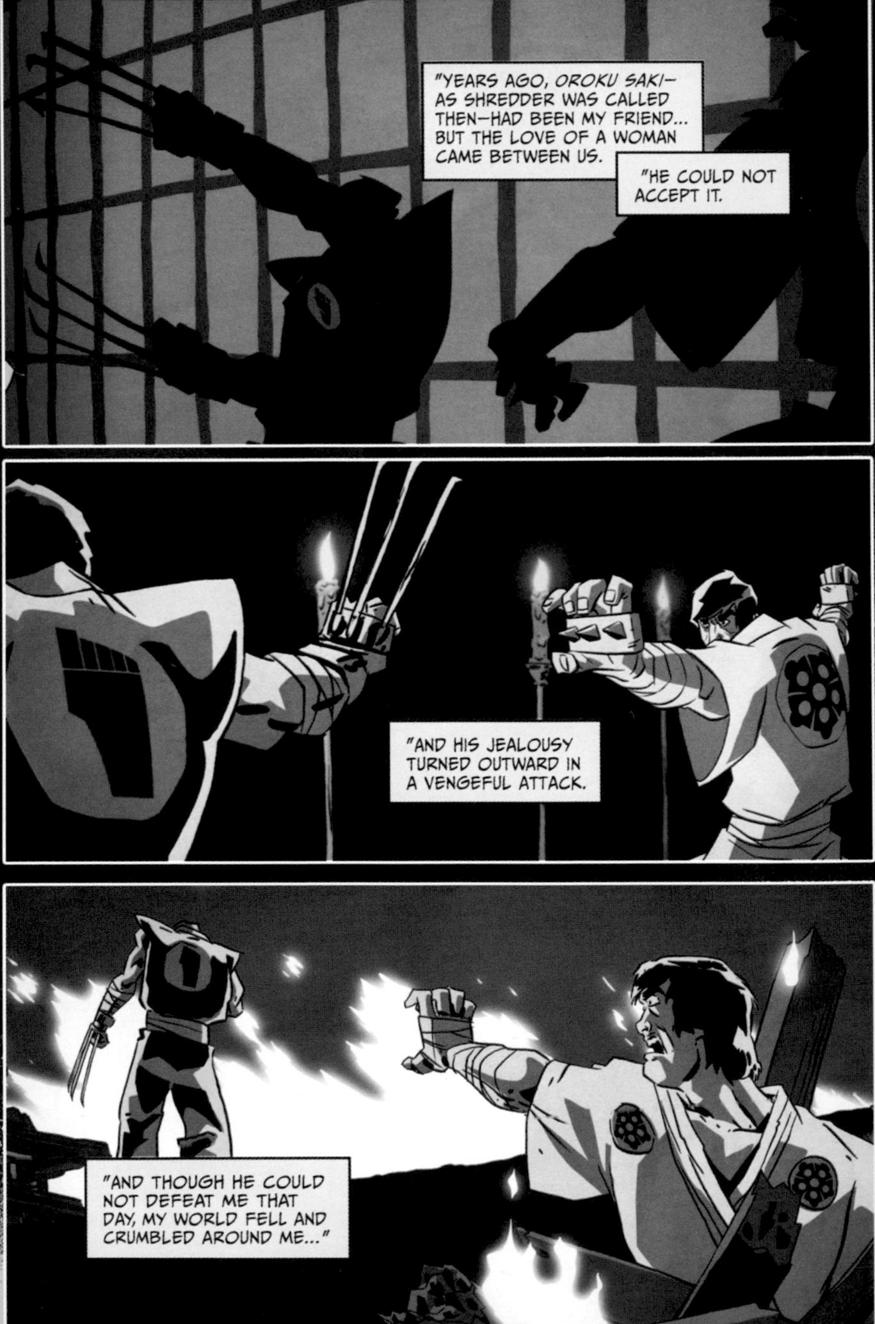
"YEARS AGO, OROKU SAKI—AS SHREDDER WAS CALLED THEN—HAD BEEN MY FRIEND... BUT THE LOVE OF A WOMAN CAME BETWEEN US.
"HE COULD NOT ACCEPT IT.
"AND HIS JEALOUSY TURNED OUTWARD IN A VENGEFUL ATTACK.
"AND THOUGH HE COULD NOT DEFEAT ME THAT DAY, MY WORLD FELL AND CRUMBLED AROUND ME..."

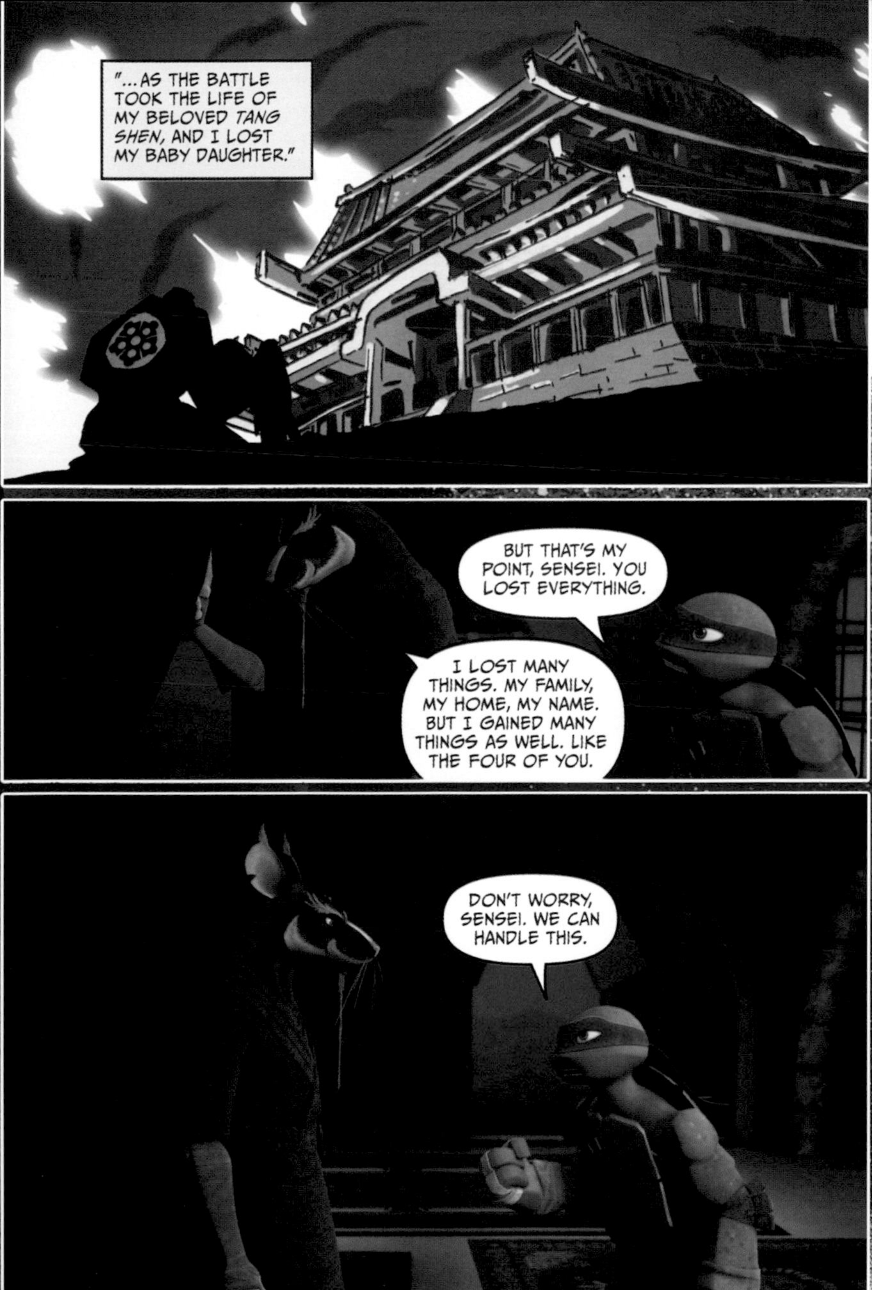
"...AS THE BATTLE TOOK THE LIFE OF MY BELOVED *TANG SHEN*, AND I LOST MY BABY DAUGHTER."
BUT THAT'S MY POINT, SENSEI. YOU LOST EVERYTHING.
I LOST MANY THINGS. MY FAMILY, MY HOME, MY NAME. BUT I GAINED MANY THINGS AS WELL. LIKE THE FOUR OF YOU.
DON'T WORRY, SENSEI. WE CAN HANDLE THIS.

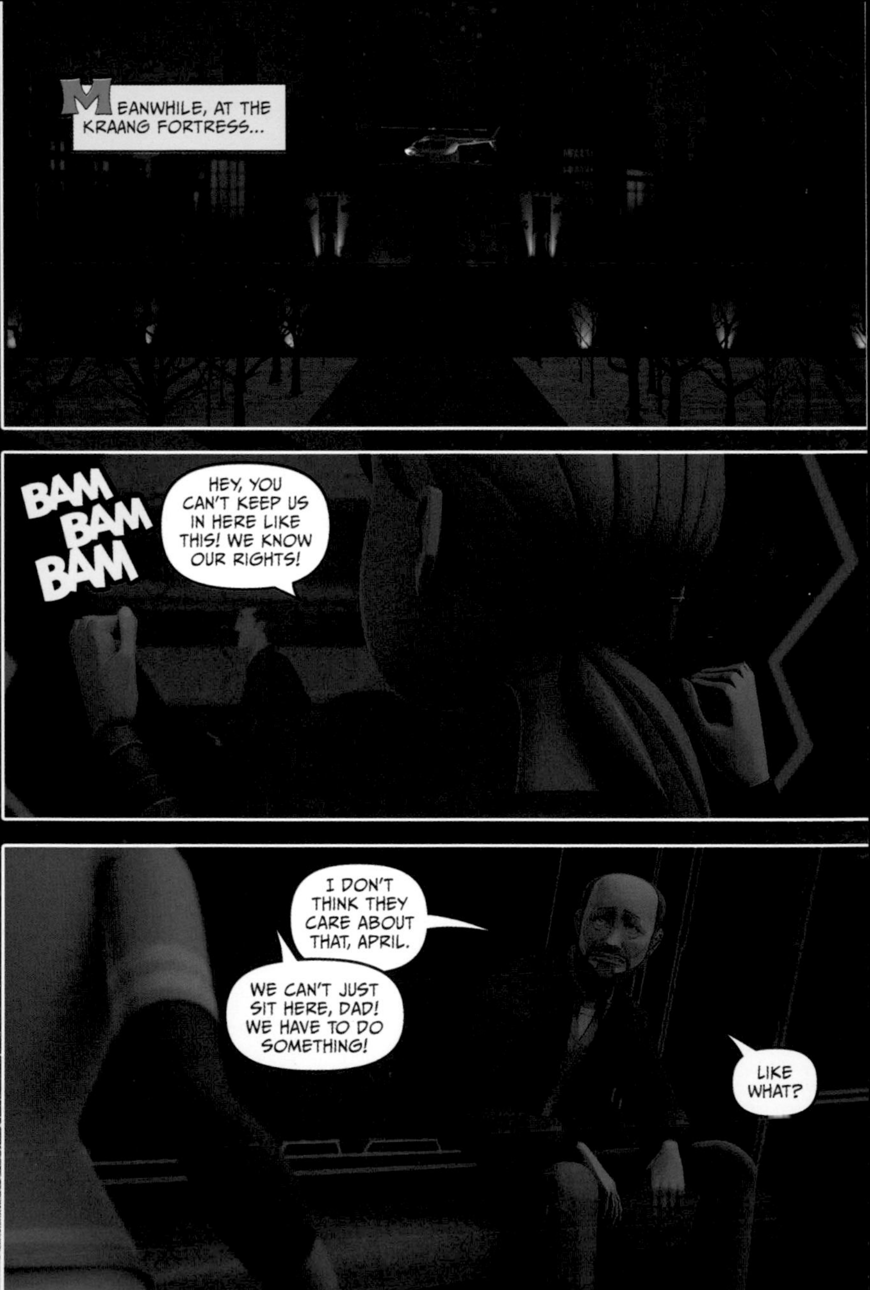
MEANWHILE, AT THE KRAANG FORTRESS...
BAM BAM BAM
HEY, YOU CAN'T KEEP US IN HERE LIKE THIS! WE KNOW OUR RIGHTS!
I DON'T THINK THEY CARE ABOUT THAT, APRIL.
WE CAN'T JUST SIT HERE, DAD! WE HAVE TO DO SOMETHING!
LIKE WHAT?

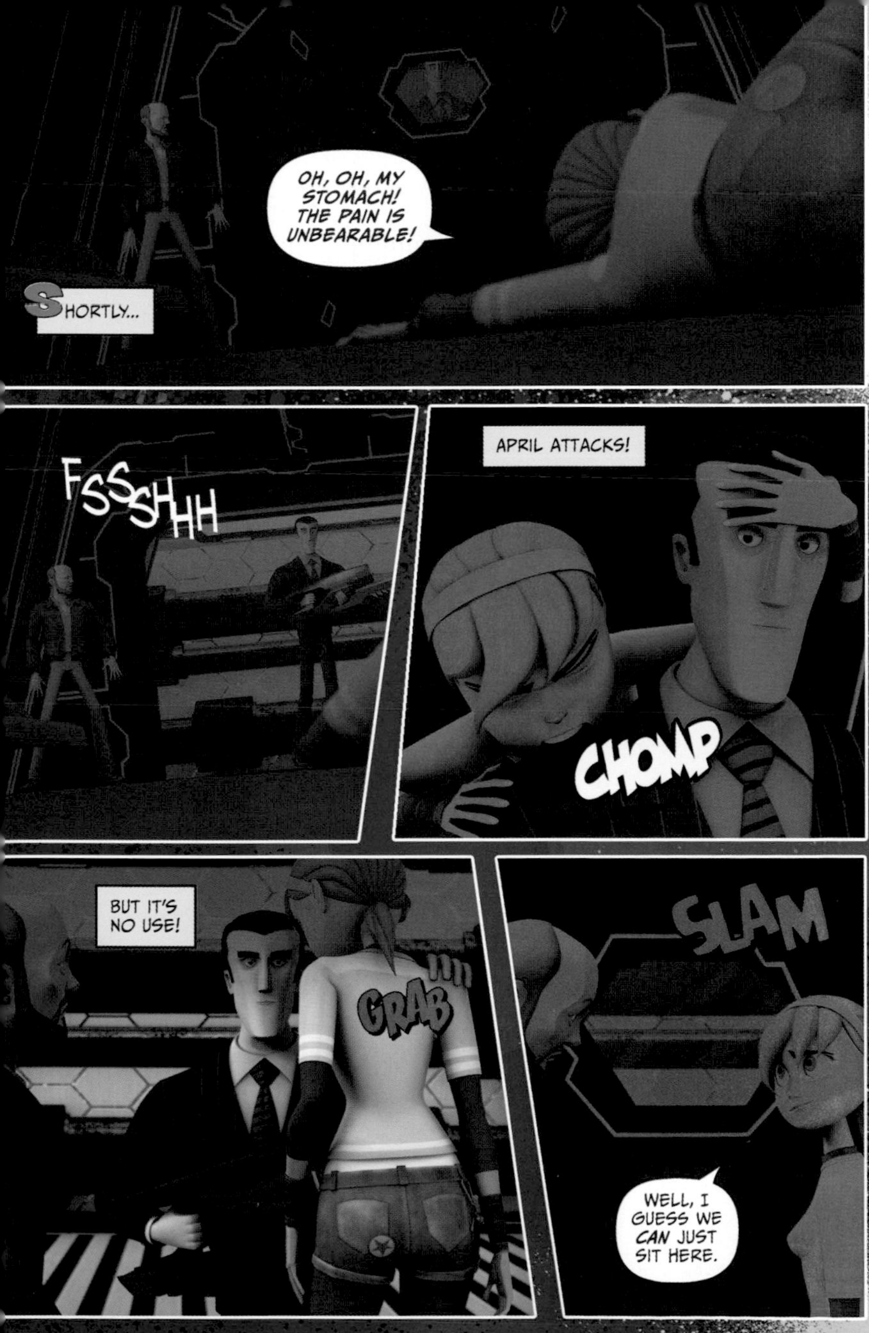
OH, OH, MY STOMACH! THE PAIN IS UNBEARABLE!
SHORTLY...
FSSSHHH
APRIL ATTACKS!
CHOMP
BUT IT'S NO USE!
GRAB
SLAM
WELL, I GUESS WE CAN JUST SIT HERE.

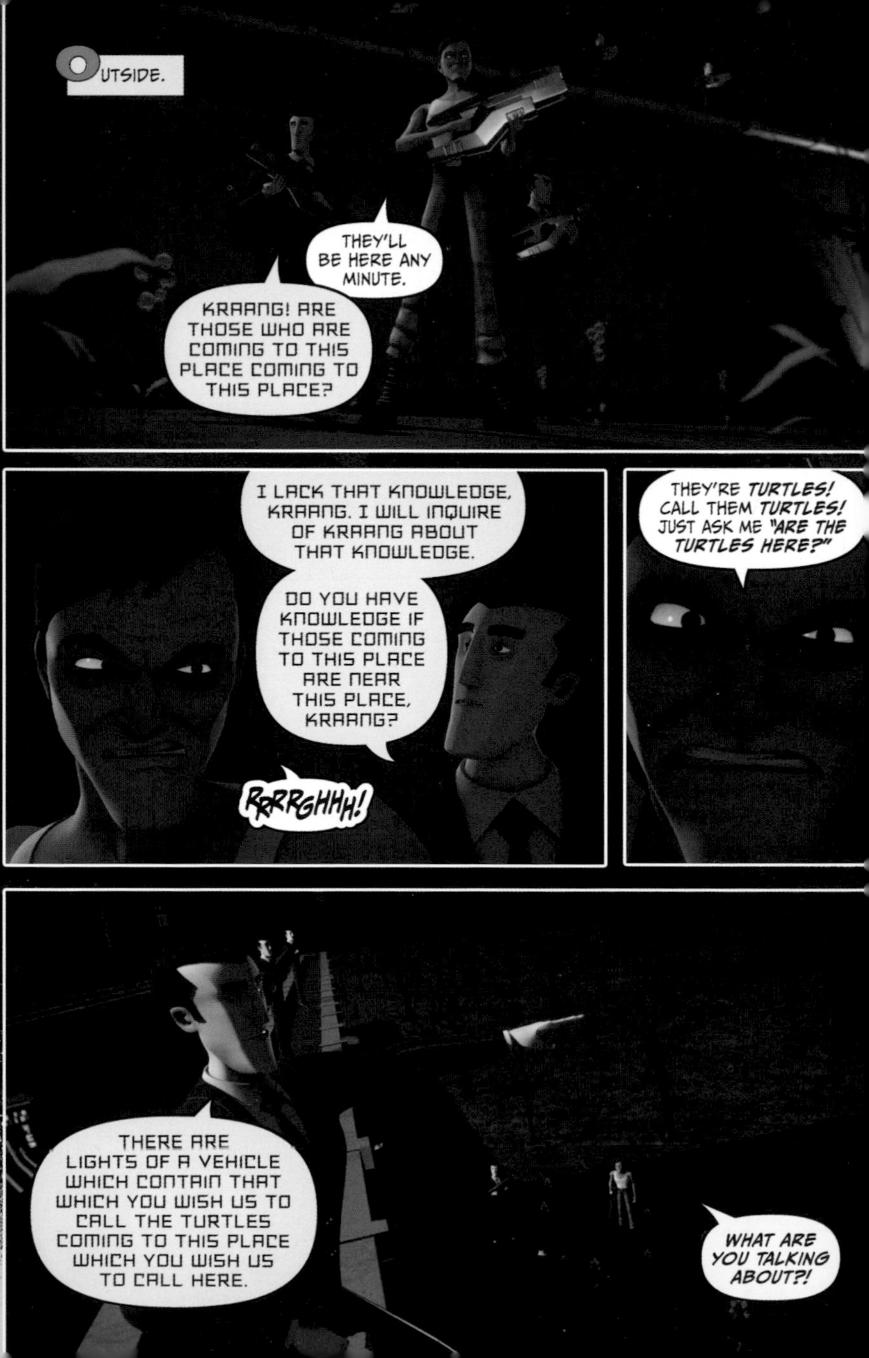
OUTSIDE.
THEY'LL BE HERE ANY MINUTE.
KRAANG! ARE THOSE WHO ARE COMING TO THIS PLACE COMING TO THIS PLACE?
I LACK THAT KNOWLEDGE, KRAANG. I WILL INQUIRE OF KRAANG ABOUT THAT KNOWLEDGE.
DO YOU HAVE KNOWLEDGE IF THOSE COMING TO THIS PLACE ARE NEAR THIS PLACE, KRAANG?
RRRRGHHH!
THEY'RE *TURTLES!* CALL THEM *TURTLES!* JUST ASK ME *"ARE THE TURTLES HERE?"*
THERE ARE LIGHTS OF A VEHICLE WHICH CONTAIN THAT WHICH YOU WISH US TO CALL THE TURTLES COMING TO THIS PLACE WHICH YOU WISH US TO CALL HERE.
WHAT ARE YOU TALKING ABOUT?!

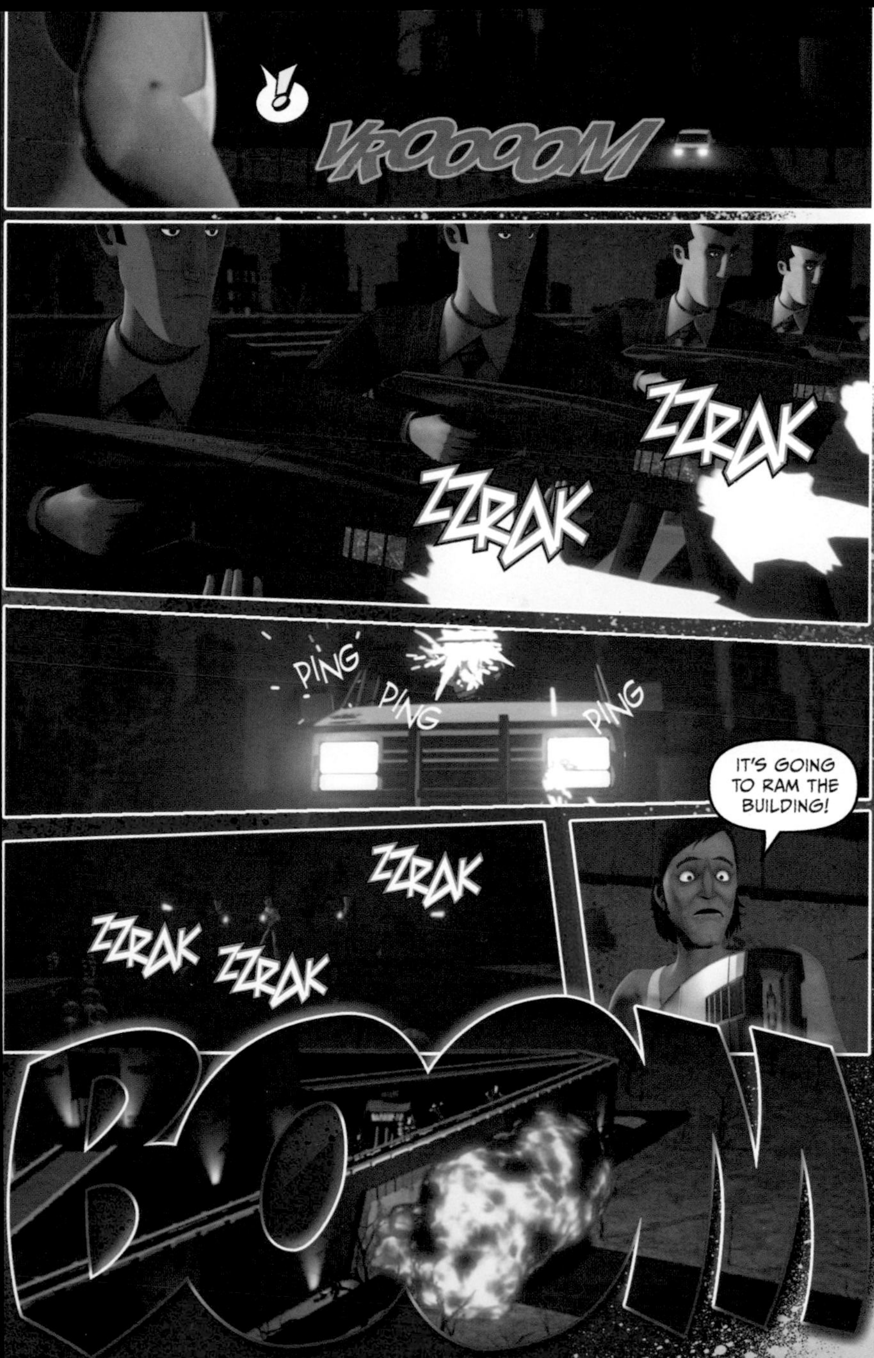
VROOOOOM
ZZRAK
ZZRAK
PING
PING
PING
IT'S GOING TO RAM THE BUILDING!
ZZRAK
ZZRAK
ZZRAK
BOOM

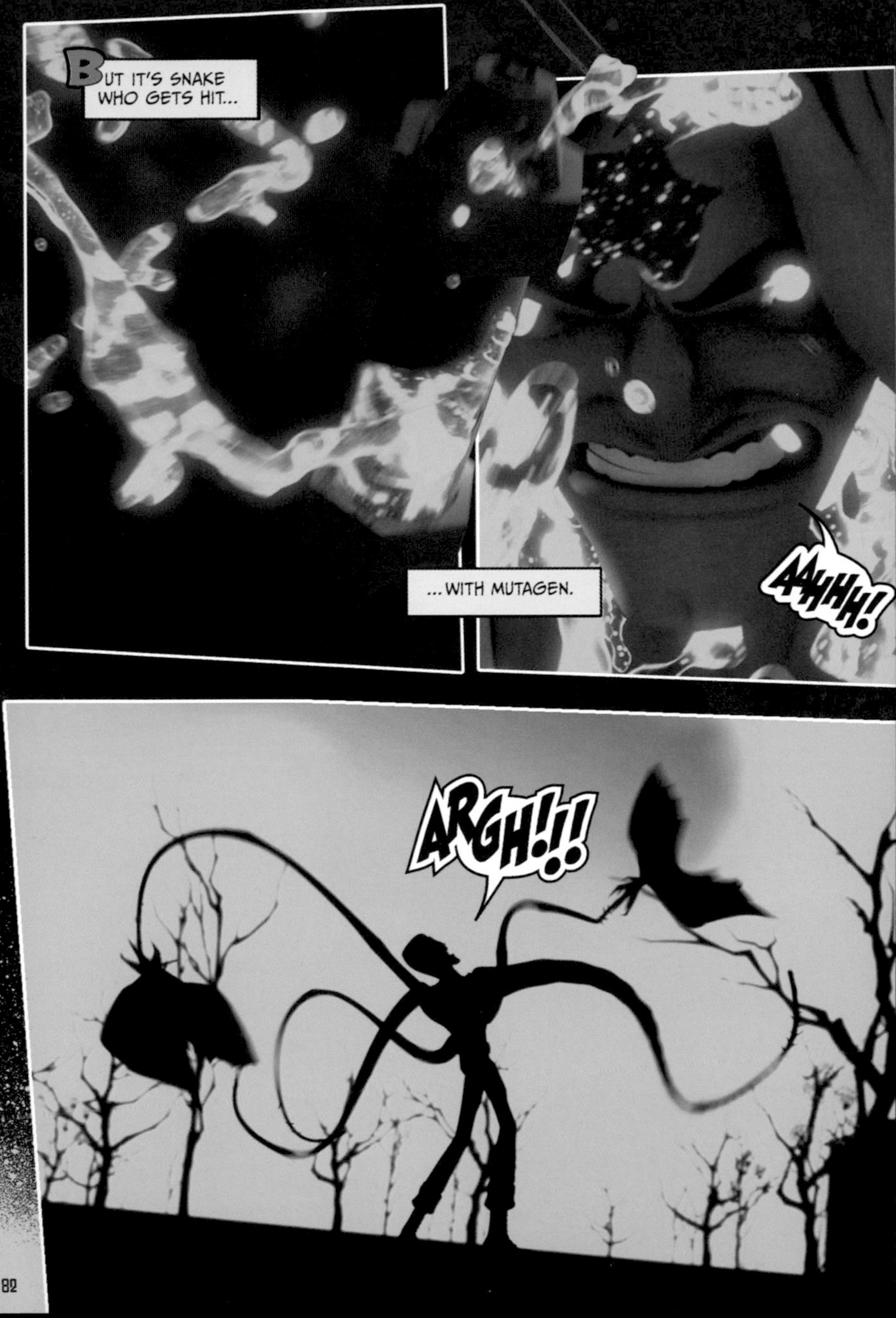

BUT IT'S SNAKE WHO GETS HIT...
...WITH MUTAGEN.
AAHHH!
ARGH!!!

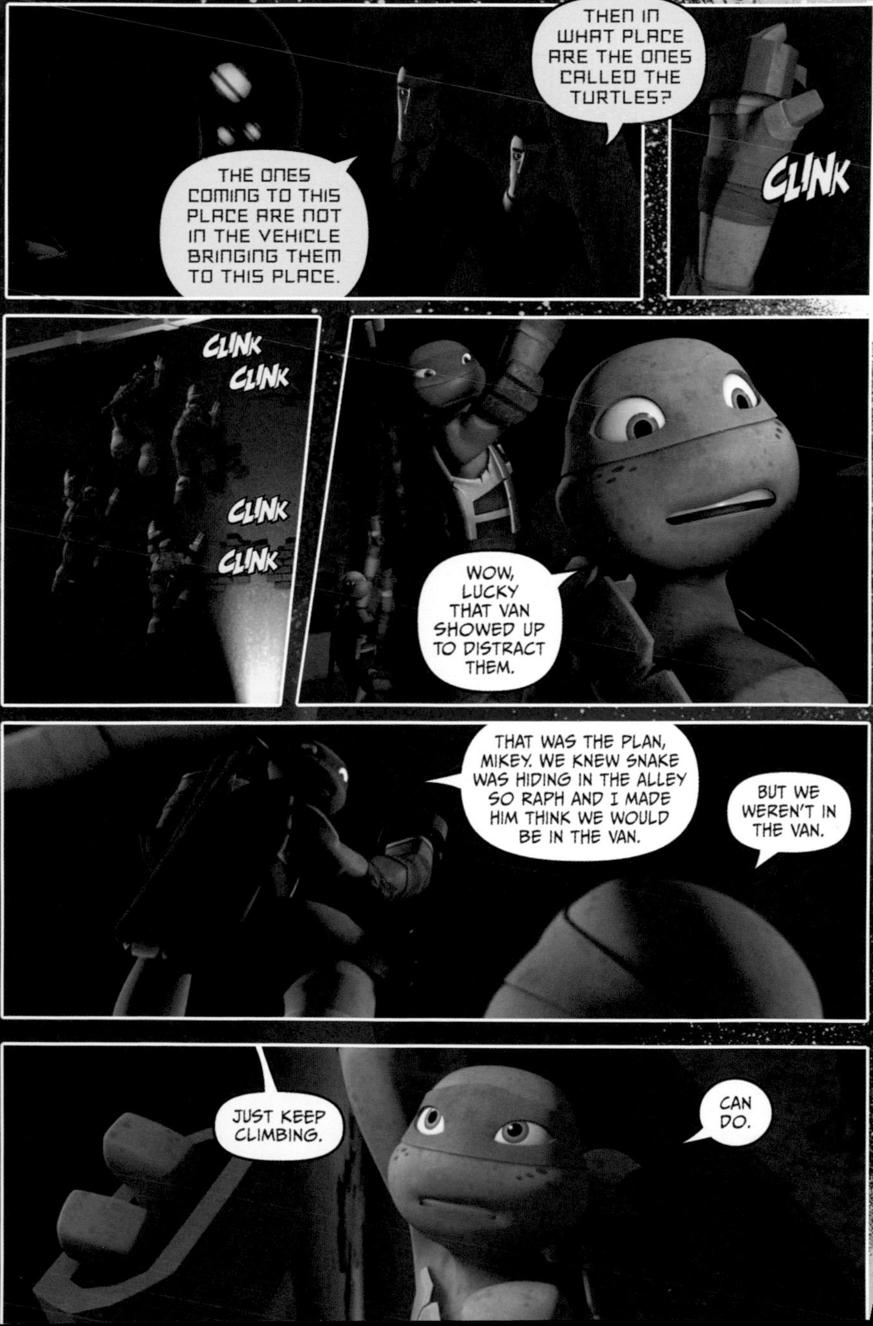
THE ONES COMING TO THIS PLACE ARE NOT IN THE VEHICLE BRINGING THEM TO THIS PLACE.
THEN IN WHAT PLACE ARE THE ONES CALLED THE TURTLES?
CLINK
CLINK
CLINK
CLINK
CLINK
WOW, LUCKY THAT VAN SHOWED UP TO DISTRACT THEM.
THAT WAS THE PLAN, MIKEY. WE KNEW SNAKE WAS HIDING IN THE ALLEY SO RAPH AND I MADE HIM THINK WE WOULD BE IN THE VAN.
BUT WE WEREN'T IN THE VAN.
JUST KEEP CLIMBING.
CAN DO.

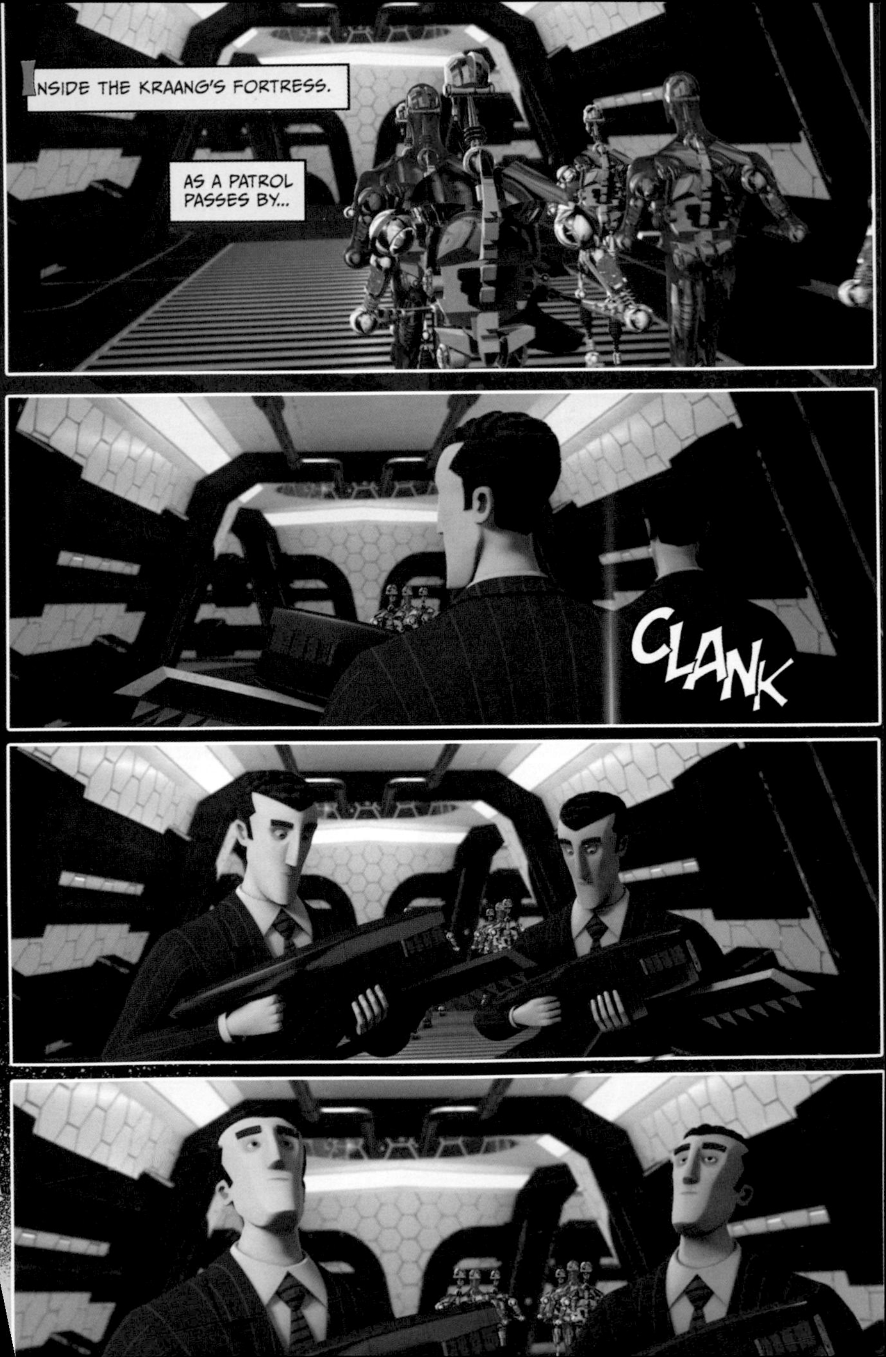
INSIDE THE KRAANG'S FORTRESS.
AS A PATROL PASSES BY...
CLANK

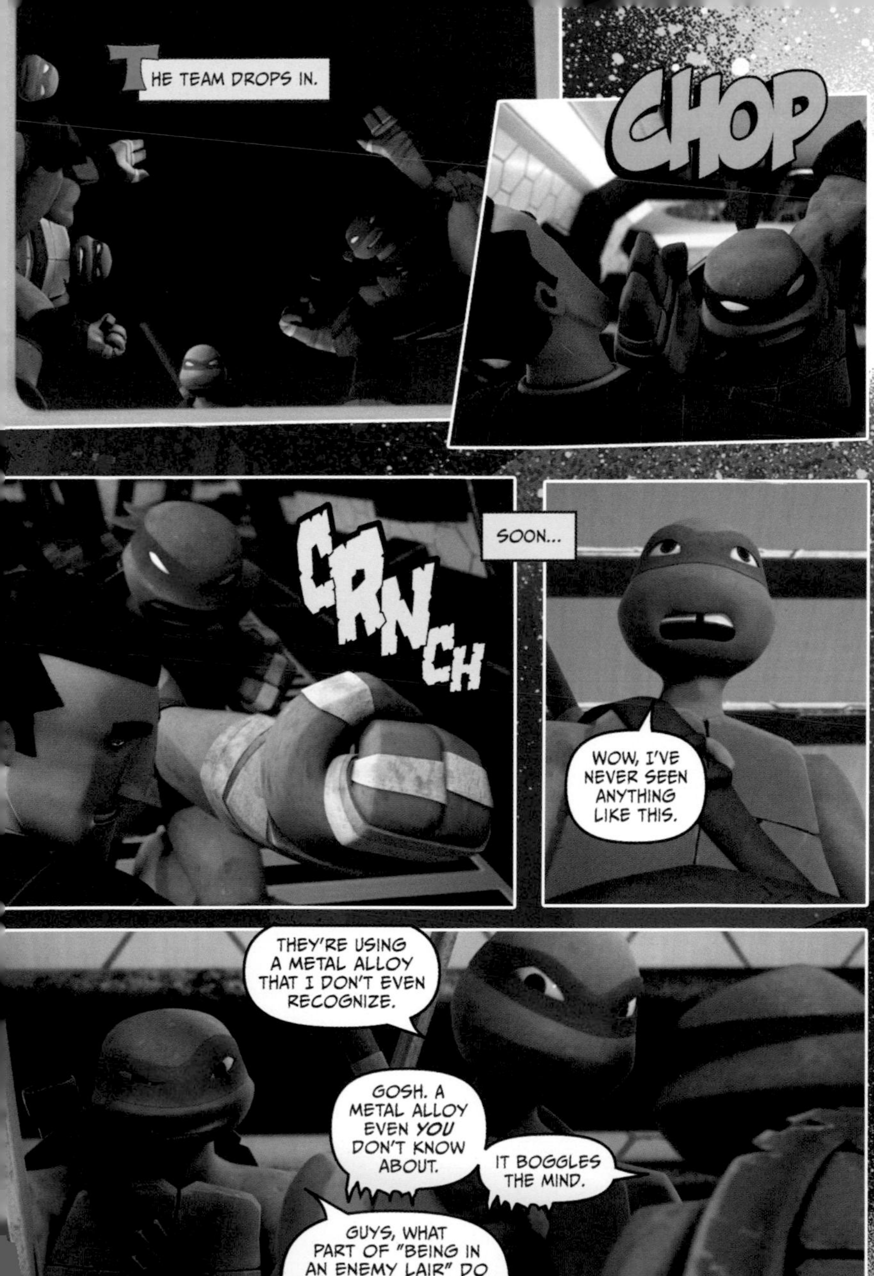
THE TEAM DROPS IN.
CHOP
CRNCH
SOON...
WOW, I'VE NEVER SEEN ANYTHING LIKE THIS.
THEY'RE USING A METAL ALLOY THAT I DON'T EVEN RECOGNIZE.
GOSH. A METAL ALLOY EVEN *YOU* DON'T KNOW ABOUT.
IT BOGGLES THE MIND.
GUYS, WHAT PART OF "BEING IN AN ENEMY LAIR" DO YOU NOT UNDERSTAND?

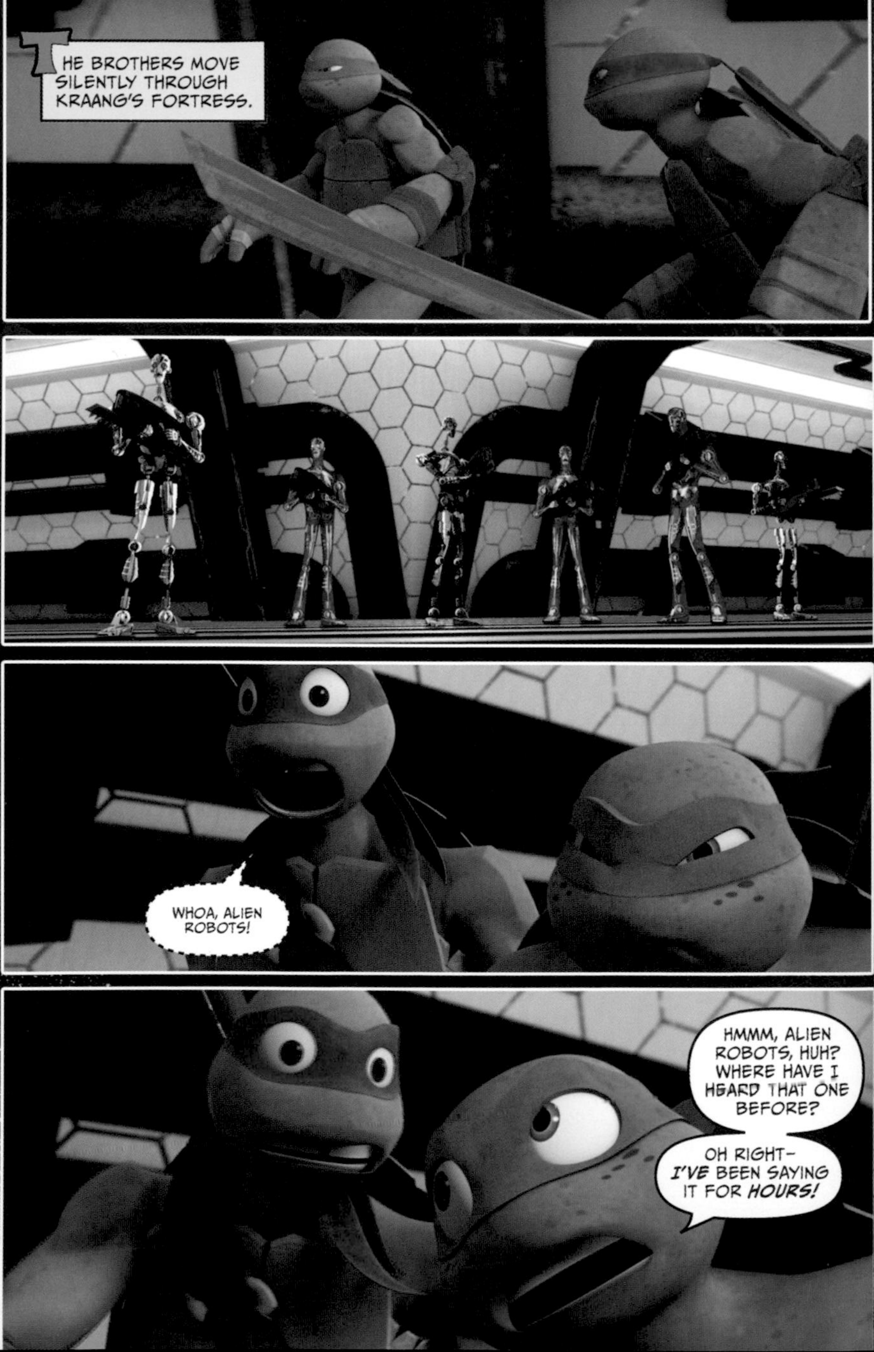
THE BROTHERS MOVE SILENTLY THROUGH KRAANG'S FORTRESS.
WHOA, ALIEN ROBOTS!
HMMM, ALIEN ROBOTS, HUH? WHERE HAVE I HEARD THAT ONE BEFORE?
OH RIGHT– I'VE BEEN SAYING IT FOR HOURS!

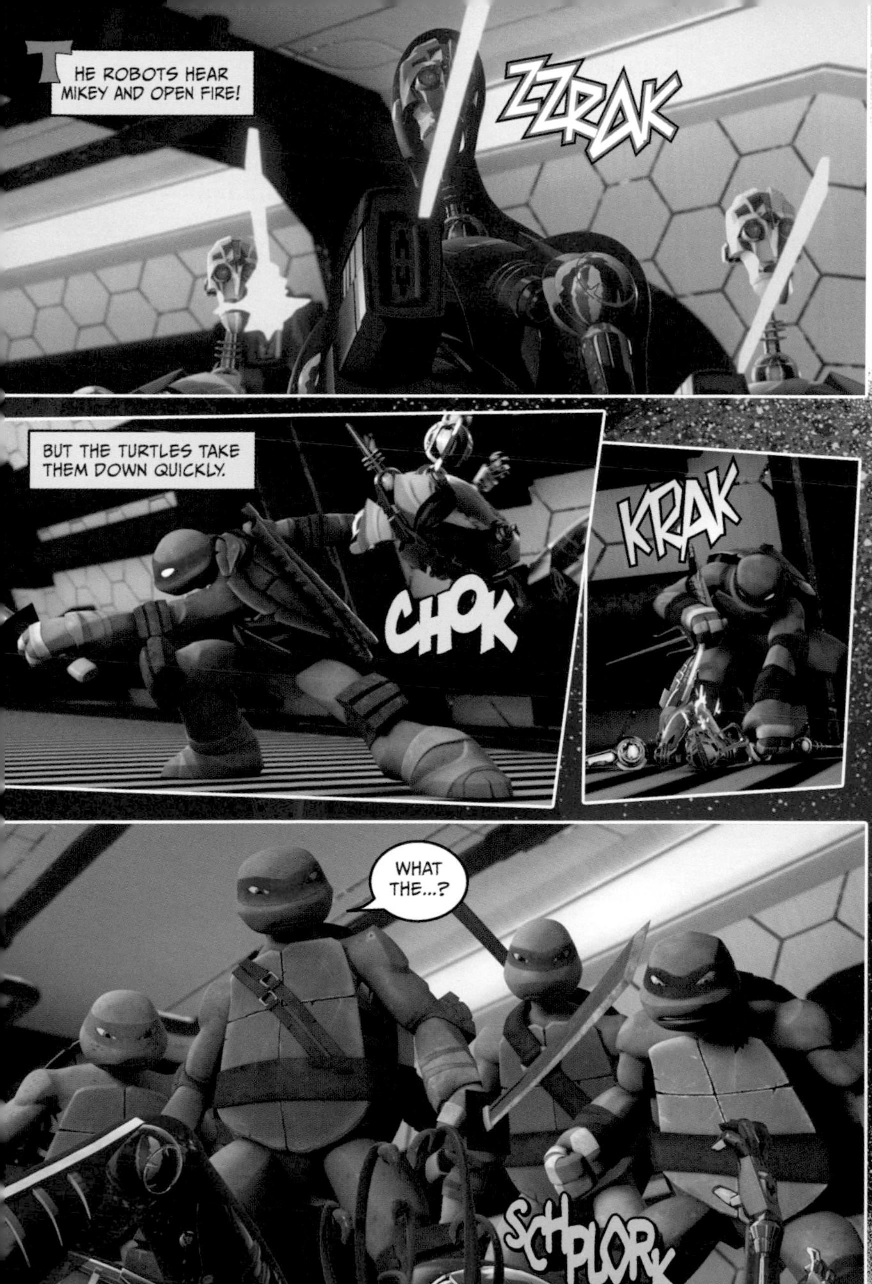
THE ROBOTS HEAR MIKEY AND OPEN FIRE!
ZZRAK
BUT THE TURTLES TAKE THEM DOWN QUICKLY.
CHOK
KRAK
WHAT THE...?
SCHPLORK

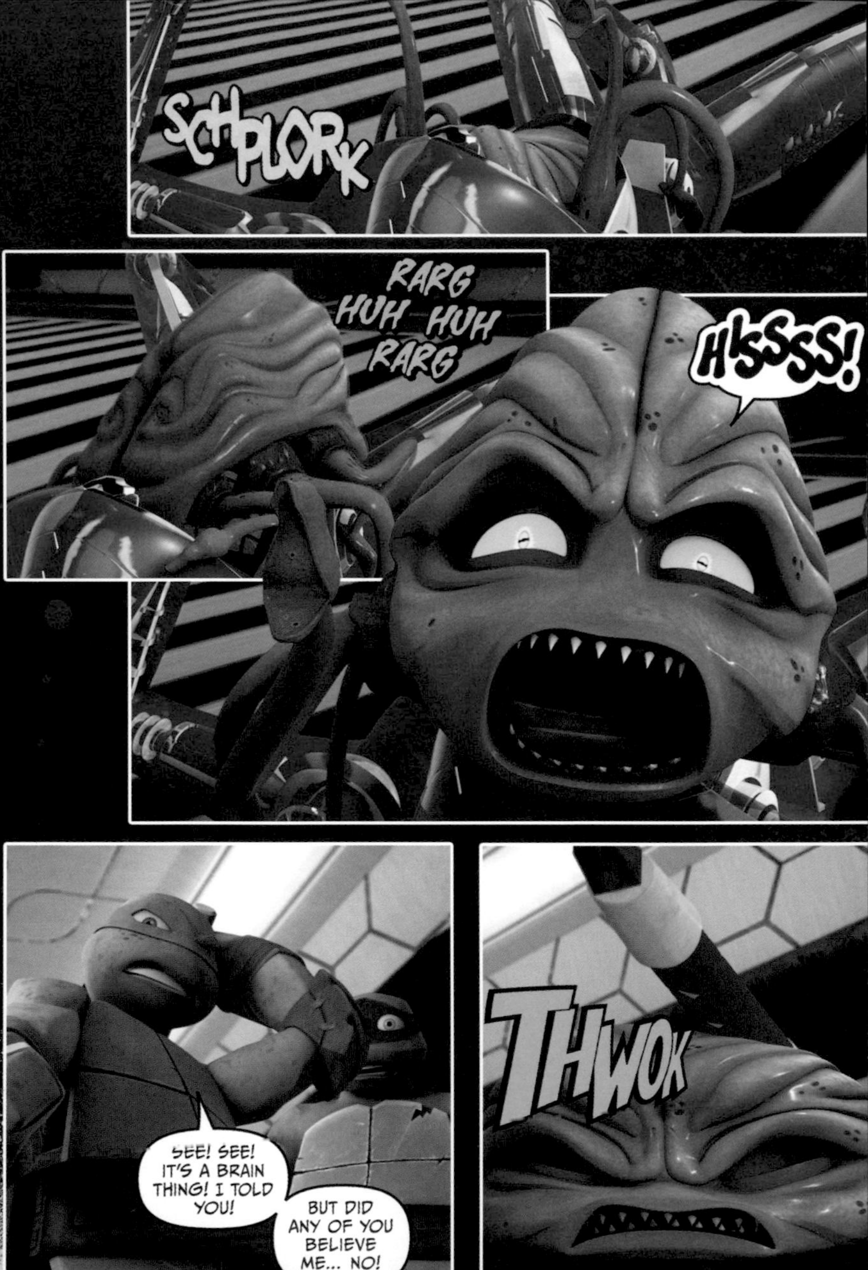
SCHPLORK
RARG HUH HUH RARG
HISSSS!
SEE! SEE! IT'S A BRAIN THING! I TOLD YOU!
BUT DID ANY OF YOU BELIEVE ME... NO!
THWOK

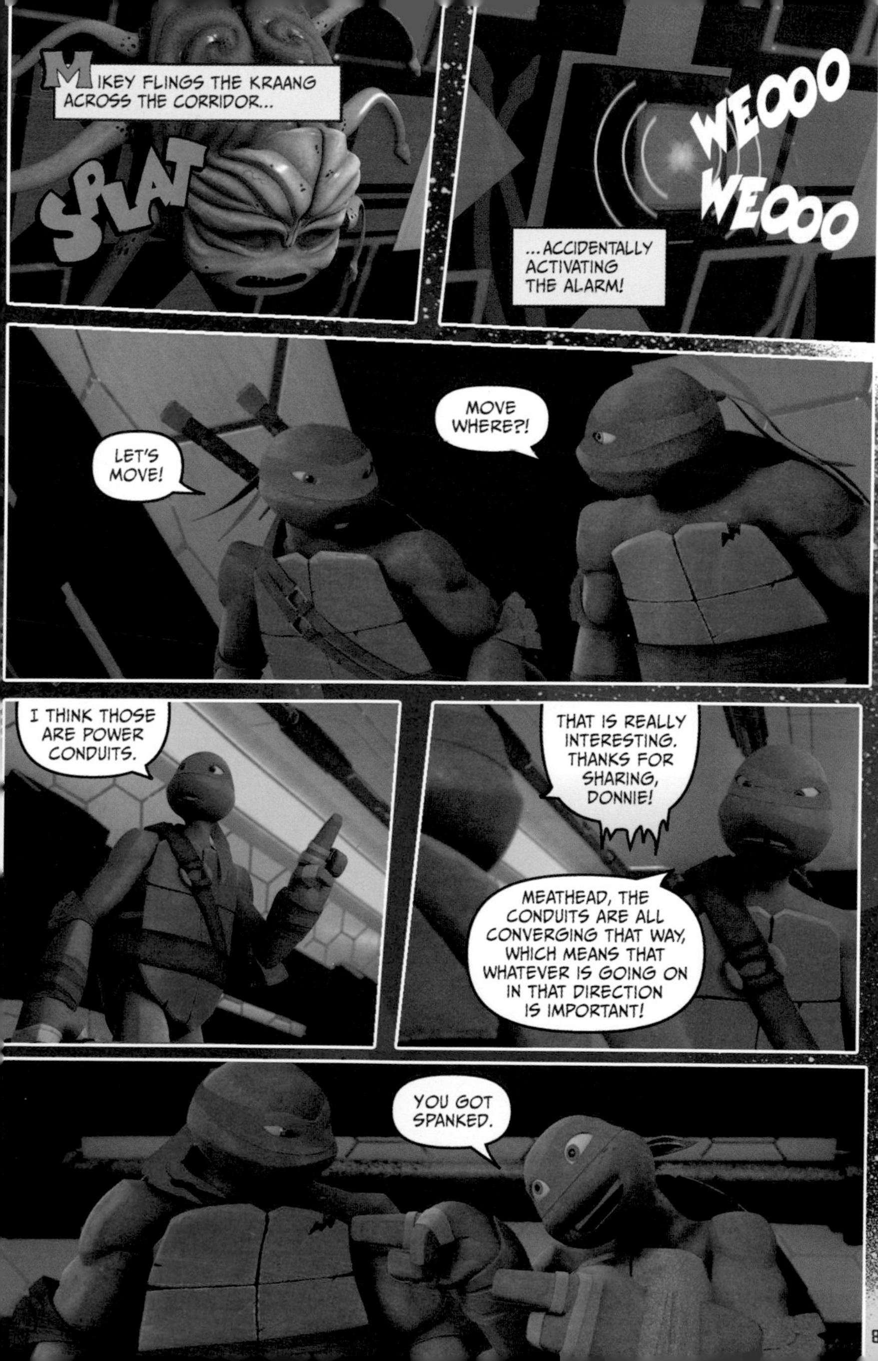
MIKEY FLINGS THE KRAANG ACROSS THE CORRIDOR...
SPLAT
WEOOO WEOOO
...ACCIDENTALLY ACTIVATING THE ALARM!
LET'S MOVE!
MOVE WHERE?!
I THINK THOSE ARE POWER CONDUITS.
THAT IS REALLY INTERESTING. THANKS FOR SHARING, DONNIE!
MEATHEAD, THE CONDUITS ARE ALL CONVERGING THAT WAY, WHICH MEANS THAT WHATEVER IS GOING ON IN THAT DIRECTION IS IMPORTANT!
YOU GOT SPANKED.

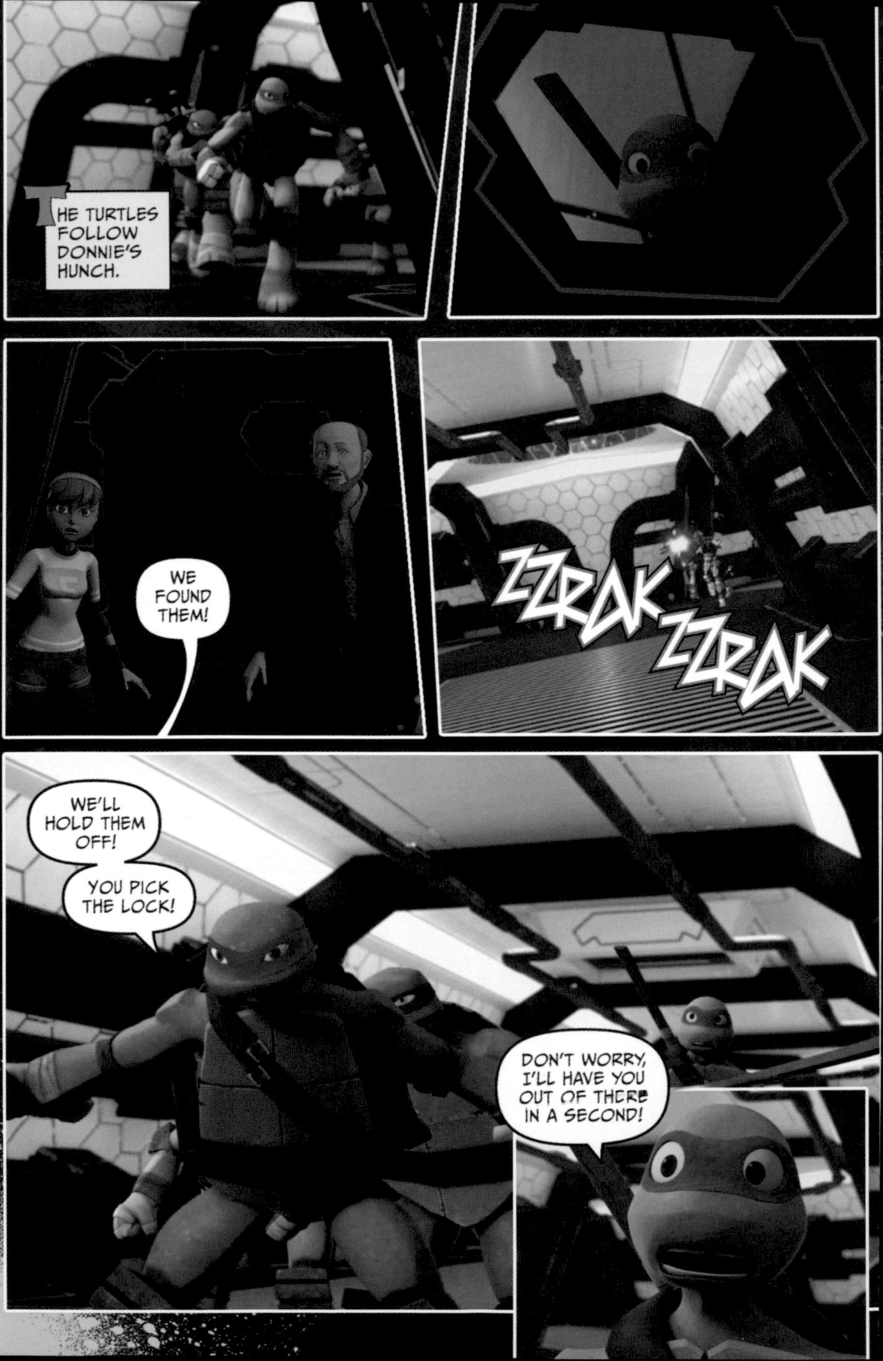
THE TURTLES FOLLOW DONNIE'S HUNCH.
WE FOUND THEM!
ZZRAK ZZRAK
WE'LL HOLD THEM OFF!
YOU PICK THE LOCK!
DON'T WORRY, I'LL HAVE YOU OUT OF THERE IN A SECOND!

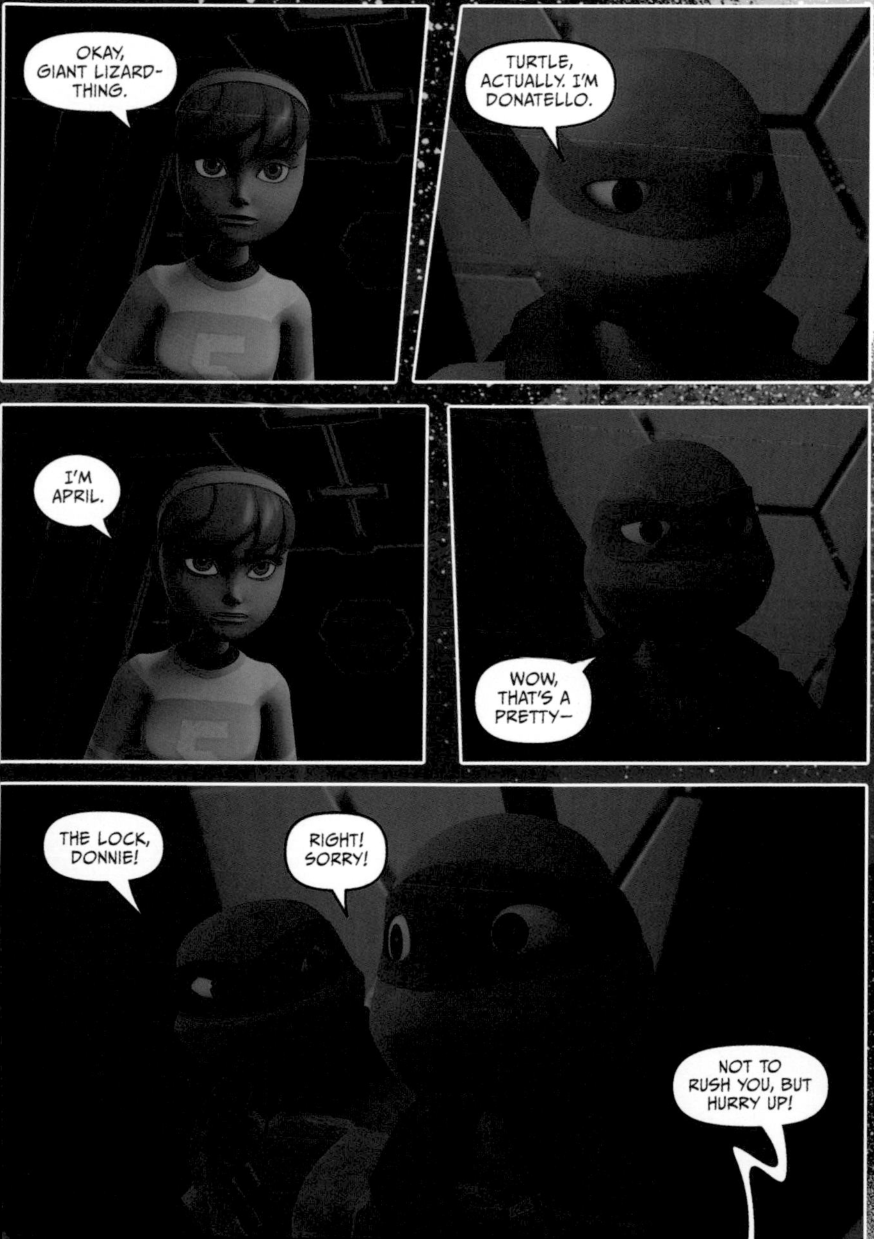
OKAY, GIANT LIZARD-THING.
TURTLE, ACTUALLY. I'M DONATELLO.
I'M APRIL.
WOW, THAT'S A PRETTY—
THE LOCK, DONNIE!
RIGHT! SORRY!
NOT TO RUSH YOU, BUT HURRY UP!

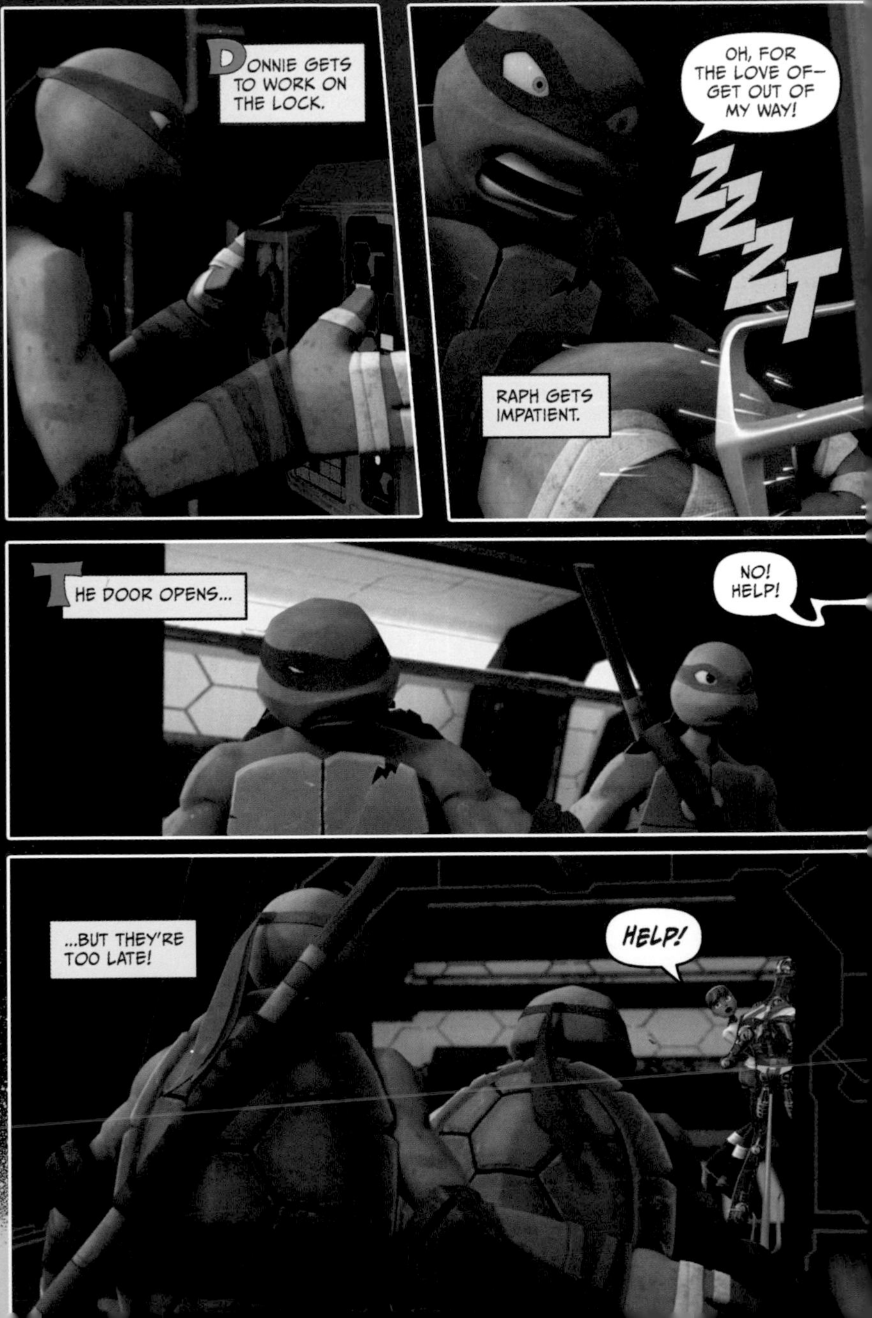
DONNIE GETS TO WORK ON THE LOCK.
OH, FOR THE LOVE OF— GET OUT OF MY WAY!
ZZZT
RAPH GETS IMPATIENT.
THE DOOR OPENS...
NO! HELP!
...BUT THEY'RE TOO LATE!
HELP!

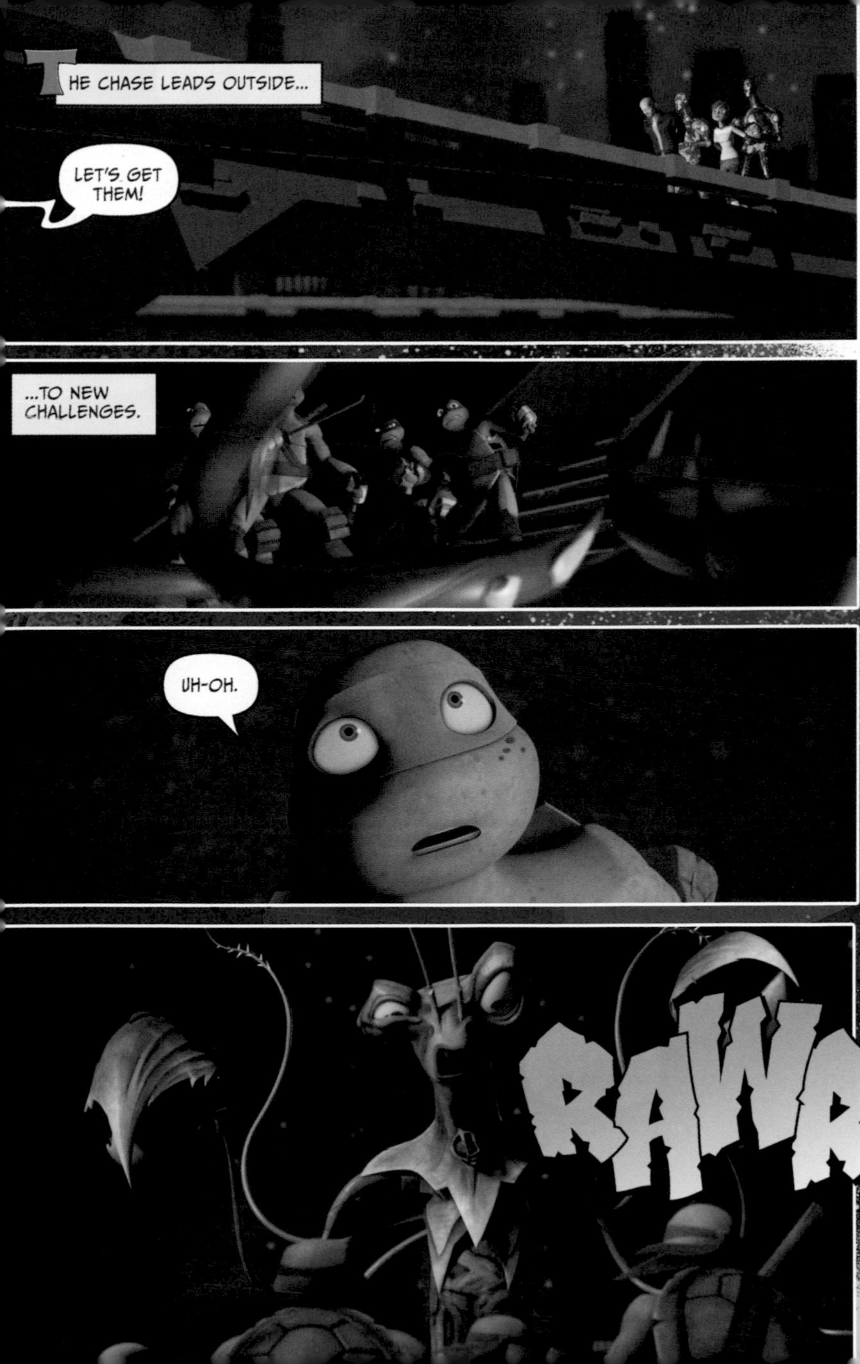
THE CHASE LEADS OUTSIDE...
LET'S GET THEM!
...TO NEW CHALLENGES.
UH-OH.
RAWR

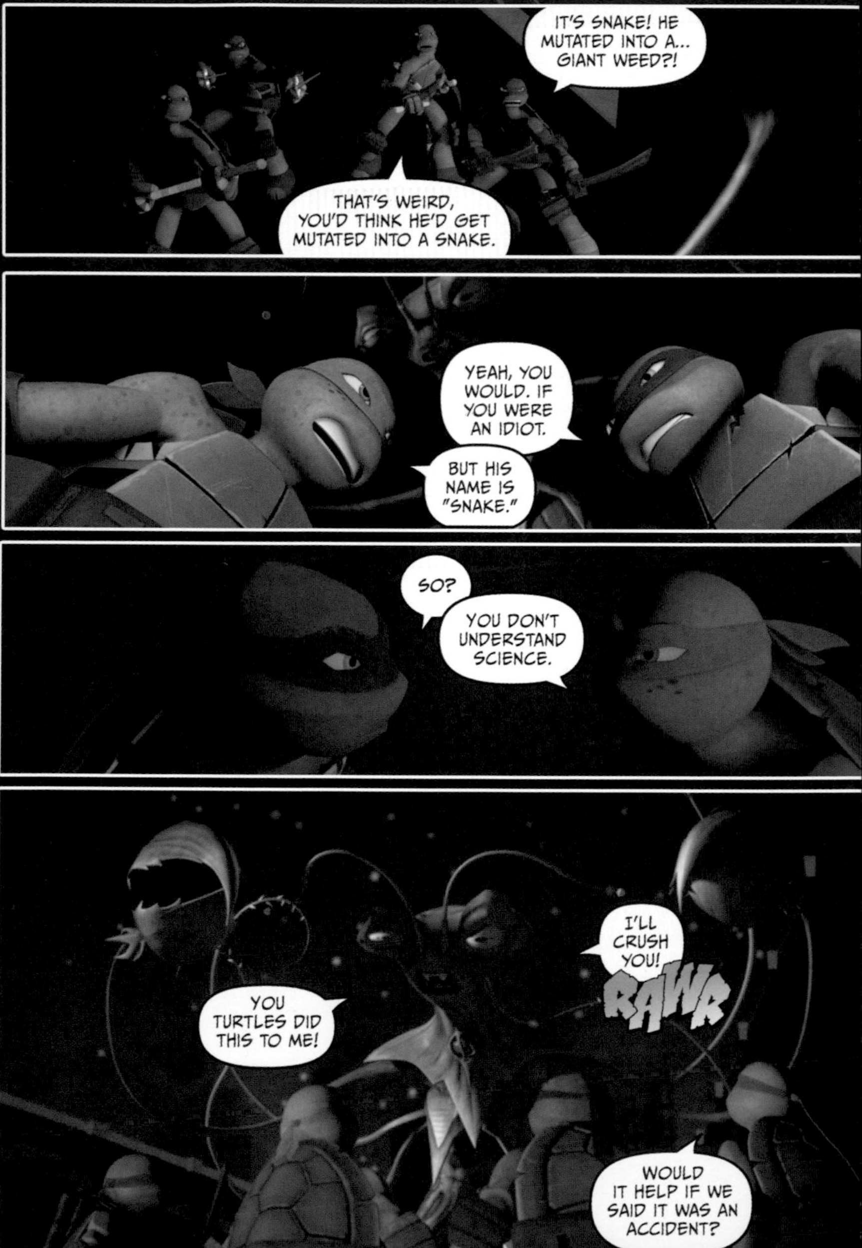
IT'S SNAKE! HE MUTATED INTO A... GIANT WEED?!
THAT'S WEIRD, YOU'D THINK HE'D GET MUTATED INTO A SNAKE.
YEAH, YOU WOULD. IF YOU WERE AN IDIOT.
BUT HIS NAME IS "SNAKE."
SO?
YOU DON'T UNDERSTAND SCIENCE.
YOU TURTLES DID THIS TO ME!
I'LL CRUSH YOU!
RAWR
WOULD IT HELP IF WE SAID IT WAS AN ACCIDENT?

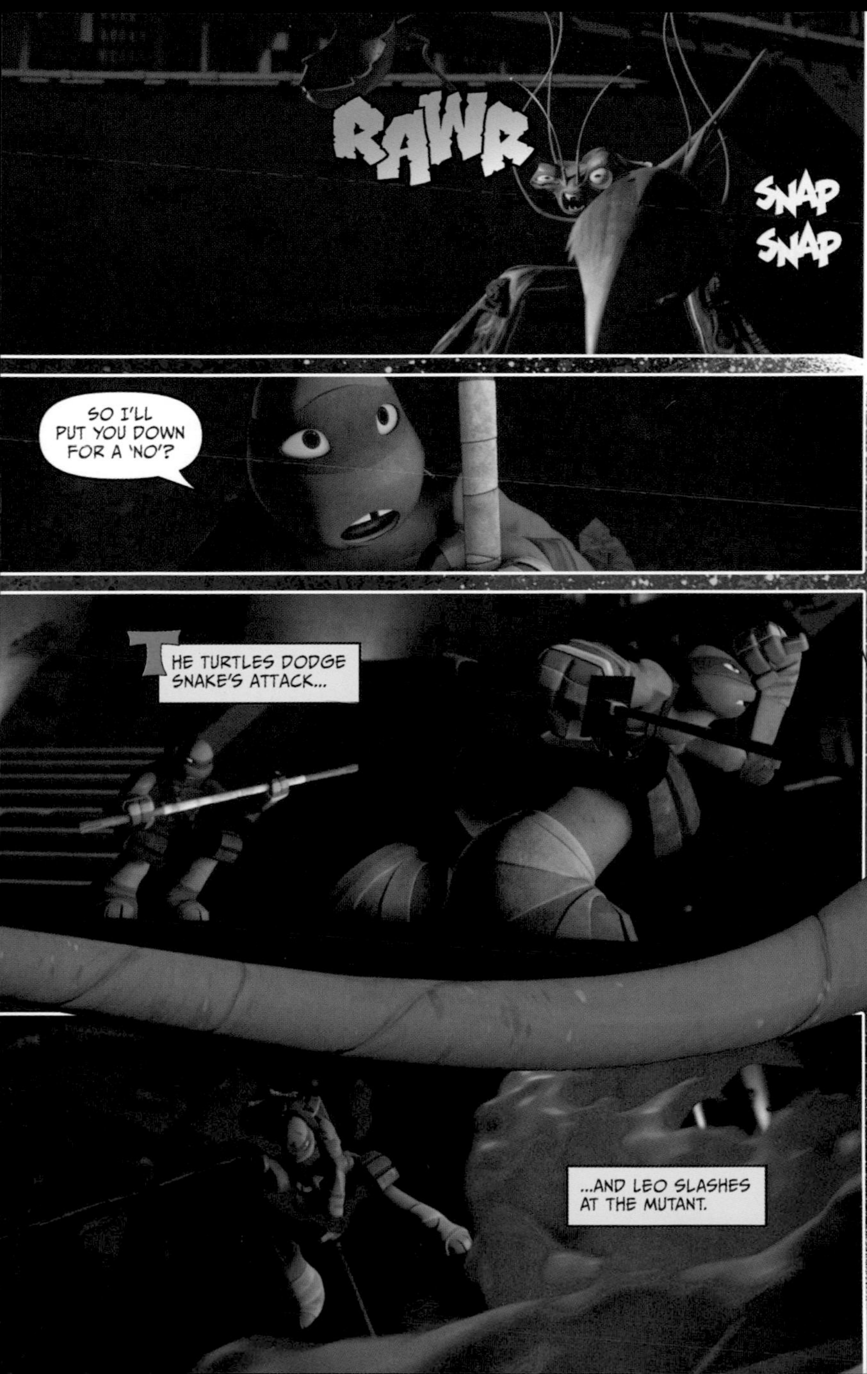
RAWR
SNAP SNAP
SO I'LL PUT YOU DOWN FOR A 'NO'?
THE TURTLES DODGE SNAKE'S ATTACK...
...AND LEO SLASHES AT THE MUTANT.

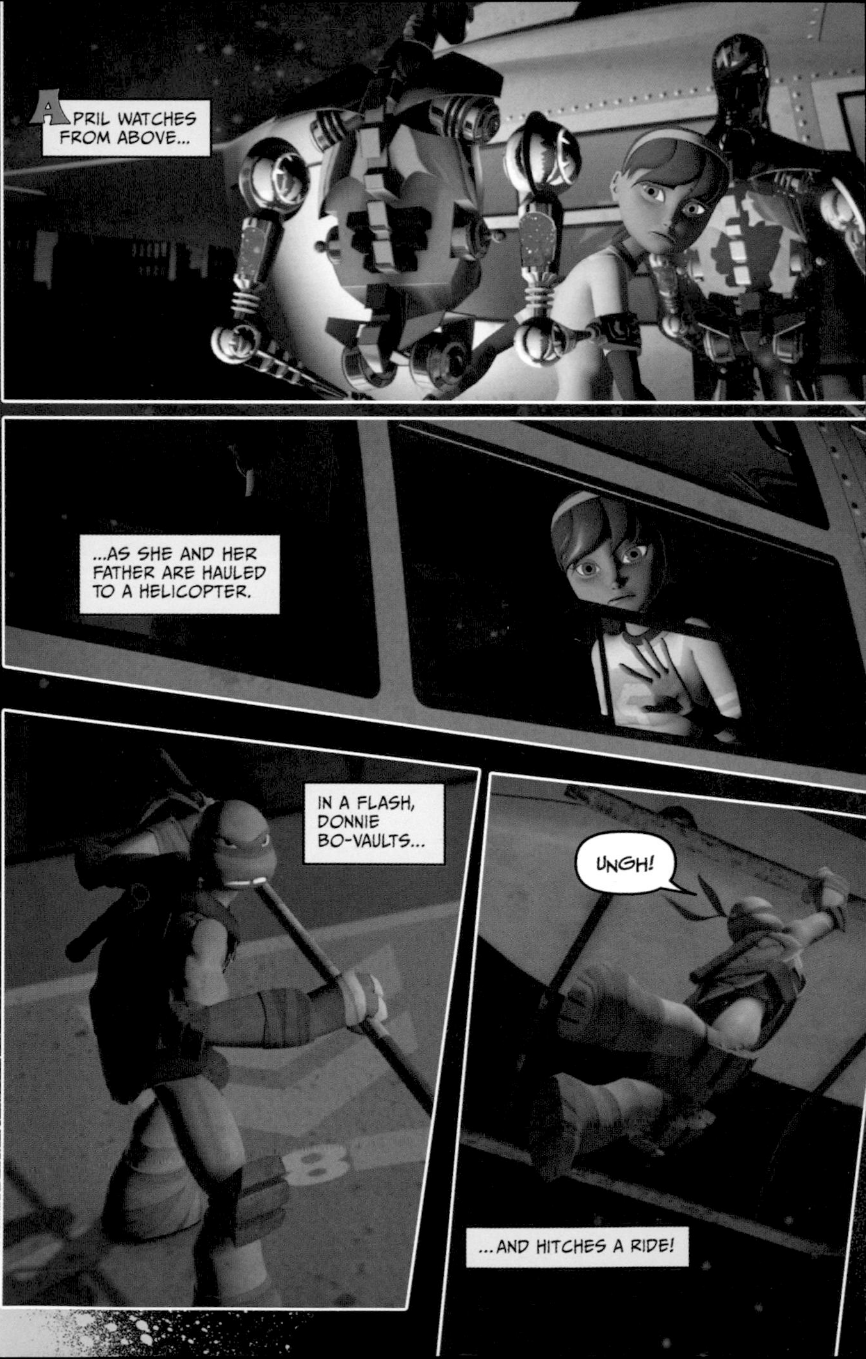
APRIL WATCHES FROM ABOVE...
...AS SHE AND HER FATHER ARE HAULED TO A HELICOPTER.
IN A FLASH, DONNIE BO-VAULTS...
UNGH!
...AND HITCHES A RIDE!

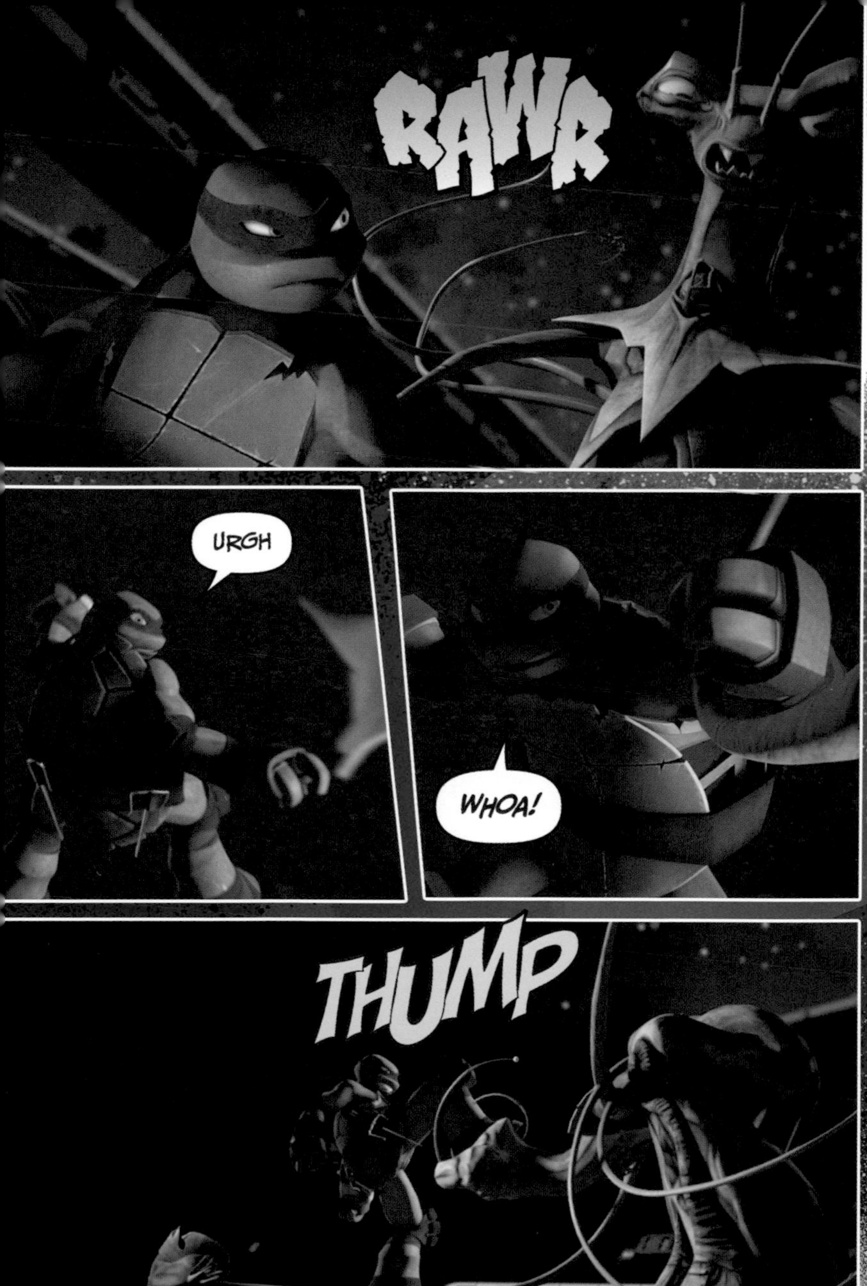
RAWR
URGH
WHOA!
THUMP

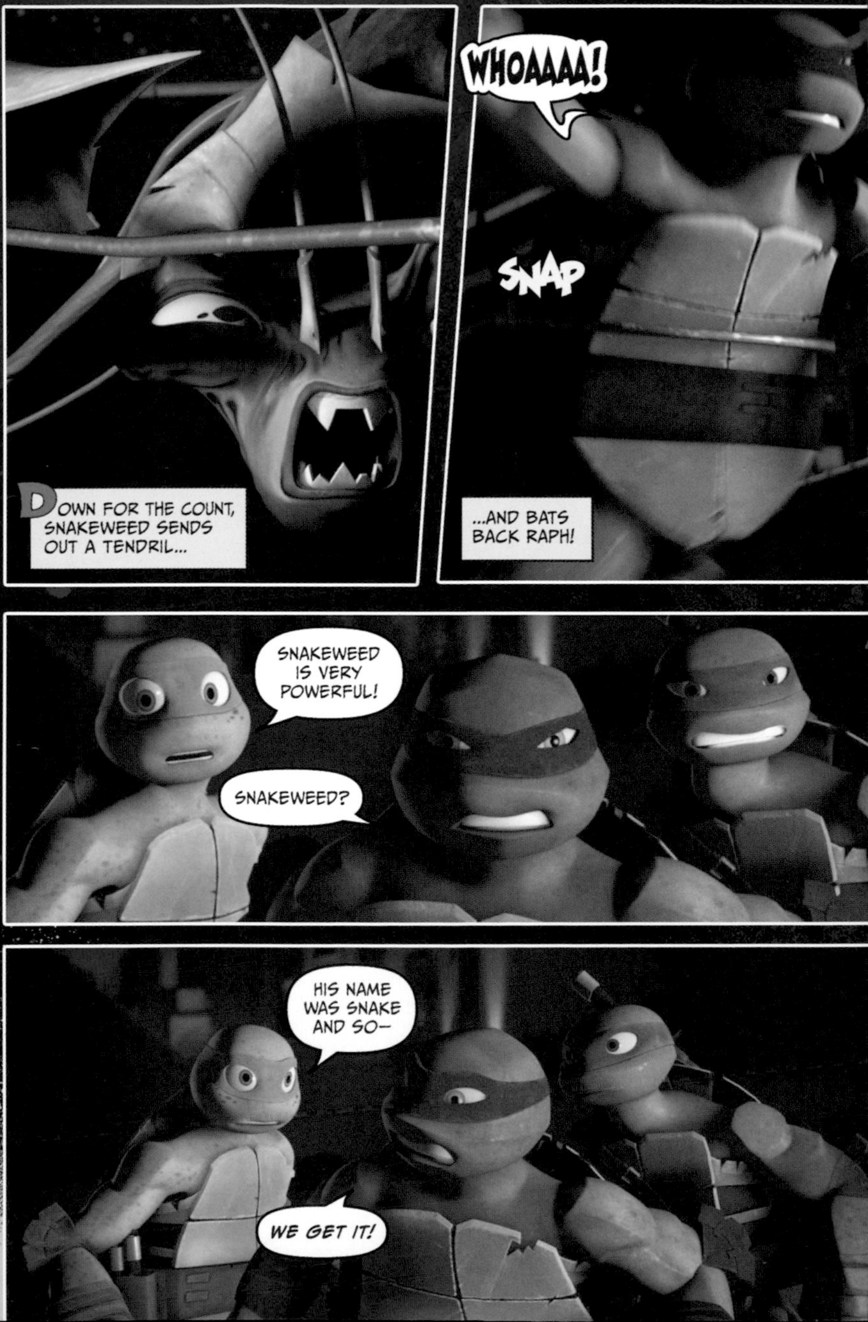
DOWN FOR THE COUNT, SNAKEWEED SENDS OUT A TENDRIL...
WHOAAAA!
SNAP
...AND BATS BACK RAPH!
SNAKEWEED IS VERY POWERFUL!
SNAKEWEED?
HIS NAME WAS SNAKE AND SO—
WE GET IT!

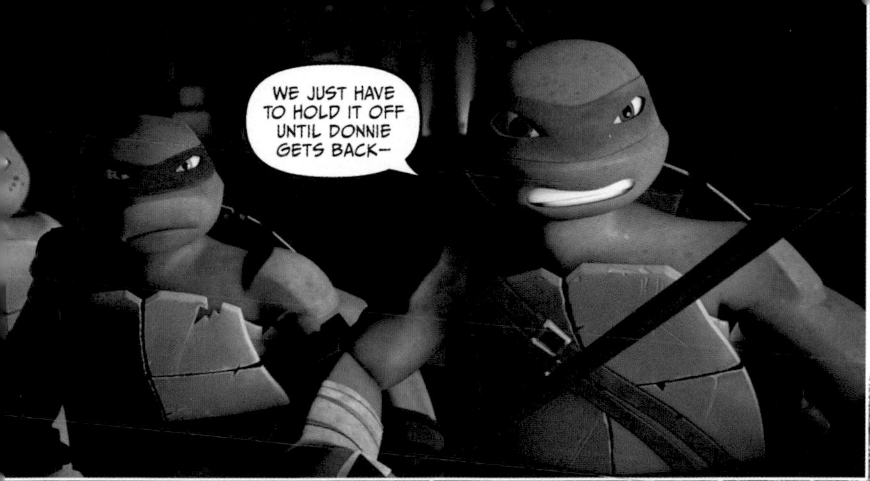
WE JUST HAVE TO HOLD IT OFF UNTIL DONNIE GETS BACK—

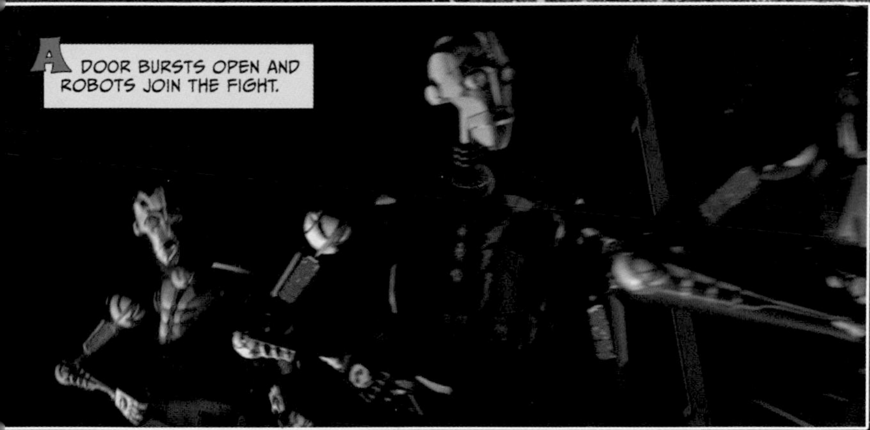
A DOOR BURSTS OPEN AND ROBOTS JOIN THE FIGHT.

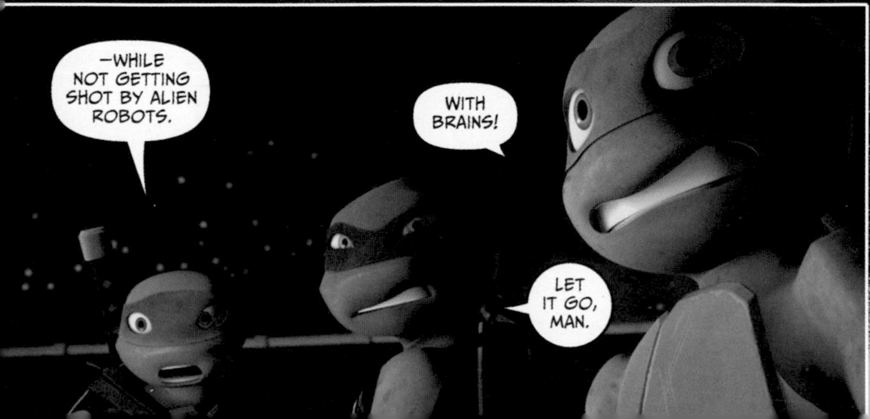
—WHILE NOT GETTING SHOT BY ALIEN ROBOTS.
WITH BRAINS!
LET IT GO, MAN.

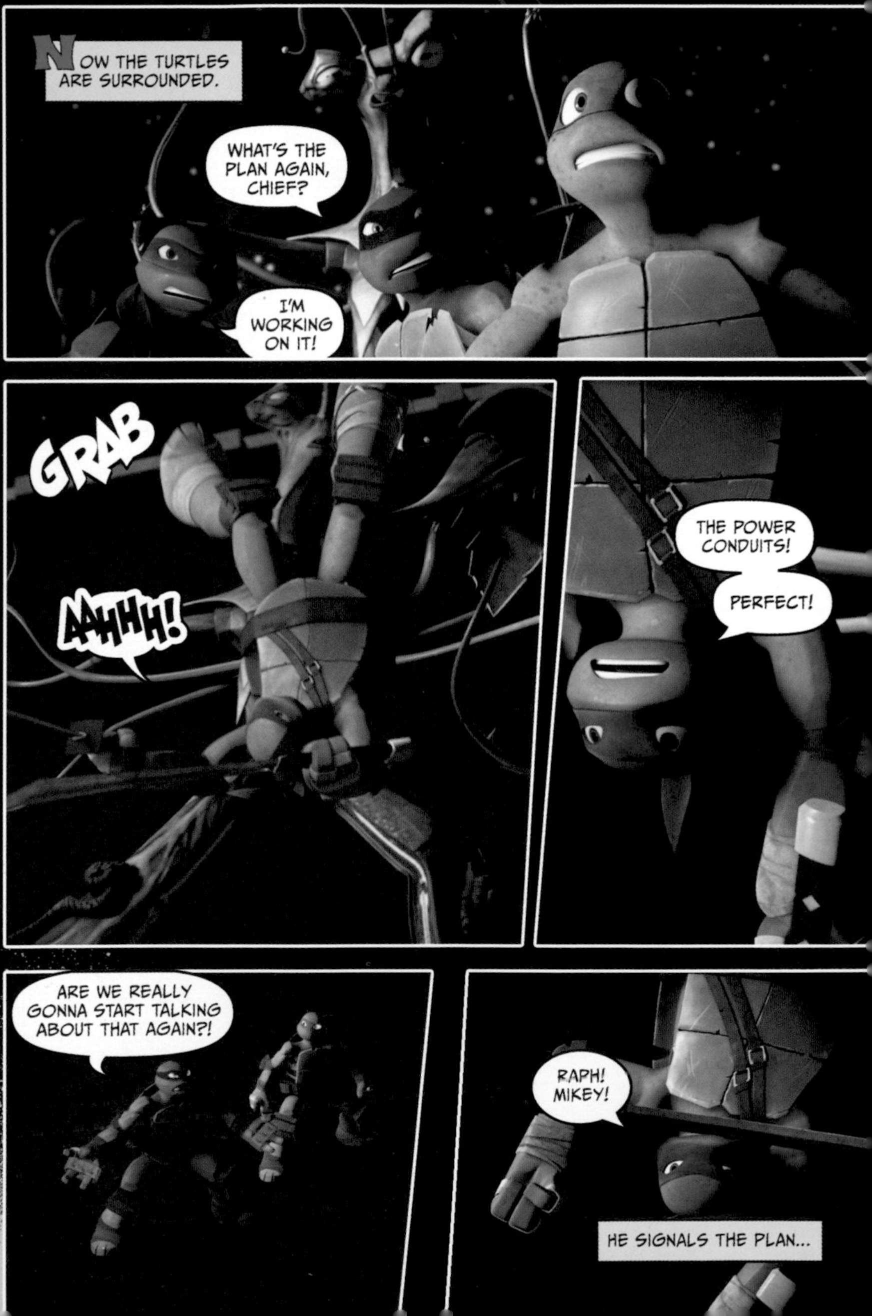
NOW THE TURTLES ARE SURROUNDED.
WHAT'S THE PLAN AGAIN, CHIEF?
I'M WORKING ON IT!
GRAB
AAHHH!
THE POWER CONDUITS!
PERFECT!
ARE WE REALLY GONNA START TALKING ABOUT THAT AGAIN?!
RAPH! MIKEY!
HE SIGNALS THE PLAN...

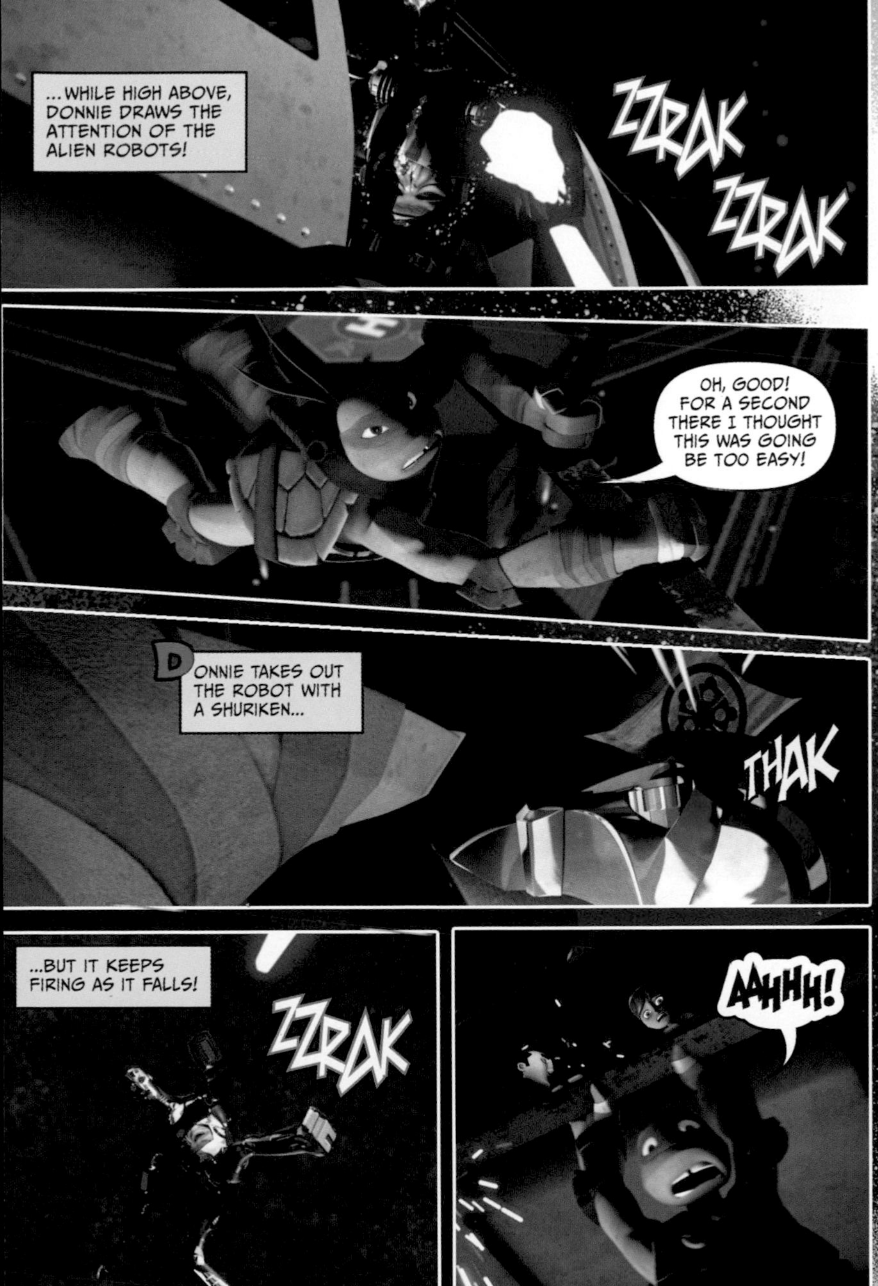
...WHILE HIGH ABOVE, DONNIE DRAWS THE ATTENTION OF THE ALIEN ROBOTS!
ZZRAK ZZRAK
OH, GOOD! FOR A SECOND THERE I THOUGHT THIS WAS GOING BE TOO EASY!
DONNIE TAKES OUT THE ROBOT WITH A SHURIKEN...
THAK
...BUT IT KEEPS FIRING AS IT FALLS!
ZZRAK
AAHHH!

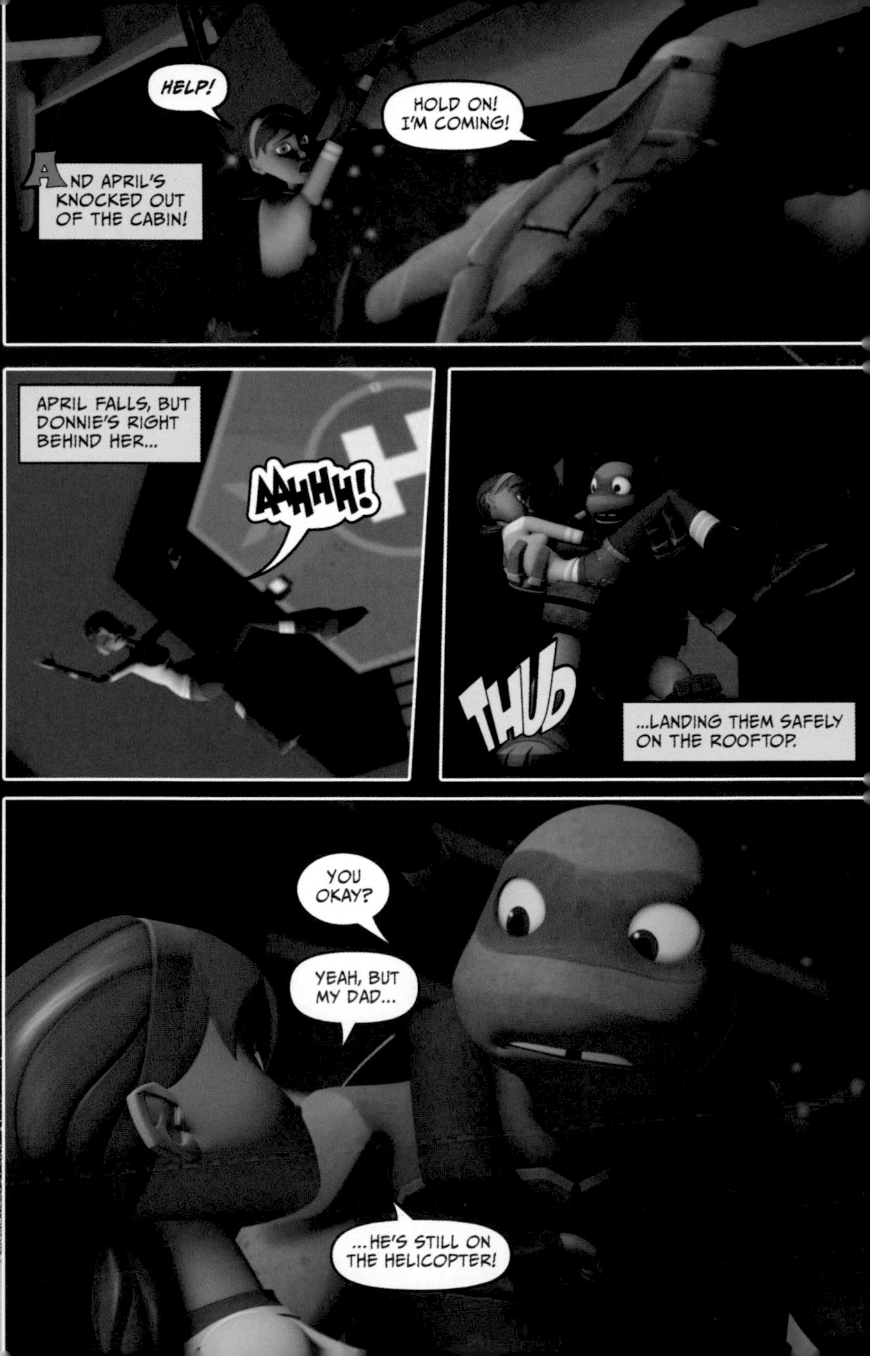

HELP!
HOLD ON! I'M COMING!
AND APRIL'S KNOCKED OUT OF THE CABIN!
APRIL FALLS, BUT DONNIE'S RIGHT BEHIND HER...
AAHHH!
THUD
...LANDING THEM SAFELY ON THE ROOFTOP.
YOU OKAY?
YEAH, BUT MY DAD...
...HE'S STILL ON THE HELICOPTER!

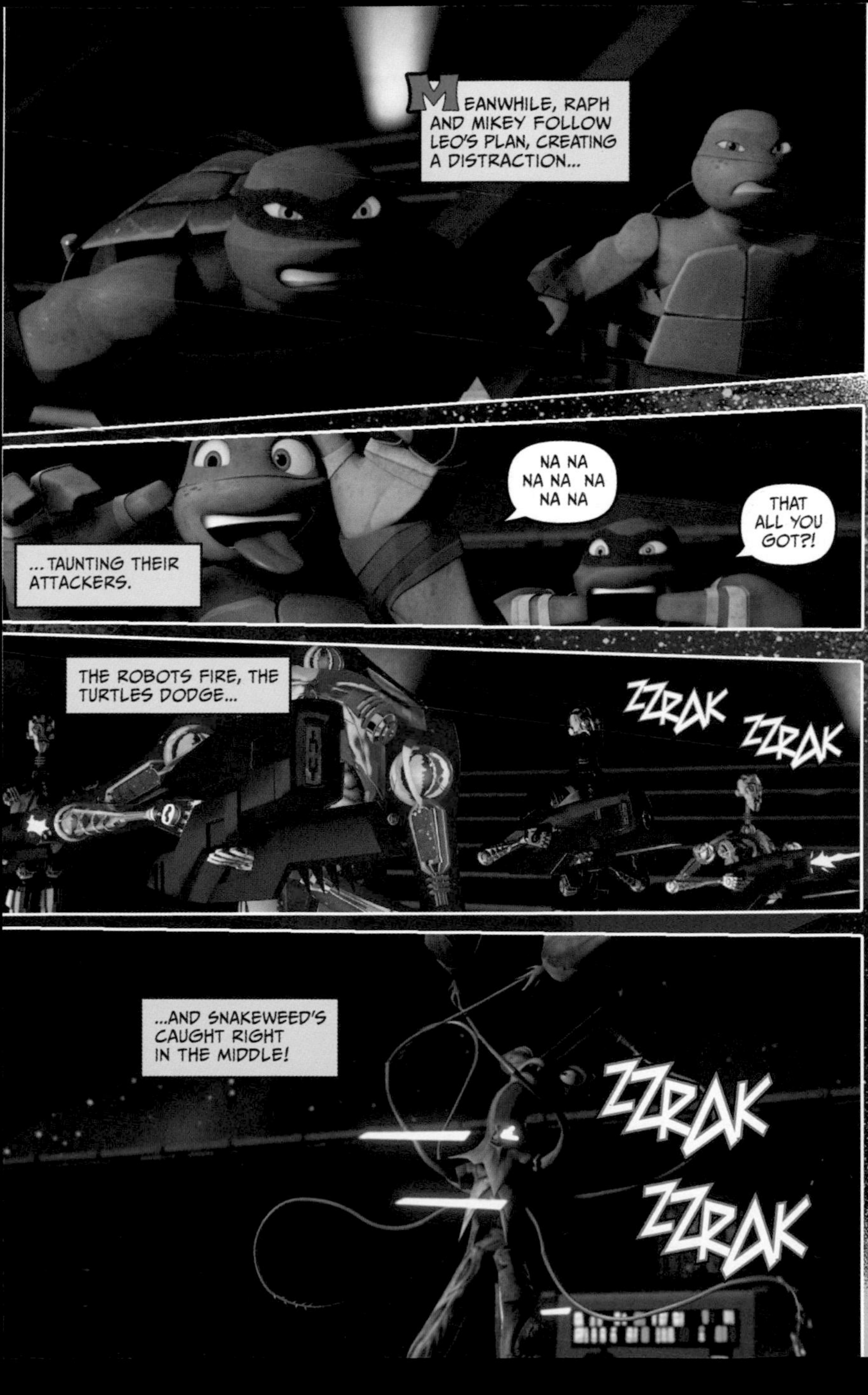
MEANWHILE, RAPH AND MIKEY FOLLOW LEO'S PLAN, CREATING A DISTRACTION...
...TAUNTING THEIR ATTACKERS.
NA NA NA NA NA NA NA
THAT ALL YOU GOT?!
THE ROBOTS FIRE, THE TURTLES DODGE...
ZZRAK
ZZRAK
...AND SNAKEWEED'S CAUGHT RIGHT IN THE MIDDLE!
ZZRAK
ZZRAK

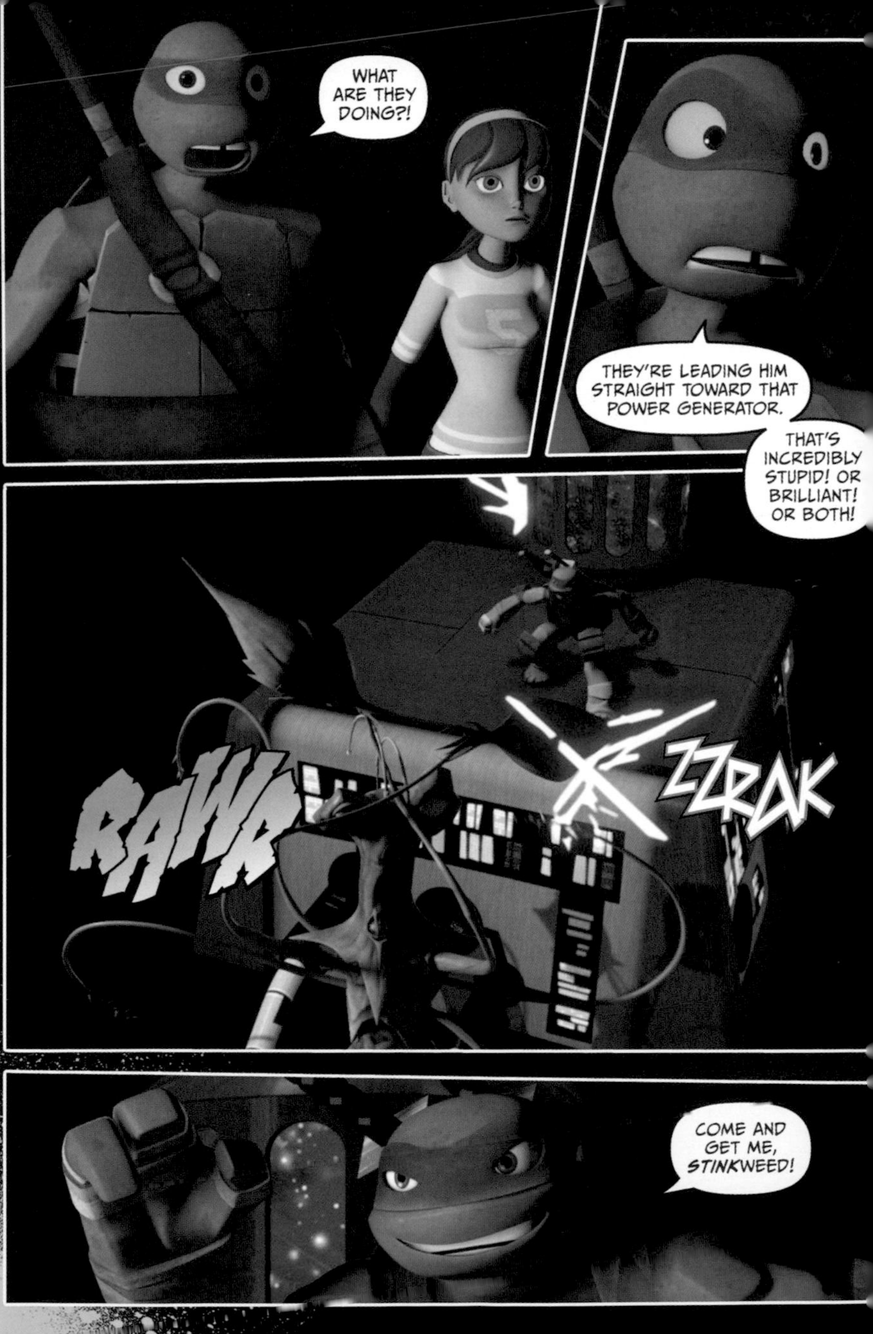

WHAT ARE THEY DOING?!
THEY'RE LEADING HIM STRAIGHT TOWARD THAT POWER GENERATOR.
THAT'S INCREDIBLY STUPID! OR BRILLIANT! OR BOTH!
RAWR
ZZRAK
COME AND GET ME, *STINK*WEED!

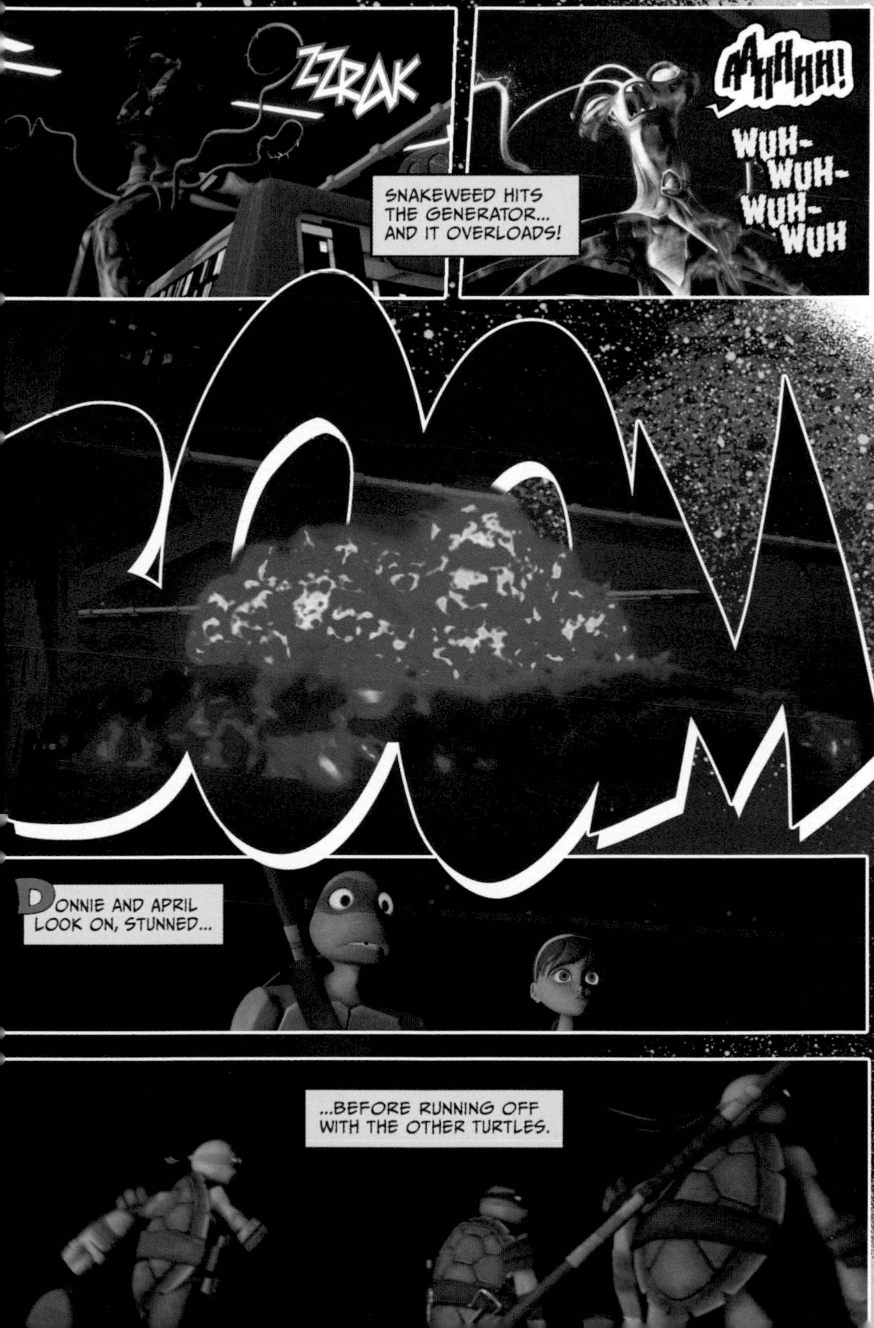
ZZRAK
SNAKEWEED HITS THE GENERATOR... AND IT OVERLOADS!
AAHHHH!
WUH- WUH- WUH- WUH
DONNIE AND APRIL LOOK ON, STUNNED...
...BEFORE RUNNING OFF WITH THE OTHER TURTLES.

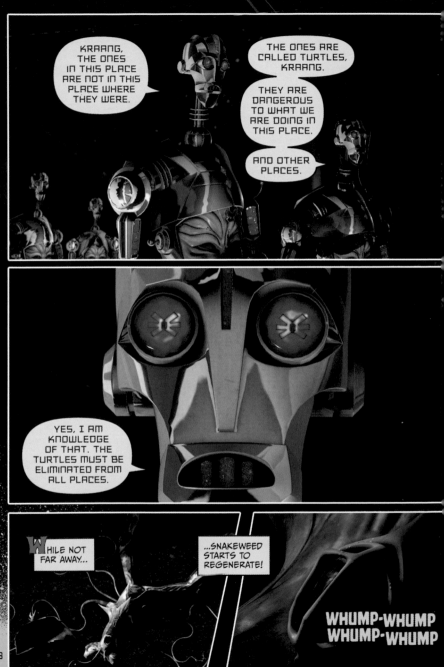

KRAANG, THE ONES IN THIS PLACE ARE NOT IN THIS PLACE WHERE THEY WERE.

THE ONES ARE CALLED TURTLES, KRAANG.

THEY ARE DANGEROUS TO WHAT WE ARE DOING IN THIS PLACE.

AND OTHER PLACES.

YES, I AM KNOWLEDGE OF THAT. THE TURTLES MUST BE ELIMINATED FROM ALL PLACES.

WHILE NOT FAR AWAY...

...SNAKEWEED STARTS TO REGENERATE!

WHUMP-WHUMP WHUMP-WHUMP

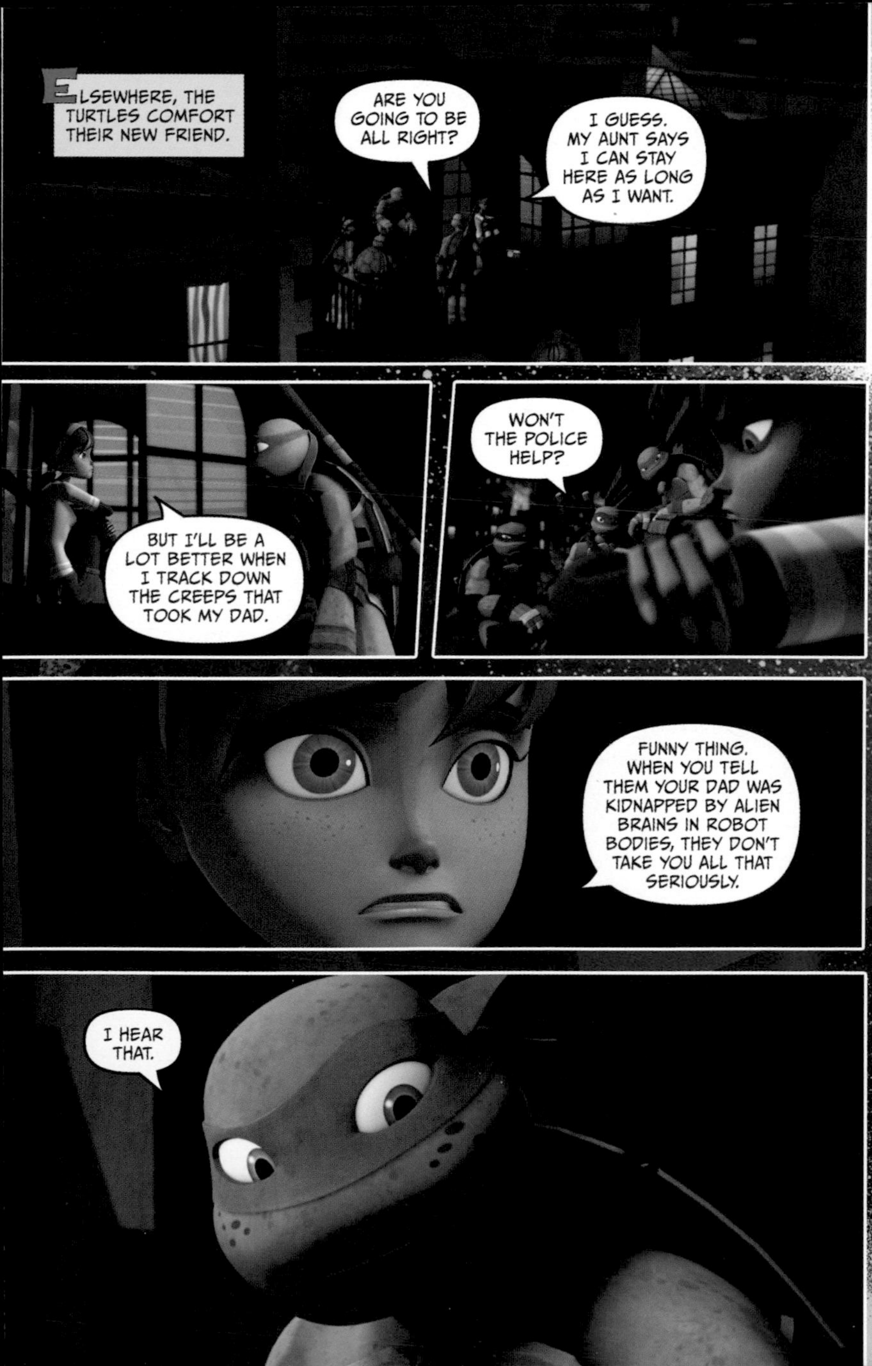
ELSEWHERE, THE TURTLES COMFORT THEIR NEW FRIEND.
ARE YOU GOING TO BE ALL RIGHT?
I GUESS. MY AUNT SAYS I CAN STAY HERE AS LONG AS I WANT.
BUT I'LL BE A LOT BETTER WHEN I TRACK DOWN THE CREEPS THAT TOOK MY DAD.
WON'T THE POLICE HELP?
FUNNY THING. WHEN YOU TELL THEM YOUR DAD WAS KIDNAPPED BY ALIEN BRAINS IN ROBOT BODIES, THEY DON'T TAKE YOU ALL THAT SERIOUSLY.
I HEAR THAT.

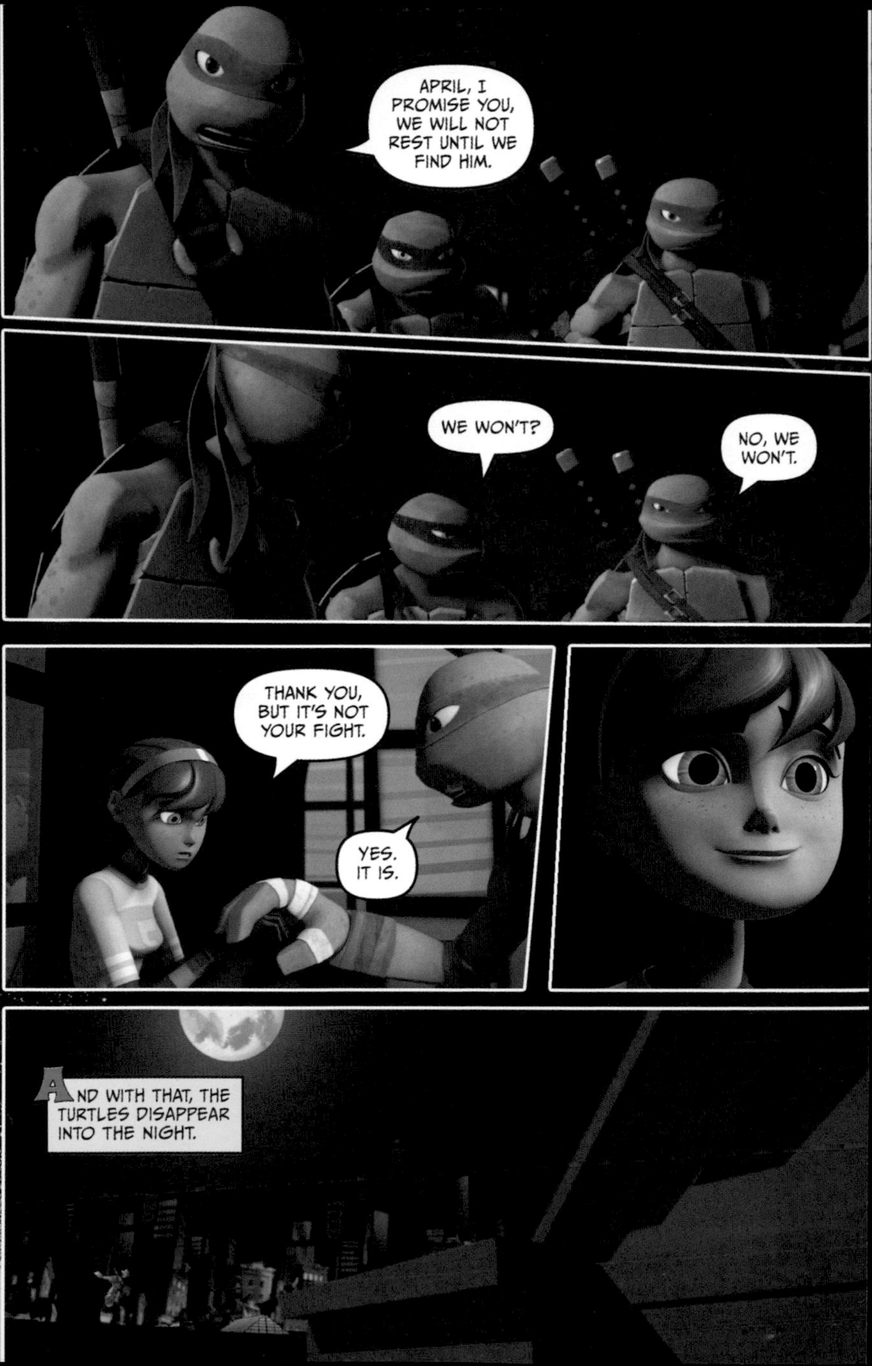
APRIL, I PROMISE YOU, WE WILL NOT REST UNTIL WE FIND HIM.
WE WON'T?
NO, WE WON'T.
THANK YOU, BUT IT'S NOT YOUR FIGHT.
YES. IT IS.
AND WITH THAT, THE TURTLES DISAPPEAR INTO THE NIGHT.

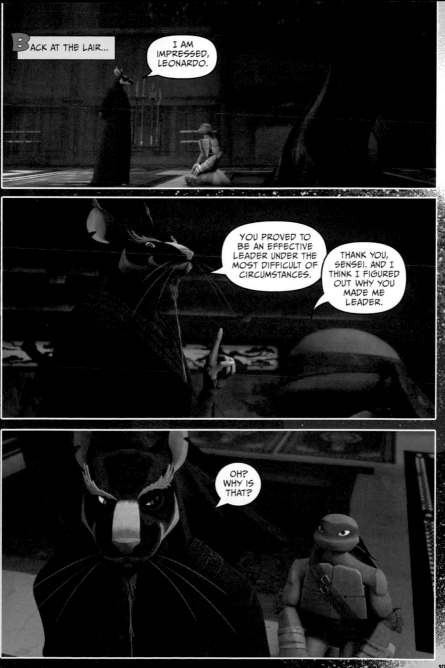

BACK AT THE LAIR...

I AM IMPRESSED, LEONARDO.

YOU PROVED TO BE AN EFFECTIVE LEADER UNDER THE MOST DIFFICULT OF CIRCUMSTANCES.

THANK YOU, SENSEI. AND I THINK I FIGURED OUT WHY YOU MADE ME LEADER.

OH? WHY IS THAT?

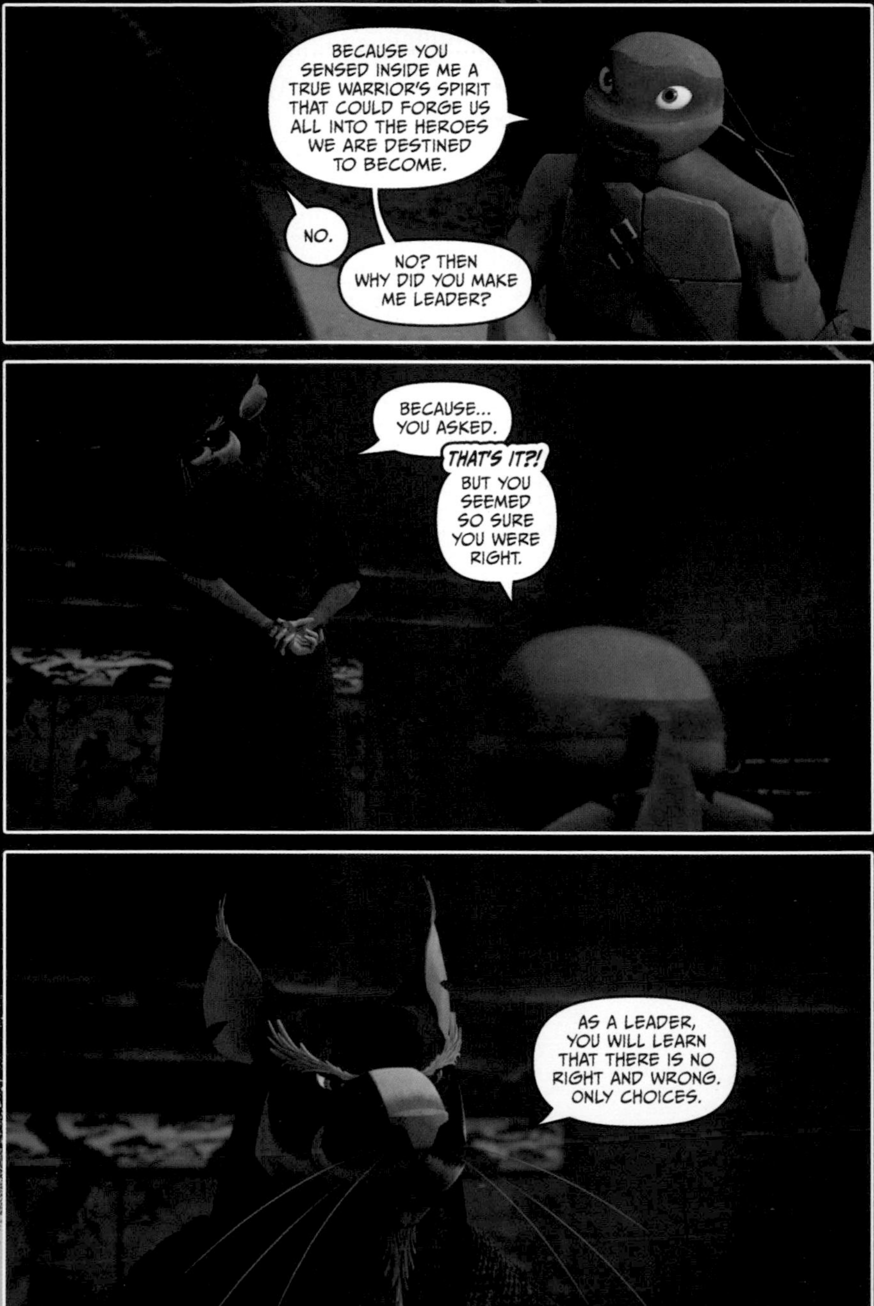
BECAUSE YOU SENSED INSIDE ME A TRUE WARRIOR'S SPIRIT THAT COULD FORGE US ALL INTO THE HEROES WE ARE DESTINED TO BECOME.
NO.
NO? THEN WHY DID YOU MAKE ME LEADER?
BECAUSE... YOU ASKED.
THAT'S IT?!
BUT YOU SEEMED SO SURE YOU WERE RIGHT.
AS A LEADER, YOU WILL LEARN THAT THERE IS NO RIGHT AND WRONG. ONLY CHOICES.

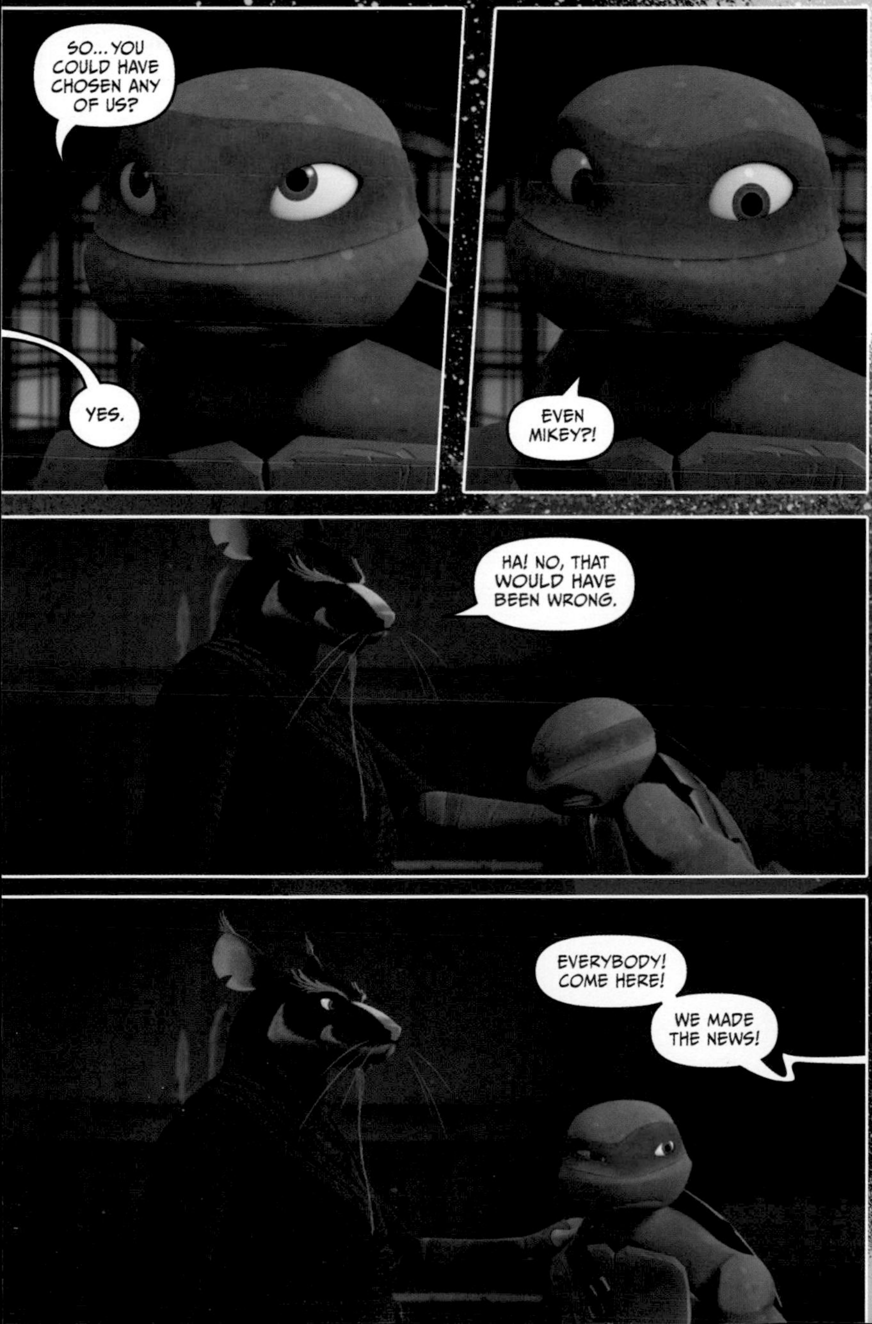
SO...YOU COULD HAVE CHOSEN ANY OF US?
YES.
EVEN MIKEY?!
HA! NO, THAT WOULD HAVE BEEN WRONG.
EVERYBODY! COME HERE!
WE MADE THE NEWS!

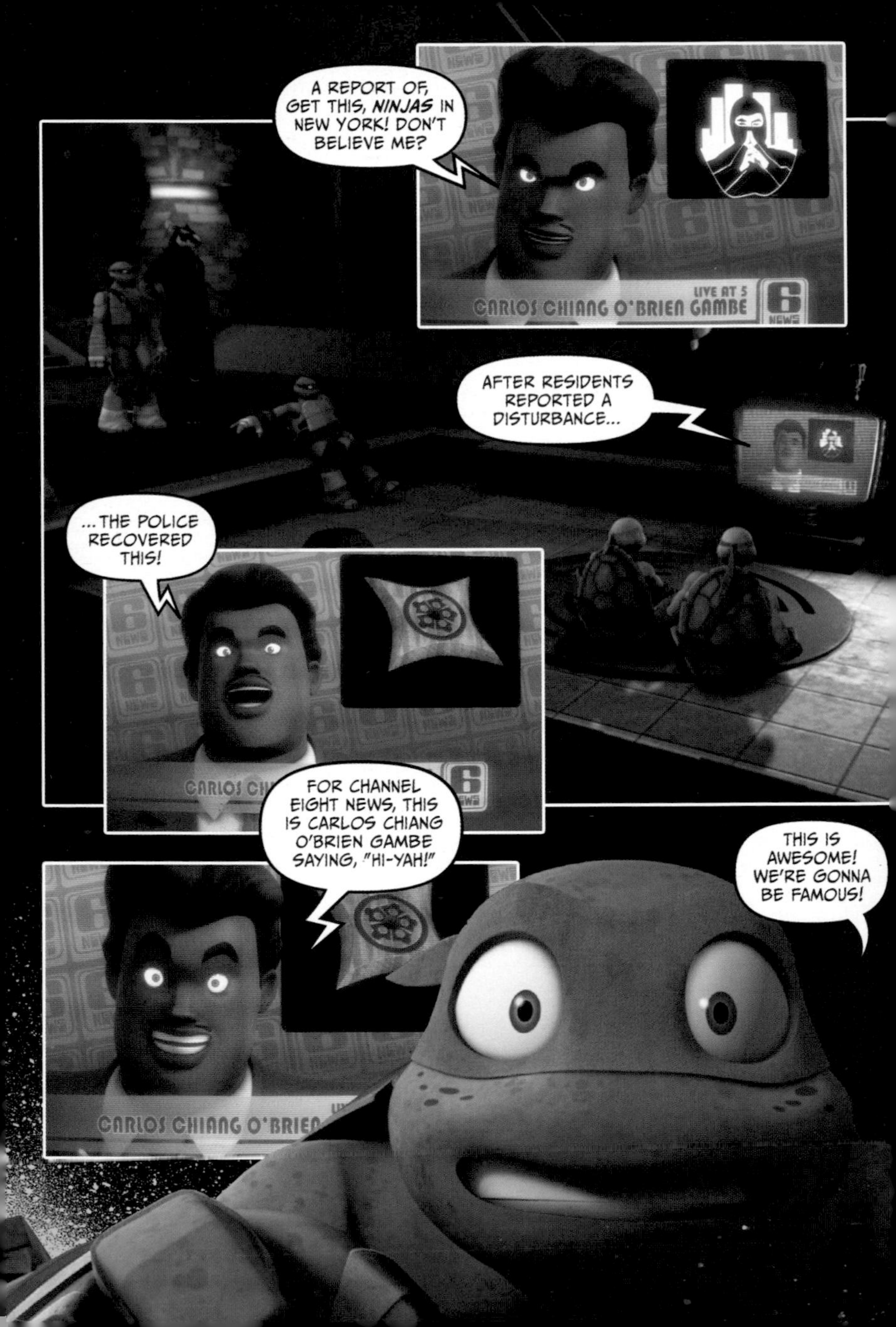
A REPORT OF, GET THIS, NINJAS IN NEW YORK! DON'T BELIEVE ME?
LIVE AT 5
CARLOS CHIANG O'BRIEN GAMBE
6 NEWS
AFTER RESIDENTS REPORTED A DISTURBANCE...
...THE POLICE RECOVERED THIS!
FOR CHANNEL EIGHT NEWS, THIS IS CARLOS CHIANG O'BRIEN GAMBE SAYING, "HI-YAH!"
THIS IS AWESOME! WE'RE GONNA BE FAMOUS!

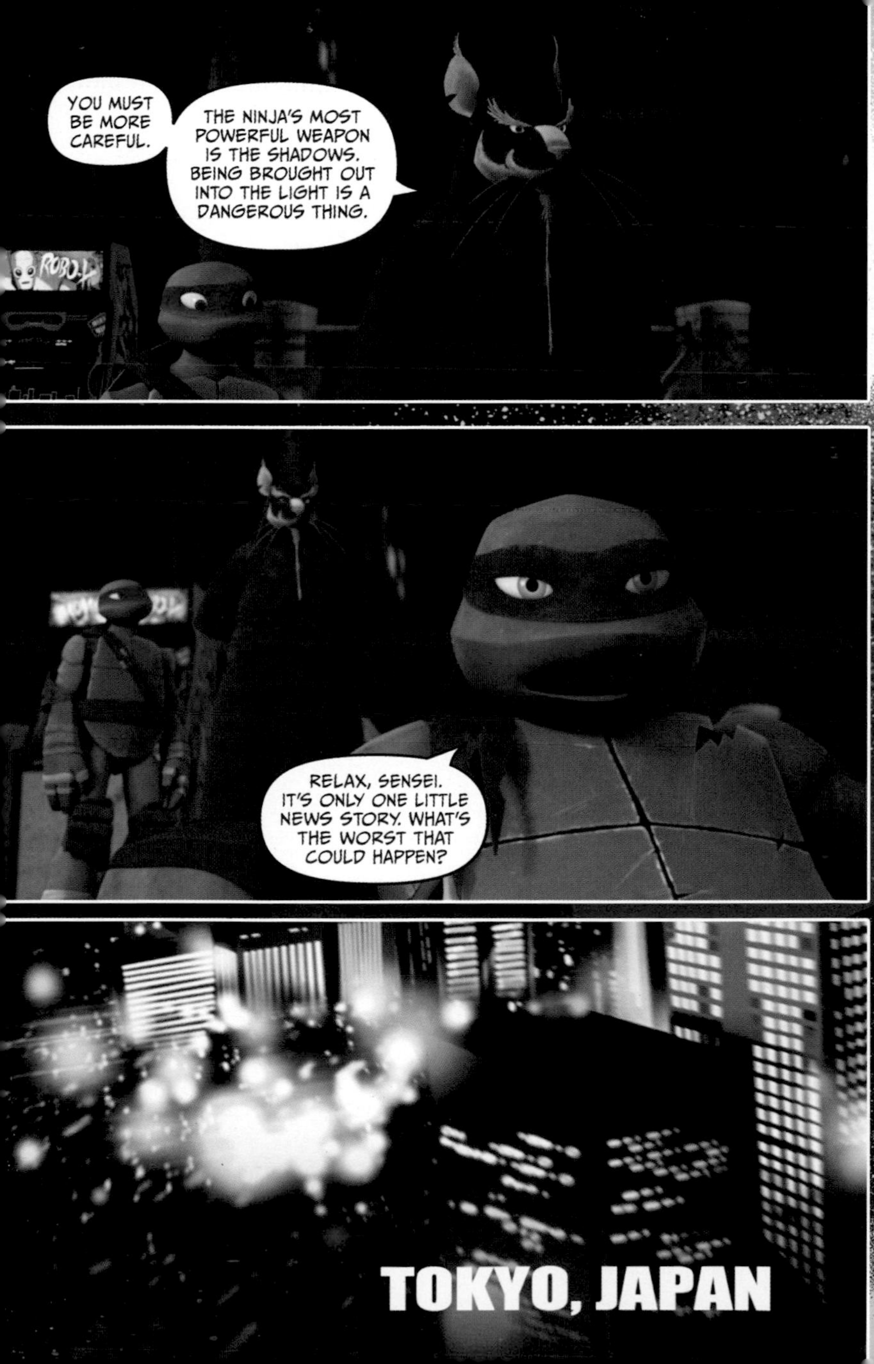

YOU MUST BE MORE CAREFUL.
THE NINJA'S MOST POWERFUL WEAPON IS THE SHADOWS. BEING BROUGHT OUT INTO THE LIGHT IS A DANGEROUS THING.
RELAX, SENSEI. IT'S ONLY ONE LITTLE NEWS STORY. WHAT'S THE WORST THAT COULD HAPPEN?
TOKYO, JAPAN

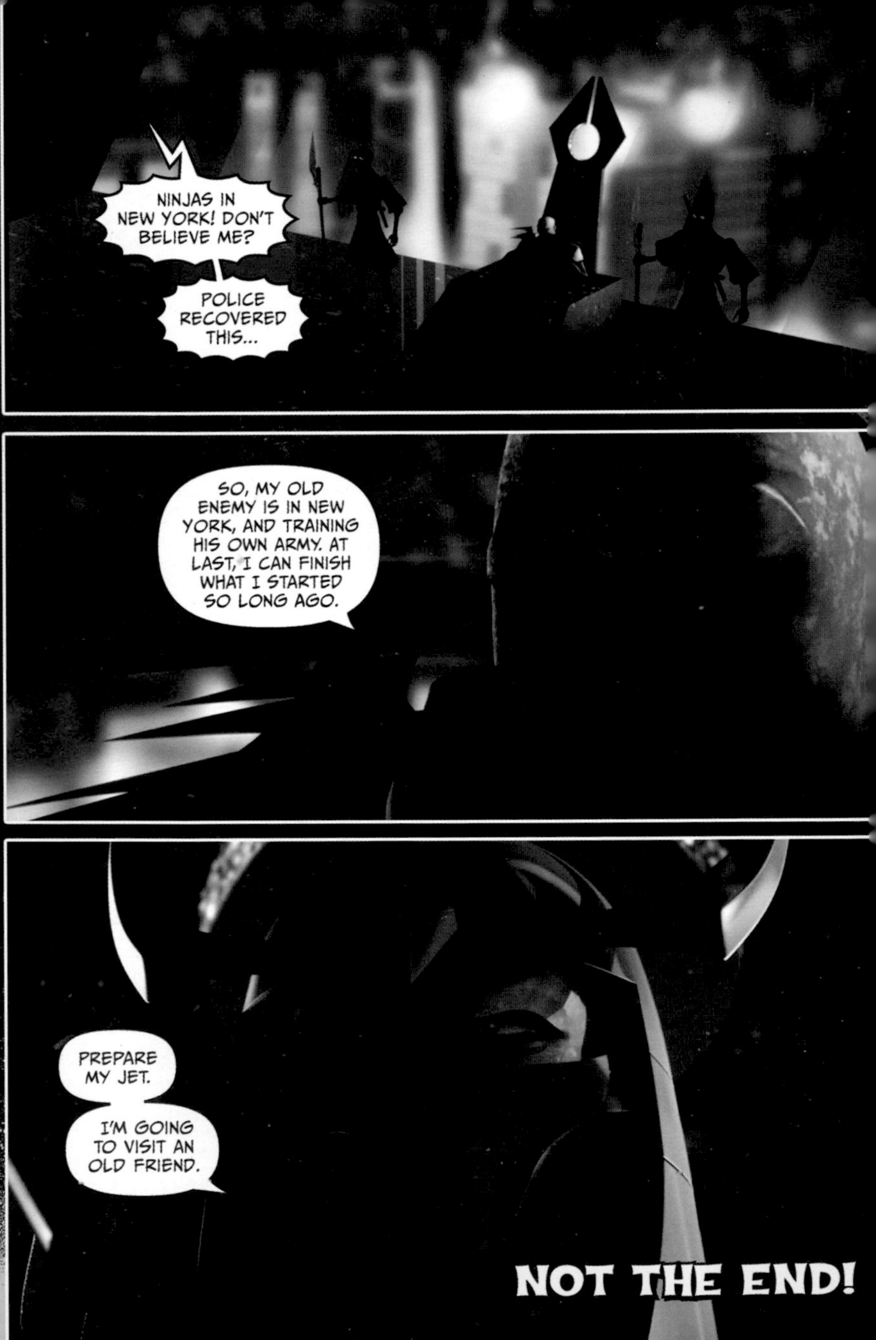
NINJAS IN NEW YORK! DON'T BELIEVE ME?
POLICE RECOVERED THIS...
SO, MY OLD ENEMY IS IN NEW YORK, AND TRAINING HIS OWN ARMY. AT LAST, I CAN FINISH WHAT I STARTED SO LONG AGO.
PREPARE MY JET.
I'M GOING TO VISIT AN OLD FRIEND.
NOT THE END!